GOD SAVE THE QUEEN

FORTY-SEVEN STORIES

PORTRAIT OF AMERICA, VOL. II

G. Lowell Tollefson

Preface

In bringing out this second collection of short stories, I find myself confronted with a problem: How can I, in this complex modern age, justify my persistence in the use of a simple narrative style?

To explain it, I ought to begin by saying that my narrative method derives from the observance of a principle almost too obvious to state. It goes like this: since it is always hard to make things clear for a reader, I should bend all my efforts toward doing so.

But this point of view often runs counter to what many people have come to expect, since obscurity and complexity are the characteristics they've grown used to in contemporary literary works. For this reason, my method has brought me into conflict with what has long since become established as an accepted practice.

The term for this practice is *self-expression*. Many readers seem to be of the opinion that an artist is in the business of simply expressing his or her self. But when this idea is taken too seriously by critics and big name writers, it can create a self-consciousness which leads to obscurity and even intellectual arrogance. Then, by becoming the established practice, it restricts those who are coming into the field. To be recognized, they must do the same thing in the same way.

The problem is that, while some of these works have become standards for imitation, they're not required to involve the reader in simple, unpretentious and honest emotion. This is because they don't draw freely upon emotions. Instead, they appeal almost exclusively to the intellect. But I want to go against this lack of commitment to a communication of feeling. I would rather pursue a full-blooded engagement with life.

So if a work of art isn't to be limited to a simple exercise in self-expression—especially if it should turn out to be intellectually pretentious, emotionally unengaging and obscure—then the question arises, what should it be? That I hope to answer.

* * *

To begin, I say a work of art (literary or otherwise) is an expression of an artist's deepest emotional response to everyday experience. That response is sincere because it arises from his most profound and simplest emotions. That is to say, it originates in his intuition. In this way, it becomes a work developed inside the very core of human nature. So it expresses, not the individual idiosyncrasies of a single person, but the way *any* person might respond to experience if he were attentive to genuine emotions.

To go further, we could say that an artist responds to experience in terms of a universal human feeling. This involves something more than simple emotions. It's a complex of emotions held together by an idea for the sake of establishing a mood. To illustrate what I mean by this, I will, for the sake of clarity, draw upon a work from the medium of painting.

In Rembrandt's *The Apostle Paul*, the play of golden light over the apostle's face, the shadow over his eyes and mouth, the rough beard, fibrous enough almost to be felt—all these concrete details create the visual impression that a strong man is deeply engaged in inward purposefulness and thought.

The head resting on the hand, the eyes appearing not to focus on anything, the pen held without present employment, enhance the perception that all relevant action is inward. Then, by means of the softly dramatic lighting of the whole picture, the bare furnishings of the room and the apostle's clothing are cast mostly into shadow, while his facial features and hand holding the pen are brought out into bold relief.

As a result, an overall emotional effect is created, which moves our perception of the painting into a contemplative mood much like that of the apostle himself. We feel, not only that we're observing a man who's buried in thought (the subject of the painting), but that deep thinking is important. It's a necessary activity in spiritual human beings.

This feeling then becomes the mood that governs the whole composition. It tells us how we should feel about its subject. It is also an expression of the artist's emotional response to this subject: first to the thinking apostle, then, by extension, to thinking people in general. It's a subject taken from everyday experience.

As I said, the emotion isn't simple. It is mixed and imprecise, as one might expect of several different emotions brought together by an abstract idea to express a mood. In other words, what happens here is that an idea about the subject is held in the mind of the artist. It produces a feeling in him which he directly conveys through his artistry to the viewer of the painting. The feeling is one of reverence.

The artist does this by using concrete visual details to express his own emotional response to the subject he's painting. The emotional response, being governed by his idea, usually consists of more than one elemental emotion. Reverence, in this case, would include a feeling of both awe and respect.

The idea is also general, as general as the mood into which it is converted. This general character gives it a universal quality. It is universal in that it concerns all men. It concerns the general meaning of some moral aspect of life, as it is applied to an individual experience.

I say moral because it's an idea about human behavior. It can be about an action or a motive, or both. We have in this painting the contemplative act of the apostle, which also implies a motive on his part: the conviction that what he's about to write requires careful consideration.

The mood of the painting goes even further in moving the viewer's mind into a reverential attitude toward the apostle and his motive. While looking at the painting the viewer is, at least temporarily, imbued with his own motive about life: men ought to be like the apostle. *It is in this last aspect, the mood, that every work of art takes a moral position, even if its subject should somehow be morally neutral.*

The complex nature of this general emotion, or mood, which includes feelings of awe and respect in this painting by Rembrandt, thus has its correlative in a similar complexity of the idea. In this case, the idea would be that Paul was both a good man and a thinker. We admire him for the kind of person he was and for what he accomplished. So we recognize that his goodness and thoughtfulness must've been the traits that brought about these accomplishments. Unconsciously and intuitively, we conclude that other good men in important situations like his, or perhaps in any situation, should be thinkers too. Thus our own mood of reverence toward him.

Besides this painting of the apostle, we can observe the same sort of artistic mode of expression in a literary work, a play by Sophocles.

In the Greek tragedy, *Oedipus the King,* the overall character of a man's existence is defined by the problem of his overreaching pride and his consequent, inescapable encounter with fate. On the other hand, who he is as an individual, how he expresses this pride, and the particular manner in which fate disposes of him are details that belong to his individual experience, to which this universal condition applies.

Such an abstract and universal idea as this connection between pride and fate is translated by the playwright into something that is felt. It becomes a mood: the tragic mood, full of admiration, horror and awe. This is accomplished through the magic of his talent, his ability to handle the idea in terms of specific actions in the life of a king.

Here is the point: the mood concerning pride and fate is directly expressed through the way in which the subject is handled. In other words, the subject is King Oedipus and what he does: his prideful acts lead to his downfall. The way in which they do so provides us, the viewers, with an insight into the connection between pride and fate. Due to the playwright's skill in handling the dramatic situation, that connection is felt to be a strong one, and we're left with the conviction that it's inevitable, even morally necessary.

* * *

So why do I say that modern art and literature don't always do this? I mean that they don't always give us a clear and unambiguous interpretation of life. The emphasis here is on both *interpretation* and *life*.

I'm not denying that the paintings of a brilliant innovator like Pablo Picasso can be fun. But he doesn't convey sincere feeling, because he refuses to communicate with or take his viewers seriously.

Note, for instance, a painting from his early years: *The Old Guitarist*. It's enigmatic. It's cold. So we might ask, is something in life at issue here? Does it offer us a way of looking at life? What is the interpretation of it? How is it presented to us, so that we can relate to it? In answer to these questions, all we can find in it is a wall of intellectual and emotional ambiguity.

Or try the later *Woman Weeping*. We sense in this second painting what we suppose to be the anger and alienation of the artist, perhaps in reference to the bombing of Guernica by the German Air Force at the beginning of the Spanish Civil War. This is reputed to have been of great concern to Picasso at the time of his execution of the painting. But if this is so, then why does the painting evoke in the viewer a desire to laugh? Surely Picasso knew it might have this effect. It's hard to ignore it.

This is what I mean by fun. We experience here a kind of intellectual playfulness or, maybe worse, a withdrawal from the shock of real experience. There's an apparent desire to evade, or only partially express, an honest emotional response. The savage bombing of Guernica must've been extremely unpleasant news for a Spaniard like Picasso. But is the mood of the painting candid and sincere?

No. Rather than openly express Picasso's true anguish, it seems to tell us we shouldn't feel anything at all. We should, as he does, throw up before our hearts a screen of ironic playfulness in visual image making that, at one and the same time, expresses the idea of hurt and anger, while providing an avoidance of their pain.

Compare this to the one painting I'm aware of in which Picasso seems to give us an honest glimpse into his true emotions: the painting actually called *Guernica*. It's one of the great expressions of twentieth century anguish, and it stands alone among his works in genuine emotional appeal.

Such irreverence toward common human experience and feeling, as is normally the case with Picasso, is the reason I think he's harmful in his impact on contemporary taste and on professional practice. It is an attitude, born of intellectual self-involvement, which ultimately trivializes both his and his public's responses to the deeply communicative calling of his profession.

It attracts collectors, who are wealthy dilettantes who can afford to put life's most important interests aside for the enjoyment of mere intellectual play. But it turns away thoughtful individuals who can find little nourishment, little insight and subsequent personal growth, in such insincere playfulness.

Rembrandt in *The Apostle Paul,* on the other hand, takes us into the soul of the individual portrayed, into his experience, and finally into our own experience of life through him. We're engaged in life, not disengaged from it.

But painters like Picasso are not alone. There are also writers at work today, and in the recent past, who do what he has done, though I won't enumerate them. Some are thoroughly uncommitted to a direct engagement with life, others only partially so. Either way, such performances are an expression of insincerity, of a preoccupation of the writer with himself, rather than with the world.

It's not for me. I feel compelled to insist, as I've done in this preface, that art is emphatically *not* simple self-expression, the record of one individual's personal quirks, ideas or games. It is never so irrelevant to life. It's also not an exercise in intellectual puzzle-making and puzzle solving.

It's something deeper, broader and more lasting. It reaches into those intuitions, or elemental emotions, in our nature which we share with others, not only now but in any age. And because it's a product of the desire for a true understanding of the conditions of our existence, it strongly expresses an idea, or view, of them. Therefore, it should be sincere, serious and honest in purpose.

So much is this so, that any innovation in style or technique can be no more than a necessary byproduct of the artist's interaction with his material. He may search out new forms of expression and ways of seeing, as he usually does in the best work. But these innovations are an inevitable consequence of his struggle to fit his ideas and emotional responses into words or paint. What is truly original and enduring is his view of life. Insofar as the material limits to his expression of this allow, the results should be clear.

That's what I've tried to do as a writer and would have tried to do as a painter, had I been one.

Lowell Tollefson
May 15, 2003

GOD SAVE THE QUEEN

FORTY-SEVEN STORIES

PORTRAIT OF AMERICA, VOL. II

G. Lowell Tollefson

Contents

Part One

Second Chance

Jonathan Swayze had spent the whole of his life in Lancaster, Pennsylvania, a town of sixty thousand souls surrounded by rolling green farmland. Philadelphia was sixty miles to the east, but he had been there only twice: once in his childhood to visit an ailing aunt, whom he never saw again, and once again in his early twenties to answer the call of the draft. At the armed forces testing center he had been found physically unsuitable for service, and they had classified him as 4F. That was that.

John became an electrician and belonged to the union, which meant that he generally had steady work, either in Lancaster or in one of the surrounding towns within a forty mile radius. He now lived where he had always lived: in the northwest part of town with his wife, Jean, also a lifelong resident. In their early thirties, they had no children. For reasons he never understood, Jean had lost all but a perfunctory interest in sex and had become emotionally distant around the sixth year of their marriage when she had suffered a second miscarriage. For another six or seven years he had been making excuses to himself for the endless train of sensually seditious thoughts, fantasies and erotic feelings passing through his mind. It was an exhausting process, since he would indulge no more than thought in such matters, until one day a twenty-four year old divorcee moved into the house next door. She was attractive and accompanied by a child of six, a quiet and unobtrusive boy.

What was John's surprise when he discovered that this young woman was immediately attracted to *him*? At such close and unavoidable proximity it was inevitable that they should readily strike up a warm acquaintance. They "fell in love." That is, they found an outlet for certain mutual cravings which might easily be assuaged without undue regard to complications. A torrid affair went on for six months, then abruptly began to cool, all without the knowledge of Jean or special interest of the boy. Once their passions were seen to abate, they found themselves in frequent disagreement, until finally Julie, the young woman, in apparent exasperation, expressed her opinion that they ought to see less of one another.

Two years passed. They no longer saw one another at all, and Julie had eventually taken up with another man. John had assumed it was over, swallowed both his regret and any remorse, and had gone on with his life without recourse to an unnecessary confession. Then, on an otherwise unremarkable warm summer afternoon, as he arrived home early from work, he found Julie sitting alone on his front porch. He could see she had been crying.

"What's wrong?" he asked, sitting down next to her with his feet on the front steps.

"Danny has been hurt." Her blue eyes shown through the sparkle of her tears.

"Your boy?"

"There was an accident on the school grounds."

"Is he alright?"

There was a pause. "Yes." She put her hands to her face and pushed back her short, blond hair. "He's in the house. And some stitches in his head. It just gave me a good scare."

"I can imagine." He wanted to put his arm around her, but the occasion for such gestures had long since passed. Besides, they were in full view of their neighbors. It might have occurred to him to ask why she was sitting on his front porch. It did not. He sat for several minutes in silence while she stared out across the street, lost in her own thoughts.

She sniffed, raised her head, and rubbed her hands over both arms as though she were cold—an unconscious gesture he had observed on numerous occasions in the past when she was under stress. "I think," she said, straightening her blouse and tugging at the ends of her shorts, "I think you're the only person I could turn to at a time like this." She smiled. "I'm sorry. I just needed to see you. I'm okay now." She got up, brushed the dirt off herself, and went into her house.

The crisis this simple act set up in the heart of that man was indescribable. In a moment everything had returned, all the old passion and interest. But also with it was a condition of regret such as he had not felt the first time—something like sorrow for the undeclared injury he had done to Jean. He felt he could not do it again. Besides, there was the boyfriend.

In the days that followed John discovered that the boyfriend was no longer a part of Julie's life. And Julie had unmistakably renewed her interest in him. Her smiles, her gestures, which seemed to confront him at every turn, were like a warm summer shower followed by birdsong. He could literally feel them on his body. His pulse quickened and would not settle into a normal rhythm until some time after each encounter. His blood coursed through his veins. He felt like a man once again—a man in desperate need of a woman. Accordingly, his imagination was awash with vivid and arousing images. If anything, this attraction was stronger than it had ever been before. Reconquest carries with it, not only the sweetness of old memories, but a new vindication.

On a Friday morning perhaps a week after the encounter on the porch, Jean remarked casually to her husband at breakfast before leaving for work, that he hardly seemed to be eating. That afternoon John came home early, arriving before Julie. He found the front door to her house unlocked, a habit he had chided her for during the interval of their prior romance. He went inside and sat down in the front room. When Julie came in, he stood up to greet her.

"John. I didn't expect to find you here."

"Where's Danny?"

"He's with his father for the weekend." Julie was holding a bag of groceries. "Let me put these away. I'll be right with you." She went out of the room, then returned, having opened the neck of her blouse and looking as fresh as morning dew. "What can I get you?" she asked.

"Nothing." John was still standing. "Nothing's changed," he said. He felt a trickle of cold sweat on his back. "Has it?"

"No," Julie answered softly. She came up very close to him. He could smell the scents in her hair and on her body. The soft shoulders and arms. She looked up into his face.

He stepped back. "Julie, I wanted to say, I don't think we should do this again." It irritated him that his voice had a pleading tone. He wanted to appear calm and in command of himself. The look of shock and sudden horror in her eyes put his tongue in his throat. He thought he saw a flicker of anger in her eyes. They became dull. He knew there was disappointment and pain.

Julie looked at him in silence, her eyes filling with tears.

"I'm sorry," he said. He went out the front door.

Behind him he heard her say, "I never should have let go of you the first time."

God Save The Queen

Mavis Washington came home to North Philadelphia late every day except Sunday. In winter it was usually after dark when she got there. She worked long hours and was tired at night, yet she had to fix dinner for her fifteen year old son, Steve, and do laundry. This afternoon, a Sunday, after she had had time to relax over coffee and a magazine during the morning, a knock came on the weather-worn wooden door of the old brownstone where she and her son lived.

"I got it, Ma." Steve opened the door.

"Hello, Steven. Daryl Carpenter's the name." A tall black man stuck out his right hand. It was a big hand. Steve took it.

"May I come in?"

Steve moved out of the doorway. The man had a trim mustache, high cheekbones, broad forehead. His facial expression was confident like his speech. "I believe your mother will be expecting me," he said.

Mavis came into the room. Daryl was standing just inside the door. "Steven!" she said. "You didn't offer Mr. Carpenter a seat."

"That's okay, Mavis." Daryl took a seat in the living room.

For perhaps an hour and a half Mavis and Daryl chatted, while Steve occupied himself upstairs in his bedroom. When he came back downstairs, Daryl was gone.

"Who's that?" he asked.

"A friend."

He looked at his mother. She went into the kitchen, and he followed her. Busying herself putting cups and saucers into the sink, she began filling it with warm water. Then, turning around, she said, "Steven, how many times I got to tell you to keep that fridge door shut?"

Steve got up from the table, where he'd sat down with a glass of milk, and pushed the refrigerator door shut. This was done in a manner which indicated that his trim, teenage body was heavier than the refrigerator itself and more difficult to move.

Mavis dried her hands on a dishtowel and sat down at the table across from him. "You're probably wondering …" she began.

Steve turned up his glass of milk, then set it on the table. One side of the glass was stained white. He watched the liquid run slowly into the bottom of it before looking at his mother. "I figured it out," he said.

"Figured what?" Mavis was startled. "We met on the Girard Avenue bus a few days ago, and I invited him to drop by!"

"It's okay, Ma." Steve got up, put his glass into the sink, and left the kitchen.

Mavis sat at the table for several minutes, then got up and pulled the garbage bag out of its receptacle in the cabinet under the sink. She closed the top of it with a twist-tie. Stepping outside into an alley, she set the large, white, plastic bag into a metal container, clamping a lid firmly onto the can. Though it was the middle of March, it was a cold winter day, a day when the sun was bright but not warm.

* * *

Daryl Carpenter's father was a professor of American Literature at a small liberal arts college in Buffalo, New York. As a graduate student at George Washington University he had met and married a German girl. Daryl, their only child, grew up in a black, middle class suburb of Buffalo. Though not the scholar his father was, he was encouraged to get an education and had majored in financial management and marketing at Temple University in Philadelphia. After graduation, he obtained in the same city a position in marketing research for a manufacturer of men's woolen outer garments.

Sitting alone in his apartment one Saturday morning a month and a half after his first visit to Mavis' house (he'd been over to see her a number of times since), he was enjoying a breakfast of black coffee while reading the paper, which he'd picked up on the way home from work the previous afternoon. Setting the paper down and drinking his coffee, he philosophically observed to himself, "I'm in love with her?"

* * *

At three in the afternoon he got off the Girard Avenue bus. A wind whipped up some debris on the avenue as he crossed it. When coming to see Mavis he always felt tense. Quite a few store fronts in North Philadelphia were heavily barred after hours. There was almost always trash in the street. There were broken windows in some of the buildings and boarded up doorways. In fact, one entire row house building he'd seen in a white, Ukrainian neighborhood a mile or so south of where he was now was crumbling to the ground, unused and abandoned. Both sidewalk and street here were freely and alternately used by people, parked cars, delivery vans, stray dogs and trucks. There weren't many vacant lots, so the buildings pressed in like walls on either side as sunlight filtered down from above. Moreover, perhaps due to age or the smooth cobblestone paving of some of its streets, parts of North Philadelphia always had a damp feel, no matter how dry the season.

As Daryl proceeded along the west side of Thirty-first Street, he could see a group of preteen boys playing stickball halfway down the block. They were in the middle of the road. When he got to them, one boy hit a line drive. The surprised pitcher missed catching the deflated rubber ball as it whizzed past his ear, struck a wall and lolled back into the street. The bases were so close together, in spite of home plate and second being located on opposite sidewalks, the batter traversed them all in less than half a minute. In the middle of this makeshift diamond lay the brown carcass of a dog, which had been there awhile and was stuck to the concrete like an old leather glove. Daryl passed through the game as unnoticed as an x-ray, turning a corner and arriving at Mavis' door with the concrete stoop leading up to it.

When Mavis came home several hours later, he and Steve seemed to be on good terms. They were laughing when she entered the house, and the TV set was on, but neither of them was watching it. "Daryl," she said. "I didn't expect to find you here. Is something wrong?"

"No. Steven and I were just talking."

* * *

"No dude going to come on my block what's not invited." The boy, in his mid-teens, was smoking a joint. He handed it to another boy. The home rolled paper at the unlit end of the marijuana cigarette was wrinkled and wet. The other boy took it and inhaled, closing his eyes and holding the smoke. This other boy was named Damian. He was Steve's friend.

"Them Puerto Ricans is as bad as the whites," Damian said, opening his eyes and handing the joint on to the next boy. "Worse. The honkies buy and the Puerto Ricans only want to sell."

"They all bad," a third boy chimed in, "but we the baddest of them all."

They all laughed. There were seven boys standing on the corner in front of a boarded up store. It was a warm night in May, close to two in the morning. All seven of them were sharing one joint. But there were several bottles of alcohol making the rounds: Thunderbird and port in green bottles. One boy stepped back with a bottle under the glare of a street light, turned it up and began to guzzle.

"Hey, gimme that!" Another boy stepped forward and tried to snatch the bottle away. The first boy moved further into the street, out of reach. He turned it up again, then threw it down empty, smashing glass all over the pavement. There was general laughter, and a slap fight ensued. Two boys began to sing, "God Save the Queen."

Queenie was the name of the one who had broken the bottle. He was a big fellow, seventeen years of age and known for his high spirits. He wore an afro that stood several inches high on his head and made him look even bigger. The boy with whom he was tussling was tall and thin, quick on his feet. He got one slap in after another and appeared to be a better fighter. Queenie grabbed the tall, thin one, who was called Mo, and put him in a headlock. Shouts, laughter and whistles ensued. All five of the other boys were chanting, "God save the queen."

Suddenly a second story window went up with a bang in the row house across the street. A middle-aged woman, large, heavy breasted, round faced and very angry, leaned out. "What's matter with you boys?" she shouted. "Ain't you got no homes? Git! Git out of here before I call the police!" She slammed the window down with another bang, muttering something unintelligible. The boys did not leave. But the woman's abrupt intrusion did have the effect of quieting them down. They returned to the street corner sidewalk in front of the boarded up store.

These boys called themselves the Thirty-third Street Gang. Their rivals, from the same general neighborhood, were called the Girard Avenue Gang. The two gangs were small. Each of them had about twenty members, including hangers-on. Some boys in one gang had friendships with those of the other. But they were generally divided by the leadership they coalesced around. The leader of the Thirty-third Street Gang was Queenie. Queenie was the only true flash point of enmity between the two groups of teenagers, for he was the bitter opponent of Leon, the leader of the Girard Avenue Gang.

Damian had only recently been drawn into this new circle of friends, who were not at all like Steve and thought of him as a mama's boy, often taking pleasure in deriding his character in Damian's presence. At first Damian tried to defend his friend, but this generally increased the jibes. So he finally resolved the dilemma with an habitual shrug of the shoulders, a sheepish grin, and would occasionally add a comment or two of his own. Steve knew of this and, though their friendship continued, a strain had opened up between them.

Damian never asked himself why he had become associated with the gang. There was a girl, Michelle Peters, who held his interest. She was pretty, popular with most of the kids at school, and had once been Queenie's girlfriend. She had a way of turning her head when Damian glanced at her from his locker in the school hallway, or across the gym floor at PE. He lay awake and thought about her at night, and he had seen her associated with members of the gang. He wanted to find a way to get to know her better.

* * *

Mavis didn't like the idea of marriage, having once been burnt, and Daryl had moved in with her only the week before. Living with a man, though, wasn't much different from being married. There was, for her at least, the same growing attachment, and, as with any relationship, she assumed, the same petty annoyances. She thought about these things now, as she drove south on Interstate Ninety-five with her son.

"How you get Daryl to give you this car?" Steve asked. He was sitting on the passenger side in front, lolling, enjoying the comfort of well-appointed, thickly cushioned, leather seats, with his elbow extended conspicuously out the open window. At that particular moment he would have liked to have had a cigar in his mouth to improve his prosperous image in the eyes of those who might catch sight of him.

"He didn't give it to me. He loaned it."

"Nice wheels!"

"He makes good money."

"What's he do?"

"I don't know, son. He never talks about work. Something to do with men's clothing and marketing."

"If I was going to marry somebody I'd want to know. He might decide to move to Mongolia or someplace with his company."

Mavis laughed. "I don't think so. But why not? You don't want to travel?"

"Not to no cold desert. That's where Genghis Khan come from. Now that man traveled! You suppose they use traveler's checks back then?"

Mavis laughed again. They drove for awhile, looking at the fertile green country of the northern Chesapeake. They went through the Baltimore beltway and continued along the stretch of freeway that runs between Baltimore and Washington, D.C. It was noon and, as soon as they got past the beltway, the traffic was almost bumper to bumper at sixty miles an hour. Then they hit the Washington beltway, and that was even worse. They had to go around the city, as on the rim of a spinning wheel. South of Alexandria, they entered the Virginia countryside. "Whew!" Mavis said. She took her hands off the steering wheel and flexed them. They were as stiff as pottery. Her fingers were sore. "No wonder the government's acting so crazy!"

It was Steve's turn to laugh.

From the freeway Richmond appeared to be a city made all in red brick—old brick. They passed it on the east side. It looked dingy from the road, as though the buildings were cliffs composed of dark soil and showing their reddish iron deposits. Then there was Petersburg. Virginia leveled off after this, and there was a single sign leading to Norfolk, Portsmouth, Suffolk and the Dismal Swamp. The surrounding forest was thick in pine.

Across the State line North Carolina became dark with forest and the trees seemed taller. This Southern coastal wood, filled predominately with long-leaf and loblolly pine, looked primeval in its density. Once in a long while, stuck in a clearing of the woods, after they had turned off onto Federal Route Seventy toward New Bern, they saw an occasional, weathered, old, gray boarded, frame house. One stood facing the road with its front porch collapsed completely to the ground on one side. They would catch sight of these shacks in their headlights for a fleeting moment, as it was dark now. Then there would be a wall of forest again.

Late in the evening, they pulled off onto a dirt road that led into a large clearing of fields out of sight of the highway. Near the edge of these fields, they drove up to an old farmhouse, which was not in much better condition than some of the ones they'd seen on the road. Even in the dark it was apparent that the house had not seen paint in many years. Mavis shut off the car engine and headlights as the front door of the house swung open onto the porch, flooding the wooden porch and the driveway with light. "Mavis honey!" a voice called, as a tall, gaunt, gray haired woman came out to the porch steps.

Behind Martha Washington, Mavis' mother, was her father. Sam was built small and wiry like his daughter and was several inches shorter than his wife. He stood in the doorway of the house, gnarled hand on either door jamb, a grin on his face. When he smiled with distinct pleasure, as he did now, the smile extended to his ears. Though his gums were receding, leaving gaps at the base of his teeth, he still had all of them. They were stained yellow and brown from what his wife called "his nasty habit of chewing tobacco," which he prepared himself from the product of his fields.

"Mavis, honey, you look wonderful," Martha shouted. "And how's that boy? Damned if he don't look the part of a man already. Bigger'n his ma." Martha hugged Mavis as her daughter reached the top of the porch steps. "Good to see you, honey."

Steve went past them and shook his grandfather's calloused hand. "Evening, Grandpa."

"Evening, son. Come on in. Rest yer feet awhile."

"I been riding all day."

"Then rest whatever's aching."

Steve felt his grandmother's arm pass around his waist. He turned and looked at her as she went into the farmhouse with her daughter.

Lying in one corner of the living room, as they entered tromping noisily on the loose wooden boards of the porch, was a big brown dog in the fourteenth year of its life. It lifted its head slowly, glancing sideways at them and growling out of the white corner of one eye.

"Chip, you old bear, how ya doing, boy?" Mavis said approaching him. Recognizing her, the dog's tail began to move, but with no great energy.

"He be dying on us any day now," Sam commented matter-of-factly.

"Poor old Chip," Mavis said, crouching beside the wood stove the dog was lying next to. She stood up, pulling off the sweater she'd drawn over her shoulders against the cool night air and handing it to her mother. "Where's Tom and Jodi?" she asked.

"Oh, they out somewhere, being late, as usual. At some friend's. I told them you was coming." Martha spoke with irritation as she took her daughter's sweater and put it in the closet of the hall that led off toward the bedrooms at the back of the house.

Mavis looked around. Nothing had changed. There was a chest of drawers made of oak, large and beautifully carved, though the dark brown finish was scratched and chipped, showing the blond wood beneath the varnish. It ought to have been in a bedroom but stood in a corner of the living room adjacent to the one occupied by the dog and wood stove. On top of the chest of drawers were pictures of herself, her brother and his wife Jodi. They were in large metal frames. There was also a smaller five by eight snapshot of Tom in his Marine uniform, wearing the Purple Heart he had received in Vietnam. The room was filled with furniture, most of it old, heavy and ornate. The couch, whose upholstery was worn in places, was brightly covered with a red and yellow afghan Martha had made. There were too many knick-knacks. The walls had once been papered, then painted over white, the paper buckling and coming loose in places under the many coats of paint. A smaller dining area the width, but not the length, of the living room was to the left of the front door. Beyond that the kitchen. In the dining room was a rough board table with wooden chairs, functional and heavy in construction, made by Sam. Shelves had been built along the wall of the dining area opposite the front door. These were covered with plates and kitchen utensils. The kitchen led off through a door.

Tom and Jodi came in about forty minutes after Mavis and Steve had arrived. They were in fine spirits. "Hello, Mavis," Tom said, entering the house, his eyes bright with good feeling. Jodi was behind him. They had been discussing something before opening the front door. Mavis hugged him. Steve got out of a chair and shook his left hand. Tom's right arm had been replaced by a prosthetic limb, the hand of which was a metal hook that looked like a claw. Steve glanced uncomfortably at it. "I saw firewood out there. Expecting a storm?" Tom asked, glancing toward his father who was seated in the living room.

"We can use it to smoke the hog I butchered this morning," Sam said. "Wood's green."

"That oughta bring the volunteer fire department," Tom said.

"Swamp hickory's what I got. It be good enough." Sam had a one five five millimeter shell casing his son had obtained for him and which he used for a spittoon. He unloaded into it. Martha grimaced.

"Sit down, son," Sam said. "Take a load off yer feet."

Jodi came in the door with a two year old girl in her arms and her belly large with another child. Even in her present condition, she was noticeably well-proportioned, a spirited woman with small, even teeth. Martha always thought of her daughter-in-law as a girl because she was five years younger than Tom, who was twenty-seven. "Let me help you with that child, girl," she said, going over to the door with her arms extended to receive the baby. Little Helena was asleep.

"I'm okay, Mom."

"Tsst. Don't be silly, honey. Give me that child. Old grandma got something for this baby out in the kitchen."

* * *

A few days later Martha and Mavis were alone in the house. Steve and Tom were in the fields with Sam, helping him cut the tops off the tobacco plants so they would grow fuller leaves. Jodi had driven into New Bern with Helena to shop.

"Jodi be a restless young lady," Martha said, breaking the silence of their housework. The interior of the house was cool and dark, as none of the lights were on. "Sometime it worry me with the problems Tom been having."

"What problems Tom been having, Ma?" Mavis asked, busy with a feather duster while lifting the framed photographs off the chest of drawers, then setting them back into place.

"Oh, you know ever since he come back from the war, he be in one job and out another." Martha spoke between the sweeping motions of her broom.

"Well, if they'd give him decent work. A man's got his self-respect," Mavis said.

"Ain't much to be had around here. And he ain't always needed on the farm."

"Well, I know all this anyway," Mavis said. She was dusting elsewhere in the living room now while her mother swept the dining room and kitchen floors. They had their backs to each other and were talking across the house.

"You knows what you been told," Martha said grunting. "But you ain't heard all of it. I figured you got enough to worry about raising a teenage son in the city. But I just don't know what to do. And Sam, he's no help, always saying, 'Leave them be. They be all right.'" Martha, who was in the dining room, set her broom down and pulled out a chair. She sat down on the chair and put her hands over her face.

"You okay, Ma?" Responding to the sudden silence, Mavis turned around. She came over and put a hand on her mother's shoulders.

Martha removed her hands from her face. "I'm fine." She made an effort to smile at her daughter. "I didn't want to mention this," she said. "You got enough worries of your own."

"Tom and Jodi been fighting?" Mavis asked.

"Something awful. Just the last few months. Tom's been out of work the whole time. And he done a little more drinking than he should. Said things he shouldn't."

"Like what?"

"Oh, I don't know. Just nasty words. He seem to get the idea Jodi fooling around on him."

"Do you think it's true?"

"Nah! It's just Tom's mind. Feeling down about hisself because of not having work. He told Jodi one night, right in front of me and Sam, that she only marry him out of pity, that his metal arm make her sick."

"Poor Jodi. Poor Tom."

"She was good and mad. Stormed out of the house with little Helena and didn't come back for two days. Stayed at her folks' place."

"What Tom do?"

"Nothing. Jest moped around till Jodi come back."

"But you said last night he got a good job prospect now. That's what make him and Jodi so giddy."

"Yes, praise the Lord! I pray Jesus make him settle down now and find some contentment in his heart. Jodi too."

"He's a good man, Mother. I know how he is on the inside."

"I know it too, honey. I carried him in this here body, and I sucked him from these old tits. Lord, they wouldn't keep a starving crow alive now." Martha pulled on the front of her dress as if to emphasize that what had once filled it out was now lying down on the job.

Mavis laughed. She bent over and hugged her mother in the chair.

* * *

When Mavis and Steve left for their return trip to Philadelphia at the end of two weeks, Tom had been two days on his new job.

* * *

One night, as was not at all unusual, Mavis worked an extended twelve hour shift. She started home on foot from downtown at two in the morning, since there were no buses running at that hour, and it was not until she had gone west a ways on Girard Avenue and then had begun crossing it to enter her own neighborhood, that she saw something which disturbed her. Four black youths, walking spread out single file, came down Thirty-first Street and crossed Girard, slipping out of sight into Fairmount Park on the south side of the avenue. They had gone through a clump of bushes that fronted a growth of trees. The bushes and trees being lit by a street light, the park that was beyond them was dark.

What on earth could those boys be up to? she thought. She was now just crossing Girard herself, traveling in the opposite direction, about halfway between Twenty-ninth and Thirtieth Streets. "It don't look good," she said to herself under her breath. "What they be up to?" She paused on the north side of the avenue, after reaching the corner of Thirtieth Street.

A second group made its appearance. There were four or five boys in this group. She couldn't see them clearly, for to keep herself out of the light she had retreated a ways north on Thirtieth Street. They proceeded directly up Girard, coming, as she had, west from the direction of Girard College, walking nonchalantly in a group but without talking. When they got to where the other boys had entered the park, they disappeared into it too. These events were disturbing. Though she could not make out any faces in the second group as they passed briefly within her view at the corner of Thirtieth, she thought she had recognized her son's friend Damian in the first. The second group didn't appear to have seen her, for she kept herself well into shadow, out from under any street light. But she wasn't sure about the first.

Walking back to Girard, then on to the corner of Thirty-first Street, she felt an impulse to cross over the avenue and see if she could at least hear something, but she thought better of it and continued toward home. Then she heard shouts. Realizing they were coming from the park, she returned to the corner, thinking herself crazy for doing so. No sooner had she reached it, than she heard a gunshot and saw the boys exploding out of the park like flushed quail. Four of them ran a block west, then north, and coalesced along the edge of the park, before disappearing in the vicinity of Thirty-second Street. The others fled east down Girard Avenue and darted into the neighborhood further on.

The boys no sooner out of sight, she heard a police siren. A single patrol car pulled up and stopped under the street light directly across from her and next to where the boys had originally entered the park. Two officers got out, one black and one white, the two who normally patrolled the neighborhood. They had apparently heard the shot.

"Oh my!" Mavis said, holding her hands up to her cheeks and feeling in them the warmth of her excitement. She couldn't think. She wanted to run, but her knees felt watery, so she continued watching the police. The white officer went into the bushes, the black officer following behind him, both with their pistols drawn. For a time, perhaps several minutes, she didn't hear or see anything but the squad car radio. The front doors of the car had been left open on both sides, the interior lit and the voice of a police dispatcher repeating, "Forty-nine, we have back-up on the way, ten forty your direction at zero three oh six hours. Forty-nine, this is City. Do you copy? What is your status, Forty-nine?" It was loud and clear in spite of radio static. As Mavis listened, another patrol car pulled up behind the first, its lights flashing. The avenue was definitely not a good place to be at this time, she realized. But she made no effort to leave.

Two officers got out of the second car and went into the park. A third and fourth police car, lights flashing, pulled up behind the first two. Before either could unload, one of the officers from the second car returned, said something to one of the officers in the third car, then got onto his own radio. Within several minutes an emergency medical vehicle arrived, and someone was brought out of the park on a stretcher and placed inside it. The medical vehicle left along with the third and fourth squad cars. The other four officers began to mark off the area leading into the park with yellow plastic tape.

Mavis retreated up the street. Once inside her house, she leaned for several minutes against the closed front door. "This Damian, he be my son's best friend!" she said to herself. "What is that boy up to?" She slept hard that night. When she awoke, earlier than usual and before Daryl had gotten up to go to work, she heard voices downstairs. Two boys, her son and Damian, were conversing excitedly in what they mistakenly assumed to be whispers.

"I come over soon as I could," Damian said. "My grandma thinks I come in last night around twelve. She was asleep."

"Man, you in trouble now, bro. That boy die, you gonna fry."

"I didn't do it, man. I don't never pack no heat."

"Don't matter. You was there."

"I didn't do it!" Damian insisted.

"Who did?"

"Martin. Martin Farris. You know him?"

"Sure I do. Skinny little dude. I knows him. Whew! Little Martin done it. That's crazy, man."

"You don't tell nobody I told you who it was. You hear?"

"Yeah, I hears you. These lips is sealed." Steve made a sign of zipping up his mouth.

"I make them big if you don't." Damian held up his right fist.

"Cool it, man. Hey, why he wanta go and do that anyway?"

"He crazy. Only I didn't know it. Queenie, he surprised too. We both run like hell, thinking, Why he wanta go and do that?"

"So what happen, man? Don't make no sense he just shoot him for the fun of it."

"We was having a little disagreement."

"Bout what, man?"

"Nothing. It was Leon and some of his guys. We just trying to make an agreement, so as not to cross over on each other's turf."

Mavis listened unobserved from the top of the stairs.

* * *

The night of the incident, after the shooting and panicked running, the Thirty-third Street Gang had regrouped in the vicinity of a warehouse complex between a frozen food storage facility and a six story warehouse building. These two buildings were about a block apart, and between them was a truck yard with a six foot chain link fence around it. The frozen food unit was also fenced, the chain link mesh topped with a roll of barbed wire. There was a booth for the day guard, situated outside the building and inside the fence. But no guard was posted there at night, since the workers were gone and the gate was locked.

Queenie, Mo, Martin and Damian met along the fence of the truck yard on the south side, directly in front of the cold storage unit, which was west of the yard. They were out of breath, but that didn't keep Queenie from getting in a few angry words at Martin.

"You fool, what you go and do that for?"

Martin stood before him, small, mute, big-eyed and bewildered.

"Now they, Leon and the police too, gonna be all over us like stink on shit," Queenie continued.

"Come on," Mo said. "Talk your stuff later. We gotta get outa here."

An eighteen wheeler, pulling into the yard late, had stopped in front of the guard shack inside the gate on the other side of the yard. As it pulled away and further into the yard, its big headlights swung across the lot, illuminating the fence near the boys. They ran down the street and on past the fence surrounding the frozen food facility. In the open, grassy area beyond, which was next to a railroad canyon, they found parked on a side track two freight cars that had once been loaded with sacks of flour. They climbed inside one of them. Queenie sat down on one of the remaining sacks of flour.

"You gonna get all white," Mo said, panting.

"I wish I was white," Queenie responded, panting just as heavily. "Then I'd get out of here."

All eyes turned on Martin. Queenie pulled a cigarette lighter out of his pocket, lit it, and held it up to Martin's face. "This the fool who got us into all this," he said.

"Uh huh," Mo added. "And now how you gonna get us outa this mess, boy?"

Martin tried to speak but couldn't find the words. A tear trickled down one cheek. Damian stood silently beside him, watching the expression on his face.

"Don't give me none of this crying shit," Queenie demanded. "We gotta think. You hear? We gotta think now. Think hard how we gonna get out of this."

"We could turn old Farris in ourselves," Mo said.

"And have him talking to the police about what we been doing. You crazy, man?" Queenie withdrew his lighter and clicked the metal top shut, putting out the flame.

"No," Mo said quietly.

The four boys sat or stood silently in the dark.

"We gotta think," Queenie repeated. After a long pause, he added, "We just have to keep our mouths shut. You hear? Nobody tells anybody nothing; the pigs gotta put it together themselves."

"You think the police ain't bright enough to figure it out?"

"They gotta have proof, bro."

"What about Leon?"

"Leon cool. He an asshole, but he cool. Anyway, he know better than talk. It's his balls too they gonna string up."

"Maybe," Mo said.

"No maybe, man! We just keeps our mouths shut. You hear?"

"I hears ya." Mo sounded a little surly.

Damian and Martin nodded their assent.

"Now," Queenie said in a quieter tone. "This what we do with the stuff. We stash it somewhere out here till this thing blows over, then we get rid of it quick. After that, we plays it cool, bros. For a while, at least."

"Okay," Mo said. "And we don't say nothing to anyone who wasn't there tonight."

"My lips is sealed," Damian said.

"That cat got a tongue!" Queenie said.

"He sure do," Mo said, slapping Damian on the back so hard he almost fell over.

Queenie and Mo both laughed. Martin stood among them in the dark in miserable silence. He had thrown the gun away in a brushy area near where they were now and hoped the police wouldn't find it.

* * *

Damian was in trouble. Though the police had not yet approached him for questioning, he was by implication as guilty as the rest. He felt bad about the shooting. Other than by sight, he didn't know the boy who lay now in the hospital. Still, he couldn't reverse course. Queenie will keep us out of this, he decided, and did his best to close his mind to worry and guilt.

When he left Steve's house the morning after the shooting, he went over to Queenie's. Queenie's mother sent him upstairs to find her son shaving in the bathroom. Damian watched with interest as Queenie pulled a razor through the white lather on his cheek. This manly exercise was still for him, as Queenie put it, "as futile as shaving a baby's butt." As he sat on the lid that covered the toilet seat and watched his older friend shave, Queenie's fifteen year old sister popped her head in the doorway.

"Hurry up, hamburger brains! I gotta get in here too." She glanced over at Damian and grinned.

It had occurred to Damian before, that Queenie's sister liked him. But she was far too dangerous a prospect.

"Keep your bra strap on, Boobs," Queenie retorted.

Queenie's sister went on down the hall in disgust.

This was before the police had picked up any of the boys for questioning. So there was a great deal of tension, since none of them knew what would happen next.

"You hear anything?" Damian whispered.

"Sure. The pigs pick up Martin this morning," Queenie bellowed, unintentionally stating what would soon be the truth, as he wiped the remaining shaving cream off his face with a towel. He held his razor under the hot water tap to clean it. "But I got to him first and cut out his tongue so he won't squeal on hisself."

"That was nice of you," Damian said grinning. He glanced nervously out the bathroom door.

Queenie looked over at him, his bare chest still facing the sink and mirror. "Don't worry. You know my sister won't talk. And Ma's as deef as a rattlesnake. If the floor ain't shaking, she don't hear it. Ain't nobody else in the house."

"Okay."

"Whatcha mean okay? Since when you running this show?"

"I'm not."

"Damn right. It's a good thing, or we'd be in worse than we are. I puts you one step ahead of old Martin Farris for good sense."

Damian swallowed this insult with a bland expression.

Pausing to study his response from the reflection he could see in the mirror, Queenie went on, "It's okay, bro. You good folks. But they's one or two I ain't so sure about." Though finished with shaving, Queenie was still engaged in the business of admiring the clean, manly line of his own jaw.

"Who's that?"

"I ain't saying, cause I ain't sure. You just keep your mouth shut, you hear."

"My lips is sealed."

On the way out of Queenie's house that morning, Damian heard Queenie's sister call to him from the bottom of the stairs, "Psst." When he reached the last stair, she whispered, "Michelle wanted me to give you this." She handed him a folded up piece of notebook paper.

He opened the note and read it.

Hi, Damian,

This thing is awful you guys gone and got yourselves into. I'm worried, too. Come and see me, okay? Or maybe I can meet you somewhere. Just make it soon. Tonight would be real good. I love you.

Michelle.

He looked at Queenie's sister. "Tell her to come over to my house tonight," he said. "Okay? I be waiting. After nine be good."

* * *

By the evening of the day after the shooting in Fairmount Park, the police had Martin Farris in custody. They had also questioned Queenie, Mo, Leon and several other members of both gangs. But they could not get a definitive statement out of any of them. So they released Martin without bail to the custody of his parents, pending further investigation. The boy who had been taken to the hospital was in critical but stable condition. He had been shot in the stomach and lost a lot of blood, but, thanks to the early arrival of the first squad car, had received help in time.

At nine fifteen that same night there was a faint tapping on Damian's front door. He leapt up off the couch, where he'd been sitting in the living room in the dark, and went to answer it. "Shh," he said as he pulled the door open slowly to minimize its creaking. "My grandma's asleep upstairs."

Michelle slipped inside. Damian closed the door behind her and led her into the living room. It was separated from the front door by a hallway. Inside the living room they could see better because a streetlight penetrated the room through the curtains.

They sat down on the couch, Damian holding Michelle's hands in his, his own resting on her bare knees. She was wearing a short, red and green plaid, pleated skirt and a white pullover top. She had done her hair up in corn rows. Her facial features were softly highlighted by the shadows of the muted light. "They pick up Queenie and Mo," she whispered.

"Who?"

"The police."

Fear entered Damian's eyes.

"You didn't know?"

"No. I been here all day, just lying low."

"Oh. Well, it's okay, I guess. They let them go."

"They pick up Martin Farris?"

"I don't know. He involved?"

Damian didn't answer. He leaned forward and kissed her. She put her arms around his neck and leaned back onto the seat cushions of the couch. He began kissing her about the neck and shoulders, unbuttoning her blouse.

"I'm sorry," he said afterwards. He had never made love to a girl before, and his efforts had been clumsy.

"That's all right," she said quietly, still somewhat breathless as she adjusted her skirt and rebuttoned her blouse. She had pulled her panties on crooked, and they were uncomfortable. They sat together, holding each other in the dark, Michelle resting her head on Damian's shoulder. "Your grandma sleep real good," she whispered, kissing Damian's neck.

"Yeah."

"I like you a lot, Mr. Damian," she said. "I wanted you to know that."

"Case I get locked up," he said glumly.

She didn't answer.

"Michelle," Damian said after a long pause. "I didn't do nothing. It was …" He stopped.

"Was who?" She lifted her head off his shoulder and looked at him.

"Nothing."

She lay her head back on his shoulder. "I be waiting, whatever come," she said. "I will always be your girl now."

* * *

On the evening of the second day after the shooting, a dozen youths were gathered on the street corner in front of the boarded up store. Among them were two girls: Michelle Peters and Queenie's sister. The girls were sitting on the curb in summer shorts and blouses. Behind them, and in front of them in the street as well, the boys were exhibiting their usual behavior. One youth, named Townsend, was ragging Queenie, Damian and Mo. He danced around them, throwing punches and remarks into the air. "Come on, bro," he said, addressing Queenie while shadow boxing in front of him, "let the brothers in on it. What the pigs got against you? How come they take you in?"

"I told you, we ain't talking bout none of that."

Townsend danced around Queenie, jabbing three times and giving a left hook to an unseen adversary. He hadn't looked at Queenie as he spoke, but when he came to a stop in front of Damian, he straightened up, dropped his arms and looked him directly in the face.

Damian stepped back.

"Hey, we family, ain't we?" Townsend said. "We all real tight." He paused, looking around. "Ain't we?" He danced on, shadow boxing.

"That be enough," Mo said, reaching out and grabbing Townsend's shoulder as he passed him. "You heard the man. Queenie say this matter closed."

Steve was on the corner that night. It was between eight-thirty and nine o'clock and still partially light out. He had been passing along the street, and Damian had called him over. Just as Mo put his hand on Townsend's shoulder, and as Damian watched him do so with a feeling of relief, an older model car, painted in primer red and sporting chromium wheels, came from behind the boarded up store and turned the corner in front of them. Its tires squealed. A number of the youths standing at the corner, including Townsend, Mo, Queenie and Steve, recognized the occupants of the car and scattered. But Damian didn't. Neither did the two girls have time to get up off the curb, as a youth stuck his arm out the right rear window of the car and fired a revolver. The thirty-eight caliber bullet struck Damian in the chest. He fell down beside the girls, as the car sped away.

"That Leon!" Queenie shouted as he ran. "He driving the car."

"Yeah, I seen him too," Mo said.

Michelle, crouching beside Damian, was holding his head in her lap. His chest was covered with blood, his eyes unfocused, blood trickling from a corner of his mouth. He stopped breathing. She looked at Queenie's sister, who was crouched beside her sobbing. Then she screamed. Several people from the surrounding row house buildings ran into the street. The heavy-set lady who had yelled at the boys from her upstairs window was one of the first. The police arrived several minutes later, followed by an ambulance. They found the two girls and Damian's body.

* * *

Steve tried to catch his breath and slow his racing heart.

"That you, son?" his mother asked as he entered the house.

"Yeah, Ma."

Mavis came to the top of the stairs, wrapped in a towel. "How come you're home early?" she asked. She could see Steve leaning on the closed front door. He didn't answer. "Son, there's something the matter. You tell me what," Mavis said, coming down the stairs.

"I'm fine, Ma."

"No you ain't. I can see it in your eyes."

"There's been another shooting."

"Another shooting!"

"Damian's dead."

"Dead. You were there?"

"Yeah."

"What happened?"

"I don't know exactly. We was just standing there, when suddenly this car come around the corner. Happen so fast, next thing I know Damian's on the ground."

"I need a cup of coffee," Mavis said.

* * *

At four o'clock in the morning, she went upstairs to wake Steve. He had gone to bed, but she had not. When she opened the door to his room without knocking, she found him twisted in his sheets, his blankets on the floor. No, let him get a little more sleep, she thought. She shut the door and went into her own room, wishing Daryl were with her. He was on a business trip. With the light on, she went over to her bedroom closet and pulled a big, brown, vinyl suitcase off the top shelf. There was another, smaller, canvas sided suitcase beside it, and she took that too. Setting them on the floor, she straightened her back and rubbed her forehead with her hand. "I feel hot," she said aloud. She sat down on the side of her bed and began to cry.

At five o'clock she entered Steve's room with the smaller suitcase and flicked on the light. "Get up, son," she said.

"Huh?" Steve rolled over blinking, putting an arm over his eyes to shield them from the light. "Whatcha doing, Ma?"

"I'm getting ready to pack your clothes. C'mon, get up and get dressed so's you can help me."

"What for?"

"Never mind what for. We got a bus to catch."

"A bus?" Steve sat up. As he did so, he recalled the scenes of that evening, fell back onto his bed, and let out a groan.

Mavis looked over at him. "Don't you go back to sleep, young man. I said get up!"

He sat up again, touched the floor with his feet, then stood up. He went out into the hall bathroom to urinate. While he was there he brushed his teeth, returning with the tube of toothpaste and both his and his mother's toothbrushes.

"Thank you, son." Mavis took them from him.

"What about Daryl?" he asked, still half asleep and feeling profoundly depressed.

"He'll figure it out."

"Figure out what, Ma? Is this because of me? I didn't do nothing last night, except run."

"That was enough."

Steve looked at his mother, who was filling his suitcase. "Okay," he said. He got dressed and started helping her with the packing.

They ate a cold breakfast, sitting across from each other in silence. At 6:30 a.m. they went out the front door, closing and locking it behind them. Inside the house, Mavis had left a note. It read:

Daryl honey,

We gone south. I'll explain when you get back and can call me.

Love,
Mavis

* * *

The sudden reappearance of Mavis and Steve in North Carolina came as a surprise to the older folks, as well as to Tom, who was sent into town to pick them up. As they pulled up to the house, Sam was coming through the front door with the dog in his arms. Mavis hopped out of the truck and went over to her dad, Steve behind her. Tom sat watching from the cab of the truck, resting his arms on the steering wheel.

"What's matter with old Chip?" Mavis asked.

"He getting too old to go on any further," Sam said.

Mavis noticed Sam was carrying a revolver in his overalls pocket. "You're not going to shoot him?" she asked.

Sam looked at his daughter.

"I'll go with you, Grandpa," Steve said.

"No, son," Sam said. "It's best you go with your ma."

"I can handle it," Steve said.

"Suit yerself, son."

Inside the house Mavis found her mother sitting in the living room. The room was unlit. In the shadows, the tall, gaunt woman looked tired. She started to get up as Mavis came in. "Sit down, Ma," Mavis said, coming up and bending over to hug her in the chair. "You look tired."

Martha looked up at her daughter with grieving eyes. "Tom and Jodi's gonna get divorced," she said flatly.

"Divorced!" Mavis exclaimed. She turned around, for she could hear Tom coming in the front door.

"I heared that," Tom said jovially. "That ain't what I said, Ma. I said we was gonna separate fer awhile, see how we liked it."

"Most near the same thing," Martha moaned.

"No it ain't, Ma."

"And how's I gonna see my little Helena? And the little one ain't come yet?"

"You be seeing them," Tom said. "They my children too."

"But the woman always gets the children, son. Pretty soon you don't see them no more. Then they grows up without a daddy. Or maybe a new daddy come along and beat them or hurt my little babies some way."

"We ain't getting divorced," Tom said. He walked toward the back of the house and entered one of the bedrooms.

"Might as well," Martha muttered under her breath.

A shot rang out. Mavis turned around. It came from outdoors on the other side of the tobacco curing barn. A single shot. Her heart sank. After a moment's silence, still standing beside her mother's chair, she asked, "What happened to Tom and Jodi?" Through one of the front windows of the house, as she turned toward her mother, she could see her father and son carrying the limp carcass of the dog out into a field. Steve had a shovel.

"Tom been drinking, saying nasty things," Martha said.

"Did he lose his job?"

"No."

"So why …?"

"I don't know. I don't know. Sometimes I think Jodi be too much woman for him. She makes him terrible jealous." Martha got up and went into the kitchen. She already had enough on her mind now concerning her daughter and Steve.

* * *

Tom and Steve floated carefully through longleaf pine into the swamp of Croatan National Forest. It was night. Spring peepers whistled from the surrounding brush. Fireflies flickered in the dark. Moving slowly, they poled the flat-bottom boat through shallow water with their oars. "Hold it," Tom said. Steve let his oar drift with the boat. As they approached a chorus of peepers—which meant a proximity of land—the frogs fell silent, their calls shifting to the stern of the boat. Tom and Steve were in a narrow defile of water. Now the lone croaking of a single bullfrog could be heard from in front of them. Tom lifted the spear he'd made from a slender shaft of bamboo and a kitchen knife blade. Steve picked up a large flashlight. The boat drifted closer to the bullfrog. "Now!" Tom whispered.

Steve switched on the flashlight. Just at the surface of the water, its long, black-barred legs splayed out behind it, was the bullfrog, its eyes red in the artificial light. Tom threw the spear.

* * *

On the way home in the truck, Tom asked, "You ever been fishing?"

"Sure," Steve lied.

"I mean salt water."

"No."

"I done it more'n once. Went for menhaden. We be coming in one evening, and a bunch of bluefish hit a school of them near the shore. You shoulda seen it. Bluefish was cutting and slashing and leaving pieces of them everywhere. The water was boiling. I never see such killing before."

They drove on. After some reflection Tom said, "You missed the shad run this year."

"You catch them on a line?"

"Naw. They comes in so thick in some of the smaller streams, all you gotta do is lean over with a net and scoop em up."

As they went around a bend, beyond which they couldn't see because of trees lining the road, a car suddenly appeared over the center line, coming fast with its brights on. Tom flashed his own brights and swerved. The car moved back into its lane and kept on going.

"I hears you almost got yerself shot in the big city this summer," Tom said.

"Yeah. I don't like to think about it."

"That's okay," Tom said.

They drove on for awhile, the walls of forest going with them. Tom pulled the truck up in front of the house and shut off the motor and lights. They got out of the truck, swinging the metal doors shut. They were both in good spirits as they stomped the mud off their feet on the wooden porch.

Martha opened the door, flooding them with light.

* * *

Martha sat upright in the crowded cab of the pickup truck, staring out the windshield. She was pressed between her son on one side, her daughter and Steve on the other, in a space hardly big enough for three. But this was of no immediate concern to her, for she was concentrating on what she would do to assist in the birth of her second grandchild. They turned off the highway a short distance from the house and bumped down the half mile of dirt road that led to the home of Jodi's parents, the headlamps of the truck rising, then dipping again into the potholes of the road amidst a swirl of yellow dust that was white in the light. All four of them were silent.

Tom glanced at his mother several times. Breaking the silence, he said, "Jodi's ma, she say she no good at this. She asked me to come for you."

"I know, son."

"The doctor don't make no house calls, and there don't be time to drive all the way in to no hospital."

"It's just as well," Martha said. She was still looking at the road.

* * *

Inside the house and inside Jodi's mind, there was only sweat, salt and pain. The salt was in her eyes and in some cuts at the corners of her mouth. Her lips were dry, and she felt Martha Washington's warm, rough hands on her belly. The hurt began at the small of her back, like an itch. Then it deepened and radiated up her spine, around her belly and into her thighs. Her legs spread apart, her knees, bent at a forty-five degree angle, were being held by Mavis. Martha's hands, just under her breasts, were pressing gently. She heard Martha's voice: "Push, honey! Push!" She screamed, grabbing the sheets in her fists, straining, gritting her teeth, groaning through them. The bedroom was well lit, but in the outer rooms of the house only a single light burned from the kitchen. The front door was open, and male members of the family were gathered in the living room in the cool, evening air.

* * *

Martha sat down in a straight-backed rocking chair near the front door of the house in which the delivery had just taken place. The door was still open, the night outside full of stars and occasional fireflies. A breeze picked up. Relaxing, slowly moving the chair in a rocking motion, she leaned her head back and closed her eyes. Her gaunt cheekbones standing high, nostrils flaring wide, fatigue scrolled over her face like a schoolroom map pulled down, she looked old the way a mountain is old, having experienced many weathers until its granite seams come into view.

"Martha, honey, won't you let me get you something?" an anxious, high-pitched, female voice inquired, startling her out of a doze. It was that of a woman in her early forties, short and stout, with a round, buttery smooth, naive looking face. She was Jodi's mother.

Martha opened her eyes and smiled. "I take a little of your tea if they's any on hand," she said.

"They is. They is, they is," Jodi's mother said jovially and minced off to the kitchen to fetch it. Presently she returned, handing the warm cup to Martha, hovering about her, eagerly watching her take the first sip.

"I'm fine now, thank you," Martha said tiredly. When the woman did not go away, she added, "It was a pleasure to be able to help."

"Well, it's your grandson too," Jodi's mother responded. "And I do thank you, Martha. Imagine! A grandson! Oh, I'm just so excited!" Hands quivering, held up near her cheeks, she turned around in a whirl and swayed off through the room.

Closing her eyes again, Martha thought, That woman is not going to raise my little Helena, or my grandson either.

* * *

The following morning she knew she'd had her fill. Her heart and mind were suffocating from worry over her son's irresponsibility and from her own personal concern for the future of her grandchildren. In fact, when she thought about it long and hard, she concluded she truly hated the way wounded pride, hurt feelings, or just plain old self-interest could enter a person's mind, seize an emotion, and drive him or her apart from others. But she also believed that an uncorrupted heart, carefully preserved in difficult times with faith and good will, could be greater than any divisiveness. If only such a condition could be restored in or communicated to her son and daughter-in-law, it would heal.

So she set out once again on foot alone for Jodi's parents' house. It was a good little walk, but that gave her time to put her mind in order, and her pace was quick. Energy seemed to rise from the hard packed, dirt road into the spring of her step. A humid odor of rich loam, coming from the tobacco fields of her own and neighboring farms, cleared her nostrils and charged her brain. A mockingbird, pouring out a profuse, mixed assortment of irreverently rasping calls and golden musical nuggets, lifted her heart. Her breathing was deep and calm. She believed that if Tom and Jodi could start over in a place of their own, looking after their children like the responsible parents they should be, instead of staying on the farm with her and Sam and letting them do half the work, things would work out better for them. They would get their heads on straight, find their self-respect and their love for each other, remembering what they valued most. "I aim to give them a little boost in the right direction," she said to herself.

When she arrived at the neighboring house, the energy that had been collecting in the excited vortex of her mind concentrated its determination in the small, steely fist that knocked on the door. (She was, for all her height, a small-boned woman.) There was no answer, so she opened the door and went in. She entered the house as Jodi, stiff and sore from the delivery and still in her bed clothes, was headed toward the front door, her mother behind her. Jodi looked a little bewildered at the sudden intrusion, her mother downright startled.

Martha, recognizing her own audacity, forced her heart to be still. "Now don't y'all go getting into a tizzy over what I got to say," she said.

Jodi's mother sat down on a chair.

"You too, girl. Set yerself a spell. It's you I come to see mainly."

Jodi remained standing. A whimpering sound came from her mother, who had a handkerchief out and was patting her face with it.

"I don't mean to bust in here like this," Martha said. "Looky here," she continued, addressing Jodi. "I want you coming home to my boy right now. No more of this fooling around. Why, christ, child! Ain't you got younguns to raise? Then what's all this messing around with getting separated and living apart? Like you was cats littering the fields with yer hollering and mating and no pa for the kittens. What you done you gotta own up to, girl, and live right. You was free to choose."

Jodi looked embarrassed.

"Well, wasn't ya?"

"Yes ma'am."

"Well, you pick up that boy and girl and get yer fanny on home to yer husband. Do you hear?"

Jodi's mother raised her arm with the hanky in it to lodge a protest.

"Hush!" Martha said, turning upon her.

The handkerchief returned to its former employment.

Martha left the house and returned home with the same energy. But when she got there, she collapsed in a chair in the living room. The room was dark and deserted, everyone being about their daily business. Martha said a prayer, asking the Lord to lend a strong right arm to the enterprise. Then she fell asleep in the chair.

Over at Jodi's place, the shock of Martha's visit took more time to wear off. Jodi's mother was in awe of Martha. After Martha had stormed back out the door, she said to her daughter, "We got to do something, honey."

Jodi, still facing the door, turned around and looked at her mother, who remained seated in the chair. "Do what, Ma?" she asked.

"I don't know. I'm just all a jitter over this. Look at me. Ain't I a mess now?" She held out a trembling hand. "My fingers is jest ashaking. Lord, whatever are we gonna do bout that woman barging in here like this?"

"Nothing, I spect," Jodi said reflectively, "seeing as she's already gone."

The mother looked at her daughter in consternation.

* * *

Daryl arrived at the Washingtons' house late that evening. As he only planned to stay for two days and return northward on Monday, he opened his mind to Mavis as soon as they were alone. "I talked to the police," he said, sitting down next to her on the edge of her bed. She was in her nightgown, since she hadn't been expecting him.

"They took you in?" She was alarmed.

"No. A detective came by the house one afternoon while I was there. He said he was hoping to find Steven."

"No. He never gonna do that," Mavis said, folding her arms and looking away. "He never never gonna do that."

"There's nothing to worry about." Daryl spoke softly, for he could see how upset she was. "They're not after Steven," he reasoned. "They just want to question him."

"They got no right."

"He's a witness. He was at the scene of the crime. One way or another …" He hesitated, sensing he was pressing too hard.

"No! He ain't never going north again."

"You can't hide him from them like this."

"I can't? I will, Daryl." She glanced defiantly at him as she spoke, her eyes black, wounded with emotion.

"Mavis, honey, listen to me. They're not after him. They just want to find out what he saw. Hiding him is the only thing that's going to make them think he's guilty of something."

"You didn't tell this detective where we at?" she said accusingly.

"No. But he's on the level. I'm sure of it. Turns out, he's the uncle of one of the teenagers who was there. He told me he doesn't usually work this kind of case, but he was put on it because no one is willing to talk."

"In that neighborhood, we close our mouth when the pigs come asking questions."

Daryl looked at her in surprise. "You're not acting like yourself," he said.

She started crying. "I'm scared," she said. "Scared for Steven."

"I know you are," he said, touching the back of her head with his hand. "But I promise you, Steven will be all right if he's telling the truth."

She was silent.

He wondered if he'd said too much. "He is telling the truth, isn't he?" he asked.

"I don't know," she said. "I think he is, but I don't know." She wouldn't look at him now as she spoke, but was staring determinedly at her bare knees, having nowhere else to direct her gaze.

Daryl reflected for a moment in silence, Mavis still looking away. He was beginning to better understand her motives. "I've never known him to lie," he said finally.

"You never knew him to be so scared." She looked at him. "Who know what he been through, what happen out there?"

Daryl reflected for another moment. "I think he's telling the truth," he said. He paused. "Why don't we ask him?" he continued. "Down here where he feels safe, he won't have as much reason to hold back, if there's anything he hasn't told you."

She nodded her assent.

* * *

Within a week Mavis and Steve returned North, arriving on a Saturday night in Philadelphia, where Daryl picked them up at the station downtown. He had kept in touch with Detective Peters, so early the next morning, he called him at home. Before he, Mavis and Steve had had time to finish a late breakfast, the policeman was standing on Mavis' row house stoop outside her front door.

"Who could that be on a Sunday morning?" Mavis wondered upon hearing him knock.

"I'll get it." Steve pushed back his chair and got up from the kitchen table.

"Wait, Steven. Let me get it," Daryl said.

Steve cast an inquiring glance toward his mother, who returned it with a look that said, "I don't know, son." Daryl left the room. Steve sat down. By the time Daryl returned to the kitchen, Steve was trying to compose his mind and Mavis was on her feet. "Why you didn't tell me?" she asked angrily. "You got that detective over here."

"I figured the sooner the better," Daryl said.

"You figured? Who said you got a right to figure? This my son, not yours."

"Take it easy, honey …"

"Don't you call me honey, you gonna do things like this behind my back!"

Daryl was apologetic. "I told you, everything's all right," he said. "Steven just has to answer some questions. They know he didn't do anything."

"We didn't come back to be tricked."

"It's okay, Ma." Steve had risen from his chair.

"I suppose you gotta do it," Mavis said, crossing her arms and pulling her shoulders in as if a draft had entered the room. She looked defeated, and Daryl felt a twinge of guilt. "Might as well get it over with," she added.

They went into the living room. Detective Peters, who had been sitting down, stood up to greet them. "Mrs. Washington," he said.

Mavis did not offer her hand. She sat down to wait for her son, who was following behind her.

"I'm not here to take your son in, ma'am," the detective said. "We just want to know what he saw." He was wearing a yellow polo shirt and blue jeans.

Mavis nodded but did not meet his eyes, for her own were still full of anger. When the interview was over, the detective told Steve he wanted him to go down to the precinct station to sign a statement, which Steve agreed to do the following morning.

* * *

But there was also unfinished business, as far as Steve was concerned. He felt he owed it to Damian to go see his grandmother and offer whatever condolences he could. So that Monday afternoon he walked the one block over to Damian's grandmother's house, passing through children running up and down the sidewalk, skating, jumping rope, playing stickball in the street. Knocking on the door, he waited with the noise of them behind him. There was a buzzer, but he didn't try it.

The door opened, a withered arm pulling it back. "Yes?" a cracking, tired sounding voice asked. The woman was short, bone thin and stoop-shouldered. With her other hand she held a blanket drawn over her shoulders, though it must've been eighty degrees outside. Steve could see her scalp through her white hair, and her veins stood out like cords on her hands. This woman had always seemed old to him, but she had never appeared so wasted. Not that he had ever paid much attention to her in the past. Recognizing Steve, the woman said in her cracking voice, "Come in."

He stepped inside. There was a musty odor of dust and a bittersweet smell of unwashed laundry in the house. He had never liked coming there. But now he noticed all the curtains and shades were drawn, and it was dark. "I come to tell you how sorry I am that …"

"You don't need to go on, son," Mrs. Jones said. "It don't matter now."

Steve fell silent.

"Would you care to have a seat?"

"No, ma'am. I don't want to be no bother."

The old woman whistled through her nose some way, as if breathing was difficult. The darkness, noisy breathing and silence against the roaring background of children outside began to build a sense of horror in Steve. As often as he had, in fact, been there in spite of his dislike for the place, he'd never seen it like this. The old woman seemed weaker, smaller, poorer, as if some part of her life had drained out of her the moment Damian had been shot. "I be going, ma'am," he said after a pause.

"Yes, you best be," the woman assented. "It don't be no good for young folks anymore," she said wistfully, as he stepped outside the door. "God bless ye, boy." She shut the door, leaving him standing on the cracked concrete stoop, facing the weathered wood of the door. He turned around and looked at the activity going on all about him. Then he walked home slowly, considering the nature of his visit. He hadn't accomplished anything, so far as he could see. He might've done better had he been a different person. But at least he'd tried. Proceeding in this manner, with his head down observing the progress of his feet, he didn't at first notice two people standing on the street corner as he rounded it. When he glanced up and saw that one of them was Queenie, his muscles tensed.

"Hey schoolboy," Queenie said. He was smiling. "Wa's up, bro?"

"Hey," Steve said.

"Jes hey, man? Ain't you got no more'n that to say? Looky here, I got my girl back now that old Damian's gone."

Steve had already noticed that Michelle Peters was the other person. She seemed transformed, changed from the pert personality he thought he remembered to a sad, dull-eyed, unkempt figure. He wondered if she was on something. Queenie had his arm around her, his big hand in the back pocket of her Levi shorts. "I see that," Steve answered. He put no emotion into his voice, and he couldn't take his eyes off the girl.

Queenie observed him with curiosity. He glanced from Steve's face to Michelle, then looked back at Steve. "You like what you see, huh?" he said. "You want in on a piece of the action too. She goooood!" he drawled. "Uh huh, and that old boy Damian, he know bout it too. He got his share the night before …"

"Shut up, man!" Steve shouted. "Shut your stupid mouth!"

Queenie involuntarily moved back one step. But to cover his retreat, he said sneeringly, "Whatcha gonna do bout it, man? You gonna kick my ass? Ha, ha, ha. Schoolboy gonna kick Queenie's ass. Whatcha think of that, Shel honey? Think he can do it?" He did not take his arm from around Michelle's waist.

Michelle didn't answer. She looked impassively at Steve.

Queenie measured Steve, calculating the threat to himself. He was certain Steve couldn't take him. But there was always a possibility he might be wrong. "Cool it, bro," he said. "No use in getting excited. I'm sorry bout what happen to Damian too."

No you ain't, Steve thought.

"Hey, bro," Queenie went on in his new, placating tone of voice, "whatcha tell that cop? Michelle here say you been to see her uncle."

"Nothing," Steve said.

"Nothing? Ain't no nothing in a mess of words. Whatcha write down for the man, bro? Gotta be something."

"I just told him what I seen," Steve said. "Bout Leon being in the car what shot Damian. Thas all."

"That goooood," Queenie crooned. "We's all in the clear now, cept Martin and Leon hisself and the kid that was with him. The one that done the shooting."

Steve saw a flicker of pain in Michelle's dull eyes. He turned and walked away, going up the cross street to the corner that turned off toward his house.

"Hey, bro," Queenie called after him, "ain't no good thinking bout it. The past is dead. Dead and buried, bro."

Steve kept on walking.

The Natural World

Nature is cruel, he thought. A biologist for the Idaho State Fish and Game Department, he was on assignment in a dry, rocky canyon an hour to the northeast of the city of Boise. A small stream trickled through the canyon, giving life to the deciduous trees along its banks, silver and green, dusty in the heat. Twenty to fifty yards on either side were stone escarpments sprouting sagebrush with gnarled, woody stems, gray-green saltbush, pale green rabbitbrush, locoweed, and early flowering buckwheat. Dennis Turner was a specialist in raptors. He was upset with John Myers, the thirty year old assistant who worked with his wife. He had seen them together on several occasions when he had come to the lab, which was in the hospital basement, to pick his wife up for lunch.

A male harrier was returning up the canyon toward him as he sat on the ground, leaning against a big boulder. Through his binoculars he could see the white patch at the base of its tail as it glided overhead, rocking from side to side on upturned wings. As the hawk made its pass, low against the rock walls, it reversed course, its gray back feathers becoming visible in the sun, and flew down the canyon in the direction of the stream flow. On the hunt, it had been far afield but had found nothing in the open desert, the sun having already forced much of the small animal life underground. It was now searching the shaded stream banks where several colonies of ground squirrels were active.

Dennis was not more than eighty yards from a loosely constructed nest, where he knew the brown female was brooding a clutch of four eggs. He laid his binoculars on the granite boulder he was leaning against to wipe his forehead with his arm. The late morning sun was intense. As luck would have it, the male made its dive, vanishing into a clump of bushes. In less than a minute, it rose again into the air, gripping a small, limp body in its talons. Its wings working like oars, it shot overhead. Up the canyon, the female rose into the air to meet her mate. He dropped the squirrel from the top of the walls and, coming up from underneath, she caught it in her talons and returned to her nest. The male went on up the canyon.

In an hour, the sun directly overhead, the female flew off in the direction the male had gone. Dennis got up and went to the nest, which was near the north rock wall, partially shaded from the noon sun. It was in a patch of reeds and grass along the edge of a marsh created by the stream. He stepped into the water. There was one hatchling. Little was left of the ground squirrel. The chick was at least a few hours old. Dragonflies were darting about in the warm sunshine. Climbing the canyon wall through a breach, he went to his jeep. Inside the jeep in a Styrofoam cooler were sandwiches his wife Jeanine had made. There was also fresh water in a green, metal thermos.

He sat in the jeep which was covered with a vinyl top, his socks and hiking boots set out on the hood, drying in the sun. Mopping the sweat off his forehead, he drank from the thermos. The ice water was cold against his teeth and made the roots ache. As he ate his sandwich, he wrote in a notebook. In the back of his jeep in another Styrofoam container was a collection of small bones and bird droppings he would take back to Boise at nightfall for analysis. It was very hot now. He wiped his forehead and laid his notebook and pencil in the passenger seat. An odor of sage in the dry heat made him drowsy. He leaned back in his seat and closed his eyes.

Jeanine would be at lunch, probably in the cafeteria, most likely with John, since he wasn't coming in to be with her today. John wasn't much to look at, he thought, but the idea of him made him angry. Getting out of his jeep to retrieve his socks and boots, he put them on and started walking toward the canyon.

* * *

Jeanine Turner, a hospital lab technician with a Masters degree in pharmacology, was five eight, almost her husband's height, slender and long-limbed with an attractive body. She had chestnut colored hair which set off a pale complexion and which she kept in a ponytail at work. The ponytail made her look sixteen.

"What is it about men?" she was saying coyly, sitting in the hospital cafeteria with her assistant. A bare room in its seating arrangements, the dining area was unornamented and cool, reminiscent in mood of the smell of alcohol in some of the hospital hallways. The chairs around the tables were made of a dull orange plastic. "They've always got to be hitting something, pursuing it, sticking a hook in its mouth, or shooting it." There was a smile on her lips and in her deceptively innocent, blue eyes. She was playfully taunting her male companion in a way he and others had come to accept as being usual with her.

John Myers took a drink of his orange juice. It might as well have been carrot juice. He was careful and consistent about such things, believing in the importance of good nutritional habits. He looked at Jeanine as he set the glass down. He could never look at her without observing her breasts. "I don't know. I'm not like that," he said. He was a thin man with a patchy beard and black eyes that seemed to be looking out of a corner, waiting for something.

Jeanine looked at him incredulously. "My husband says men have to be that way. It's what makes them able to handle women."

"I don't know what that's supposed to mean," he said, glancing uncomfortably across the bare room. She had a way of reeling him in like a fish, then mentioning her husband when he least wanted to hear of him. He knew she deployed him like a buoy to make her husband jealous. Putting a fork load of salad greens into his mouth, he pointed a finger at her. "It's women like you," he said with a mouth full of food, "that men have to treat like a quarry."

Jeanine swung her ponytail like a proud young mare as she got up. "I'm going back to work," she said importantly. She left with a smile. John finished his meal and followed her.

During the afternoon, after loading several vials of solution into a stainless steel centrifuge, Jeanine turned around, her hip brushing John's leg. "John," she said sweetly, "could you get me a few more of these little glass jars. I'm going to need them after we do the separation."

He went to gather several from under a counter, then brought them back. The room was lit by white florescent bulbs. There were numerous counters and cabinets, all very clean. Today, as was often the case, only the two of them were in the lab.

She took the jars from him, her fingers softly brushing his. They were long, manicured fingers. "You know," she said, turning to place the vials on the counter, "I've been thinking about it. You men really are all alike."

"If you mean Dennis, I'm not sitting out in the desert roasting my brains."

"I mean you and Dennis, all men, have a lot in common. You'll do anything to catch a woman in your talons."

"What about you? You seem pretty cagey with men."

"What did *I* do?" she asked. She was busy and spoke without looking over her shoulder. The centrifuge had stopped, and she was filling the new vials, wearing thin latex gloves on her hands.

"Oh nothing," John said. He was standing close behind her right arm, his breath almost in her hair.

* * *

Dennis had spent the rest of the day in the canyon. His arms and face were always red toward evening, but browned quickly. The back of his neck hurt and almost never seemed to heal from sunburn. At five o'clock a flock of magpies had shown up, converting the desert silence into the black and white feathered din of a dance hall. The sun was already throwing shadows across the canyon, and, after settling down, the magpies, flying off one by one, moved further downstream for their nightly roost, well away from the nesting harriers. The air began to cool. A breeze picked up. The female harrier was on her nest, the male continuing to feed her and the chick. At a little after seven, Dennis packed his gear into his jeep and drove off through the desert, the sun lying low on the horizon.

Jeanine would have waited until six or six-thirty to be picked up, depending upon her mood and the availability of a late ride. She didn't drive a car. If he hadn't arrived by then, she would get a lift home from one of the hospital staff. John would usually have left by five forty-five, though not always. If he was there, he would most likely have taken her home.

Dennis thought about this as he drove back to Boise through flat, dry country and an endless horizon to the south and east. There was now a dark curtain of approaching night against the mountains, the sun having gone out of sight. The sky was blue, though darkened and without any yellow. He wished John would go away somewhere. But if he did, there would be another John. The world seemed to be full of them.

A Stillness on Mercer Island

It had occurred in the rush hour traffic of morning. When Melanie Garrett had attempted to make a right turn at Third Avenue as she was heading downhill on Union Street, an oncoming car had hit her, crushing in her left fender and breaking the headlamp. The accident had been too upsetting for her to acknowledge any degree of personal culpability at the time. But now on the afternoon of the following day, she was able to concede that at least some share of the blame was hers. She should have been more careful, more alert for fast oncoming cars.

A soft-spoken, retired vice-president for an insurance firm in Hartford, Connecticut, she was known as a modest, thoughtful woman of formal bearing and considerate ways. Although occasionally gregarious, she spent so many hours alone relaxing on long walks through nature, that she and her husband, a physician, had made a decision to settle for their final years in a heavily wooded suburb, which was on an island surrounded by a lake just east of Seattle. They were both in their mid sixties.

She was tall and straight of carriage. She never stooped when she walked. Her neatly brushed red-auburn hair was cut short and carefully tinted to conceal any sign of whitening. Her clothing fit like a glove. Conservative in her tastes, she was rarely seen out of anything the skirt of which could not be hemmed at the knees, except when she wore long pants to work in her garden. Remarkably, even painfully, thin, she was nevertheless attractive for her years. Deeply freckled, she might once have sported the playful temper of a pixie were she not invariably elegant and quiet.

Working in her garden on the afternoon in question, she could not ignore the fact that she felt ill at ease, for the tension of the accident had remained with her. As she attempted to put it out of her thoughts and enjoy the pleasure of kneeling in damp soil, she began suddenly to experience chest pain, shortness of breath, dizziness and disorientation. Getting to her feet, she struggled over to her back porch, climbed up onto it, and lay down on the swing. Knowing she should go inside to call for help, she could not. So she remained nearly motionless outdoors in a cool afternoon breeze, suffering considerable pain. Twenty minutes later the symptoms eased, and she picked herself up and went into the house. She was weak, but began to feel it was over.

It was not the first time she had experienced symptoms of heart trouble. There had been something a month before. In fact, several times in the last few months. Tightness, pain in the upper chest or shoulder, but not like today. She hadn't mentioned it to her husband in the past, but this evening she did.

"Melanie, you must go in for tests!" he responded in alarm.

She did so the following morning, undergoing an ECG and blood analysis, along with other tests, but they all came up negative. Several weeks, then months passed without another onset of pain, dizziness or disorientation: not even a mild suggestion of these symptoms. So she told herself she was fundamentally healthy, believed it, and began to grow in renewed confidence. Enjoying her morning volunteer work as a docent at the Seattle Art Museum, she had made a new friend since her anomalous heart attack (she allowed herself to think of it only as something unlikely to recur). Her friend was another docent, whom she often went to lunch with at the end of their half day of work.

Ebullient and earthy, burly in manner and build, Darlene was a different sort of person. She was, above all, forthright and abrupt.

"I think Mr. Calder was just a boy flying kites," she remarked one afternoon in response to Melanie's observations on the subject. Her voice, which in confined spaces sounded like the trumpeting of a buffalo or an elephant, bellowed through the room. They were in a small café on Third Avenue. Melanie had seen Calder's work at the National Museum in Washington, D.C. "Now Mr. Pollack," Darlene continued, "went after his canvas like a bull." She snorted with pleasure. "Turn the cape and the pot of paint is spilled in a new and different direction."

Melanie laughed—as much at her friend's manner as at her humor, though she would have been loath to admit it to her. The two women were in a pleasant mood. "You know," she observed seriously, "my husband thinks all sculptors and painters are people who never grew up. He's of the opinion they should put away their chisels, blowtorches and crayons and do some useful work."

"Hmm," Darlene said. "And what would that be? I have it. I don't know about the sculptors, but the painters could paint houses."

Melanie smiled. "With crayons?"

"Well, no." Darlene thought, her head canted, a finger pressed into a heavy cheek. "Perhaps they could specialize in doing the trim."

Melanie laughed.

"That's what my husband calls what he does before he mounts," Darlene added obscenely, leaning forward and speaking in an audible whisper. "Doing the trim!" She snorted, bursting into laughter and falling back in her chair.

Melanie colored. She could not think of a response, and she hoped Darlene's whisper had not been as loud as it sounded.

Darlene reacted upon observing her friend's embarrassment. "I'm sorry," she said. "I do get a little carried away sometimes, don't I?"

"Yes you do," Melanie said. There were not many people in the restaurant.

* * *

Melanie and Dick had Darlene and her husband, Tom, over for a barbecue on a warm summer evening in June. The Goldsmiths arrived at four in the afternoon.

"Hello, I'm Dick," Dick said, walking from the barbecue grill on his back patio to the rail on the raised wooden porch attached to his house. He extended his hand.

Tom, who was standing on the porch, leaned over the rail and shook it. "I'm Tom," he responded. "It's a beautiful house."

"*We* like it," Dick said. "Come on down. I'll pour you a drink. You do drink?"

"Yes, of course. That'll be fine," Tom said, descending the porch steps and following Dick to the grill, looking up and all around as he did so. "Beautiful trees." He was amazed. The entire house, except the front, and including the stone patio below the porch, was surrounded by forest. The uneven hillside beyond the patio rose abruptly with its mantle of trees. Since no other houses could be seen from this vantage point, there was an ambiance of privacy and wildness, a smell of evergreen needles and lake air.

Dick reached toward a table beside the grill. Upon it were plates, napkins, eating utensils, water tumblers, two cut glass pitchers and a bottle of vodka. Everything that could be used to transfer plant and animal remains and the byproducts of yeast to their final destination in human consumption. One pitcher was filled with iced orange juice, the other with tomato juice. The pitcher of orange juice sweated. He poured from it into a tumbler almost one quarter filled with vodka—a stiff drink. Handing it to Tom, he said with a grin, "I should've asked. You're not allergic to orange juice, are you?"

"No. Certainly not," Tom said, taking the glass, an amused smile on his lips. He had noticed the generous helping of vodka he was being offered. A mild mannered man, he was lacking in confident assertiveness, but not without an observing eye and a crafty sense of human proportions. Melanie, who'd just met him in the house, had already formed a liking for him.

Dick turned several steaks over on the grill, their juice steaming on the red coals and filling the air with the smell of roasting meat. He was dressed in a neatly pressed polo shirt, white cotton shorts and white sneakers. A tall, slender, large-boned man with thick white hair, he looked athletic and, in his way, as regal as his wife. Tom, on the other hand, might've passed for a pleasantly ordinary person anywhere on the planet. But standing next to Dick, he appeared somewhat less than ordinary. In a mildly bemused sort of way, he felt the disadvantage.

"You've never been out here before," Dick commented.

"No, can't say as I have. It's beautiful. With the blue lake all around."

Dick glanced at the dense stand of trees that screened the house from the road, as well as the trees across it and the lake beyond, but he didn't comment upon it. "We like it," he said. He had a habit of repeating himself. "What do you do, Tom?"

"Nothing, you could say," Tom responded with a laugh. There was an embarrassed silence. "I'm a free lance writer, since retiring from a paper back east."

"You write a column?"

"No. Not exactly. I worked the copy desk for years. I write a little commentary now and then."

"Oh. I see," Dick said. He did not see. "A newspaper man."

"Yes."

"And a very good one, Darlene tells me," Melanie said from the porch, the screen door to the house closing behind her. She was holding a glass similar in appearance to Tom's, but there was little vodka in it.

* * *

It was evening. The four people were sitting on the porch, the darkened house becoming a shadowy presence behind them as daylight faded. Relaxed conversation passed between them amid raucous cries from Steller's jays hopping about the porch rail and patio deck. As dusk thickened, loons could be heard calling from the lake. Afterward, in the impenetrable blackness and hush of a night away from city lights, raccoons chirred and growled near the far end of the patio.

"I hope they're not ruining my flowers," Melanie exclaimed. Stretched out on a lounge chair, she could smell the evergreen needles in the damp lake air and felt languorous with the pleasure of it.

Darlene and Dick fell to argumentatively discussing the pros and cons of a democratic society that allowed disparities in wealth to arise among its social classes. It was a subject they might have applied to themselves. Melanie and Tom listened for awhile, then sat quietly in the night air, their thoughts drifting, remarking occasionally to one another about the natural beauty of the world around them, which they could hear and smell in the darkness, but not see.

* * *

Months passed. As winter rains came and darkened the lakeside properties of Mercer Island, the Garretts and Goldsmiths continued visiting one another often, alternating between the Goldsmiths' home in the working- and lower-middle-class Ballard area of Seattle and that of the Garretts. Spring arrived, looking much like winter, but less harsh. Then June, gloriously. When the cloud cover withdrew to reveal clear skies, the evergreen forests of Western Washington stood over the mountain ridges and blue waters like the clean white teeth of a girl. Flocks of goldfinches passed through the warm, yellow day, and rufous-sided towhees hid calling from the thick underbrush of deep, musty woods.

There was a place at one end of Mercer Island, a good distance from Melanie's home, perhaps two miles, that she would go to on summer afternoons. The walk, though long, was pleasant. The winding road was lined with trees, expensive homes like her own tucked back into the forest along it. She loved wandering meditatively about and imagining the lives lived in those houses. But she cared even more for the natural environment that was respected and preserved on the island.

At her chosen spot on its northern tip, beyond any houses, was a grassy clearing surrounded on all but its southern end by the lake. It was a peninsula filled with sunlight. Someone occasionally mowed the grass, not allowing it to get more than a foot tall, but nothing else was touched. On the west side of the clearing was an inlet from the lake, the water dark with algae and crowded with reeds, cattails and yellow daffodils, which were busily chirped and sung over by blackbirds. On the east was an abandoned, two story, red brick school building, which had been a reformatory. Inside it, in the shadows between shafts of light that entered through cobwebbed and broken windows, school papers could be seen scattered over damp floors. Outside, there were breezes in sunlight and unpruned red roses gone wild, their long canes moving in the wind against a brick wall of the building.

As Melanie walked away one afternoon, after having looked through one of the school windows, she tried to imagine what had become of the children. Just then she spotted a pair of pheasant cocks not far in front of her, for she had stopped and was standing still, turned about toward the school while caught up in her reverie. Each one was facing the other, its purplish-green neck extended, wings lowered and feathers ruffled for combat. Recognizing her sudden good fortune, she stood even more quietly, her heartbeat increasing. They were between her and the schoolhouse, which was now perhaps forty yards away. A fresh breeze off the lake touched her legs beneath her cotton dress. The cocks lunged at one another a few times in an angry flurry of flapping wings and thrusting spurs, then noticed her and darted off into the brush.

* * *

A week later during another outdoor gathering at her home, she tried in the descending darkness to describe to Tom what she'd seen, for they had become friends.

He listened quietly, the lake and forest air about him cool and pleasant in the enveloping night.

"Tom," Dick said, abruptly turning toward him and interrupting Melanie's soft discourse, "what say you and I go into the house and shoot some pool?"

They all went in, descending a flight of stairs to the game room. A standard pool table occupied one end of it, table tennis and shuffleboard the other. A dozen bottles of wine were stored in a rack along one wall, the rack having been placed under an awning to shade the bottles from direct light. Tom and Dick played several games, then the women joined them and they played in pairs. The room was well lit from the center of the ceiling.

"You're actually quite good," Darlene observed of her friend.

Melanie colored, her densely freckled features turning crimson. "I get lots of practice," she said. "Dick loves this game."

"You're not embarrassed?" Darlene responded with a snort. "Why, if I could play like that, I'd be hustling the young men."

Silence.

"Well, not like that! I mean I'd be wanting to play them for their money." She laughed.

"You've already got mine," Tom said.

They were all in a light mood. When they had tired of the game and returned talking and laughing upstairs, Melanie wandered outside onto the porch, followed by Tom. Dick and Darlene were momentarily delayed at the wet bar in the living room, pouring drinks for the four of them and humorously discussing the advantages that might be open to a demure pool hustler of Melanie's description. "Nobody in the pool hall would believe it," Darlene said. "She'd rake in the money. You could double your income!" she called out after her friend.

"I don't think so," Melanie shouted back. "They seem to enjoy this," she observed in a quieter voice, looking over the porch rail at the darkened patio. There was enough light from the house to softly illuminate the porch.

"My wife has extra muscles in her tongue," Tom observed, putting his hands on the rail and leaning against it.

"That's not very nice."

He smiled, glancing at Melanie. "It's hard keeping up with her," he said.

Observing the man, his features outlined by the light from the house and appearing intimately near in the semi-dark, Melanie felt something warm fill her chest and abdomen. It was followed by a flood of irritation. For Pete's sake, am I covetous of another woman's husband now? she thought. She knew her discomfort probably showed in the subdued light.

Tom continued almost in a whisper. "You would think people our age would only be interested in sitting by a fireside," he said.

Melanie stared fixedly into the dark. They were standing close enough to feel each other's physical presence. "I only wish it were true," she said. "We'd be better off." She turned away from the porch rail. "Let's go in," she added, walking toward the door. She met Darlene and Dick as they were coming out with the drinks.

* * *

On another stroll alone through the park at the end of Mercer Island, she thought about Tom, Darlene, Dick, herself and life in general. It gets harder through the years, she ruminated. We become suspicious, covetous and grasping with age and experience, maybe even a little desperate. So much seems to be missing, and we want what we shouldn't have.

Early one evening not long after, Dick and Darlene stepped out onto the porch and descended to the patio to retrieve a dozen baked potatoes that were wrapped in foil and set hissing amid the hot coals of the grill. The two of them, both talkative and opinionated, had become agreeable sparring partners. As they took turns, each presenting his or her side of an argument while fishing the baking spuds from their fiery bed, Dick holding a large earthenware platter to place them on, Tom, sitting in the living room not far from Melanie, quietly observed with a humorous expression on his face, "I think I've fallen in love with you."

He spoke so softly, Melanie wasn't sure of what she'd heard. Startled, she turned red and was at a loss for words. She blurted out, "I think I may be dying."

"Dying!" Tom sat forward in his chair.

"I've already suffered one heart attack. We had some tests done. They came out negative."

"I don't understand."

"I don't either." She got up, glanced awkwardly at him, then left to get something from the kitchen, where she could think and settle the motion of her heart.

When Dick and Darlene reentered the room, Tom was ashen faced.

In the days immediately following, Melanie held consultation with her conscience over the shock she'd given him. It was not that she was ashamed of her feelings. She wasn't sure she could oppose his.

Late one night, as she was preparing for bed several weeks later, she turned to Dick and said, "You know, honey, if I were to go … suddenly, I think I would like to have my ashes spread over this lake, or in some wild place."

Dick sat up. He had been lying in bed reading a book. He looked at his wife, who had sat down next to him in her summer gown. He observed her thin legs. Her arms, also very frail, most visibly at the wrists and along the bones of her hands, were wrinkled with age, especially at the elbows. Her face and neck were deeply lined. But her clear, hazel-green eyes were as full of expression and vitality as they had been the day they met, and there was something youthful in the erect way she held herself. "What makes you think you're going so suddenly?" he asked. "I thought we'd cleared that up."

"Oh, I was just saying what if."

He lay back on his pillow. "We have a good plot in the cemetery," he said. "It's been arranged. To keep the kids from having to worry about it. Remember?"

"Yes. But it doesn't matter to them where we're buried. You could hold my ashes. When we're both gone, Richard would put them where we wanted."

Dick thought about it. What would happen on either side of the grave after he or Melanie died was not something he was accustomed to expending much thought upon. "All right." He hesitated, arranging his priorities and measuring them against those of his wife. "All right. If that's what you want, I'll sell the plot back to the cemetery," he said and returned to his book, a paperback mystery.

Several months later, she began to experience pain again, usually for only a few moments above her heart or in her left shoulder. It was not severe, but it was unmistakable. She told Dick and went in for more tests. The heart specialist Dick recommended thought he detected an arrhythmia but wasn't certain. More testing produced inconclusive results, so he suggested a regimen of quiet, of minimal excitement. "That's the best I can do for now," he said. "But we should pay some heed to your advanced years."

Melanie could not have agreed more, though the phrase, "advanced years," was irritating. She loved her peaceful walks on the island, which were her way of remaining quiet and expressing minimal excitement. They were especially restful now in the fall when the leaves of the vine maples, spreading on low branches through the forest, were turning bright orange and red. They gave her time to think and simply enjoy. She did not want to pass from the earth as an unreflective person.

Her friendly relationship with Tom, one which previously had consisted of shared observations and occasional happy repartee, had cooled on the surface since the night she had shocked him with her abrupt news. He was irritated at her refusal to confront the tenor of his feelings and, frankly, upset and confused at the realization that this growing object of his affections might soon be leaving him. As a result, his conversations with her were confined to a more general plane whenever the two couples got together.

Dick had a boat which he kept at a small marina on the island. It was a light craft with a lower half deck that accommodated four people. Though not a fisherman, he was fond of the water and often went out alone in the boat. On those rarer occasions when the two couples went together, he never tired of sharing his knowledge of nautical lore. Tom, who couldn't swim, was thrilled at the opportunity for being on the lake.

They were out on what looked to be a pleasantly sunny afternoon in late fall when an unobserved change in the weather caught them far from shore and soaked them. By the time they were safely into dock, they were bone cold. Thirty-five mile per hour gusts had blown the rain in sheets onto the lower deck, and the water had been rough enough to make it a challenge to tie up at dock. They escaped to their car beneath drenched blankets. Once under cover, Darlene burst into laughter. They were all in high spirits.

"Wow," she exclaimed, "that was some gale!"

"*Is* a gale," Dick corrected, emphasizing his displeasure with it as he maneuvered his car through torrents of rain.

Tom, who was sitting in the back with his wife, began to shiver. "Can't seem to get warm," he complained.

Darlene started rubbing his shoulders. "I think he's getting chilled!" she said alarmed.

Dick hurriedly drove home, where they dried Tom off and got him into warm clothes. A bottle of sherry warmed them all and filled the evening with a pleasant nostalgia of the day's events.

Tom did develop a cold which was suppressed with antibiotics. In November, now well into the winter rains with overcast skies, cold winds and darkness, Melanie intermittently took to her bed. Weak and experiencing swelling in her lower extremities, she was suffering from heart failure. Physicians, including her husband, were disturbed that they had not foreseen it. She was given diuretics to lower the fluid levels in her body.

Tom threw off any pretense of distance and visited often, sometimes without Darlene, prompting Dick to refer to him jokingly as Melanie's second husband. Becoming permanently bedridden after several months, she remained calm, even at peace, in her worsening condition, bantering with Tom and Darlene, philosophizing, and making humorous comments in a tired voice, until her heart, worn out with the effort of hanging on, stopped beating altogether.

Second Honeymoon

At the lower elevations of the Sangre De Christo Range it had rained off and on all night until the ground was soaked and the evergreen needles of the ponderosas were left motionless and dripping in the cool, damp air. Even the coyotes were silent. Early in the morning Nolan Webber had quietly started the engine of his pickup truck and driven alone for several miles along the winding paved road following the Pecos River as it descended through its rocky canyon toward the town of Glorieta. Stopping a few miles above the town, he had caught four large rainbow trout in less than two hours. The rain had been falling lightly beneath a gray sky then, and the fish were active, as he had thought they would be, rising easily to his bait. But when the rain stopped as the sun broke through the clouds, the fishing became more difficult, the water swelling through the rocks, snagging his line in several places where the river was rushing and deep amid the protruding boulders. So he decided to gather up his fish, fishing rod and tackle box and return to camp.

"Breakfast," he shouted, grinning proudly as he clambered out of his truck back at the campsite. He was holding the fish up in front of him. They were hanging from a single, heavy, blue nylon cord attached to leaders.

"I wondered where you were," the young woman he was addressing said without looking over her shoulder. She had her back to him and was stretching outside the tent, her brown hair loose upon her shoulders. She had apparently just gotten up. She spoke as though unconcerned, but she had been upset moments before. "You could've let me know," she added, turning around, her dark brown eyes boldly embracing him. "Why didn't you?"

"I didn't want to wake you," he said.

"Well, there was a bear in the camp. *He* didn't mind getting me up."

"A bear!" He suddenly felt guilty, his mouth dropping as he lowered the string of fish.

Mollified by his reaction, she conceded, "I didn't actually see him. Just heard the noise of him getting into our food, then saw the evidence." She pointed to a large green canvas bag with a drawstring top. It was open. Cans of vegetables, meat and fruit, a loaf of bread torn out of its cellophane wrapper, and other items, were scattered on the ground. A sack of fresh jerky was strewn about.

"I told you to hang that outside on a tree," he said irritably, seizing an opportunity for feeling righteous.

"I thought *you* did it."

"Doesn't matter," he mumbled, aware that he could only keep his psychological advantage if it was left undisputed. He began gathering the food. "He didn't get much. Just a little jerky, it looks like. You must've scared him off."

"He darn near scared me off."

"I thought you didn't see him." He looked at her critically.

"Well, not much of him." She blushed. "Just his big black rump. He went off into the woods soon as he heard me unzip the flap on the tent."

"Good place for him," Nolan said, looking into the woods at the edge of the official campsite clearing. "I shouldn't've left you here alone."

* * *

Later in the morning they moved their campsite to Holy Ghost Creek, a mountain tributary of the Pecos that ran through dense forest in a steep valley and was about twenty feet wide. They had driven to another State sponsored campsite, higher and deeper in the mountains, then hiked further in, far enough to feel safe swimming naked in a pool of the stream. The trout in it were small, averaging under eight inches, fishing not much of an option. But the water was clear, the gray stones and brown pebbles beneath it looking as if they were not more than a foot or two from the surface. It was, in fact, deep and cold as ice but felt good in the afternoon heat, once they had worked up the nerve to get in and got used to it. Afterward, they set up their tent in a clearing near several large fir trees, made love on the dried brown needles in their utter nudity, and slept in the tent out of the afternoon breezes until early evening. A smell of pine pitch was in their nostrils and invaded their dreams, making them feel sticky, until the accumulated heat of the late afternoon sun woke them in their sweat.

"Man it's hot!" Nolan opened the tent flap.

Renee was sitting in a bent over position, slapping at herself, her small breasts caught in the narrow beam of light that came through the door, their nipples erect and dark against her untanned, chalk white body. She was enjoying her nakedness. She was also disputing possession of the tent with several mosquitos. "How'd these things get in here?" she asked with irritated exasperation.

Nolan could hear the microscopic whine of one as it flew past his head, but they seemed to be interested only in her. "They like tender young meat," he said, observing the smooth softness of her skin on her back, neck and shoulders, and the pleasant outline of her young breasts.

"You big lug," she responded, slapping him on the bare leg hard enough to leave a red mark.

"Ow! What are you trying to do—castrate me?"

"No. I've got enough sisters." She tied her hair back with a ribbon, straightening herself to sit upright in the subdued light that came through the blue and yellow canvas walls of the tent. There was a smug, satisfied expression on her face. Her stomach was gently curved, nearly flat, of which she was more than a little proud, while her buttocks and legs were full and round. "Put some clothes on, you beast!" she said hypocritically, admiring his long, supple limbs and noticing that he was becoming aroused.

He was very blond, and the amount of hair on his chest was light, almost unnoticeable. "Speak for yourself," he said, suddenly self-conscious about his erection.

* * *

In the evening they made a campfire and sat together on the ground beside it. The air had cooled quickly with the disappearance of the sun, and they were fully clothed, wearing long pants and jackets. It was dark, a clear darkness which nevertheless seemed thick and impenetrable under the dense canopy of trees. In a break between the trees the sky was full of stars, and in their loneliness Nolan and Renee could hear the nearby stream running clean over its rocks and smell the pungent odor of fallen needles, the cold earth chilling them, the world all about them large, crisp and underpopulated. In the morning they would be packing out to head for home.

"Nolan," Renee asked wistfully, leaning her head on his shoulder, "do you think we'll ever have one?"

"What?"

"A baby, silly." They were celebrating their fifth wedding anniversary.

"I don't know," he said. He wished she had not brought it up. Their apparent infertility, and the growing certainty that something must be wrong, made him uneasy.

"It's not your fault," she said consolingly, sensing his discomfort.

He got up and moved a log, distributing hot embers around it with a stick. They flared up red when he moved them, bursting into thin little flames that looked as light and delicate as feathers. But soon the flames were feeding on the log, which made him think of piranha. "We can't be sure of that," he mumbled. "Besides, would it be any better if it was your fault?" He sat down beside her.

"No. I suppose not. I guess I wouldn't be feeling quite so anxious if I knew it wasn't." She sighed, sat up straight and flung her hair over her shoulders. It was a rich, full head of hair, and there was a sensual redness in it in the light of the fire. A small piece of wet, green wood was fizzing and popping, throwing out sparks.

Feeling the night chill close in around them, Nolan got up again and threw on another log to make the flames burn hotter. "Want to make love by the fire?" he asked, changing the subject on his way back to her. "I can make it last all night." He was boasting to expand his chest against a growing sense of tightness within it.

"What? The love or the fire?"

"Both."

"At the same time? Anyway, I think I'm worn out," she moaned in a humorous, pathetic tone. "I'm kind of sore from overuse."

"Okay," he said laughing, but he was disappointed. Being alone with her in the woods, out in the open where everyone and no one could see them, was stimulating, and the way he felt at that moment, looking at her and thinking of her earlier, fresh out of the water, cool and naked in warm, dappled sunlight, he was sure he could have lived up to his boast.

They sat for awhile watching the flames. A chilling wind was picking up in the tree tops, passing noisily through the branches as though straining through a sieve, and sounding enough like rushing water to be confused in their ears with the flow of the stream. The fire was now burning so hot, the flames becoming large and leaping out in all directions, they had to move back several feet, getting up off the damp ground and sitting on some canvas stools they had brought with them.

"Does it matter?" he asked finally.

"Does what matter?"

"Having a kid."

"Of course it does." She looked at him with deliberate, big, sad eyes. "You know it does. To me anyway." She began to pout like a little girl.

He drew her to him. "It does to me too," he said. "I mean, does it matter for our love? We can love each other without any kids, can't we?"

She did not answer, looking at the fire. Then she said, "We're not a family," still looking at the fire.

"Sure we are."

"Not to me. You were an only child. But I have four sisters."

"So." His concept of family was offended. In his mind, to be married was to be a family.

"So, I'm used to lots of noise and activity. Without kids in a marriage, there's a bare place in the heart. It feels ... it feels empty."

"I'm sorry," he said. He was hurt that his love was not enough. He wanted her to be happy. So he added, "Maybe we could get help."

She glanced toward him, looking away again. "You mean a fertility clinic?" she asked abstractedly, feigning modest interest while feeling about on the ground with her hand in the dark. She could not conceal a smile, though her eyes were making a studied effort to see what was at her feet.

"Something like that."

"I guess," she said hesitantly, almost too softly to be heard, snapping a twig she picked up. She had been leading up to this point all evening, planning how she would do it, then altering her plans to fit changing circumstances, not wanting to make them obvious. She knew that in his mind the problem of infertility inevitably called his manliness into question. She thought this male sensitivity ridiculous, but even so it existed, and she needed to allow for it.

At that moment a coyote began yapping like a puppy somewhere in the surrounding forest, then several more joined in, yapping out of harmony as though they were peacocks screeching out of turn, one after another, then together in a jumble. They were thoroughly discordant and seemed to be searching for their voices, sounding something like tin cans rolling down a paved street. She drew a little closer to Nolan. She was not afraid of coyotes, but a woman should not lose the opportunity to solicit protection from the man she loves, especially in a moment of critical decision making, when a reassurance of her need for him might bolster his self-confidence and bring about the right result.

"There used to be wolves here," he observed matter-of-factly. "It's strange to think that the mighty wolf should lose out to something like a puny coyote. Of course, man did tip the balance."

"They're not so puny," Renee observed. She saw no harm in fearing coyotes when it was convenient.

Nolan, who in fact understood this and more of what she was up to than she realized, pulled her even closer. "I'll do whatever it takes," he said resolutely, kissing her ear and putting his tongue into it.

She accepted his attentions passively. He has no idea of what he might be committing himself to, she thought.

In the morning they packed up and drove past the city of Santa Fe, heading south into the desert toward Albuquerque. The sun was up in a cloudless sky and the red mesas shimmered in the heat, looking hot and dry.

Liberty Road

The explosion was sudden, intense. I felt it more inside of me than outwardly. Then I became aware once again of the dust, heat and now of the smoldering jeep. The front end of it was twisted and it lay off the side of the road in a ditch. Beyond it the rice paddy. For some reason I was still on the road and John lay just a few feet away from me. I began to crawl over to him, feeling bruised and the sting of sweat in some cuts on my face.

"John," I called softly, becoming conscious of the fact that I was probably being watched, "you OK?" Raising myself cautiously on my arms, I saw his face, turned the other direction. The lower jaw was missing and the nearer side was a pulp. "John!" I lay on the warm road for several minutes.

Where were the damned VC? John's rifle was laying near him. I had no idea where mine was, where my weapon was. I carried a 45 caliber pistol. Crawling past John without looking at him again, I got the rifle, then rolled off into the ditch on the opposite side of the road from the jeep. It was just me and that wasn't going to last long. The earth was damp in the ditch from the rice field seepage. It felt cool. The road seemed to blaze above me in the hot sun. These dirt roads, so dusty and miserably hot. They were so easy to plant mines in. Where were the VC?

Lying there, I thought it over. These mine incidents on Liberty Road were talmost always followed by an ambush. Yet there had been no small arms fire. No one had yet appeared out of the dense brush, the copses of trees surrounding the rice paddies on both sides of the road. I was nearly a mile from the nearest fire base, the battalion command post. I knew they had probably heard the explosion.

I began to crawl along the ditch. It was then I thought I heard voices. But then I wasn't sure. I heard them again. I crawled as quickly as I could without raising my profile above the edge of the road. I knew it was stupid to try to get away and my heart was pounding so hard I couldn't hear the voices above it now. It would be easier crawling without the rifle and I'd be outnumbered anyway, but I clung to its cold plastic and metal as if it were a lover. It wasn't the thought of using it now, it was just the thought of not having it, of not having anything.

I became exhausted after several minutes and stopped moving. Now I could hear the voices again and they were definitely Vietnamese. No one would mistake Vietnamese sounds for English. I tried to raise my head just enough to see. Three of them, one female. One man had khakis on. The other looked like he was wearing an American jungle utility uniform. He was carrying an American rifle. The woman, or girl, had a carbine slung over her left shoulder. She wore the white cotton blouse and black silk pajama bottoms of a peasant. The legs were rolled up to her thighs, as if she'd just come from planting rice in a field. They were standing over John. The man in khakis walked over to the jeep and then back. He said something and they all began looking in various directions down the road and over the fields.

"They're searching for me," I thought. How was it they hadn't seen me? Quietly, very slowly I pulled back the rifle bolt, released it and pushed the charging handle into place. A bullet popped out of the chamber. I knew John should have already had the weapon cocked, but I wasn't sure. I pushed the safety to automatic fire.

But I didn't fire. I was clearly within range but was afraid. There might be others and I'd be overwhelmed.

I waited and waited. They quit looking around and went on talking. The man in American uniform knelt down and started searching John's body. Obviously he was experienced at this. Because John's body was twisted at 180 degrees, the head came over when the man turned the body. The grisly face made me sick but I noticed the girl did not even react, and she was so young!

Then I heard the sound of a vehicle, the sound of more than one. Marines were coming from the command post to check things out. The VC searching John's body got up startled and they all started talking rapidly. That's when I opened fire, emptying the magazine in my rifle. Nineteen rounds. The three of them fell in a heap.

As the first vehicle, a small utility truck, came into sight around a bend in the road, I got up and started walking carefully toward the tangle of bodies around John. I loaded another magazine into my rifle as I walked and wiped the sweat and dust off my forehead with my arm.

Middle Age and Youth

The two Filipino workmen squatted on their heels on the bare ground, taking an early afternoon break. Nearby, the remains of an open fire exhaled a last breath, sending an occasional wisp of smoke into the air. A crumbled layer of black and white coals, lying in a shallow pit of sand, was all that remained of the preparations that had warmed the men's lunch. Behind them was the skeletal wood frame of an unfinished American style house. It had its roof on to beat the equatorial heat, but was otherwise a collection of two-by-four inch sticks, standing mostly upright. Close beside one of the men—a thin, gnarled, wrinkled, sun-blackened individual of middle age—was a large white rooster, sporting a gold and tan streaking of feathers, which extended along its back and fell like a shower of shiny silk threads to either side of its tail. The rooster glittered beautifully in the sun but had a head like a vulture, its comb having been removed, leaving a flat, red scar. Its thick, bony, yellow-white leg spurs were cut off and rounded at a half inch, so that they could be fitted with the steel, razor sharp weapons of its trade.

In his native Pampangan dialect the older of the two men said, pointing to the rooster, "He is a good fighter. He can never lose." He took an emphatic draw on a slender black cigarette and allowed its white smoke to curl into the air from his mouth, punctuating the stream now and then with perfect rings: one, two, three in a row.

"No!" The other man shook his head. A long, heavily oiled, black lock of hair fell over his broad, young, creaseless forehead. "He is not invincible. No rooster can win forever." He drew a line in the sand with his finger and looked over at the rooster. The rooster had extended its reach to the full length of the cord by which it was tethered. It lay on its breast, its bound leg stretched out behind it, its beak open, panting, moisture dripping onto the barren hot ground of the construction site.

"He will die of old age," the older man said simply, with satisfaction. He was wearing a brown tee shirt torn near one armpit from hard work, khaki trousers and a pair of black rubber sandals. His younger companion was similarly dressed. Behind them was a banging of hammers. Other workmen had already returned to their labors. "I will wager it," the older man continued. In an otherwise expressionless face, his eyes were dancing. A corner of his mouth turned imperceptibly. The wrinkles in his forehead might have increased. He reached into his pants pocket and pulled out a thinly folded wad of peso notes. "Today I have been given a week's pay. I will risk it all."

"No, Rodolfo. I have a family, and my rooster is to fight in the Sunday fair in Angeles."

"He is not invincible then, this rooster of yours?" The older man smiled.

"He is young and strong. He will fight for the first time Sunday. I think he will win."

"But you are not sure, Orley."

"I am sure. I am sure he will win." Orley got up, brushing his hair back. He looked down at the older man. "But not today."

In the afternoon the men began to put siding on the house. In a tropical country, this is a simple process, even on houses built for Americans. There were four men on the site. In the course of a couple hours Rodolfo told the other two men of Orley's reluctance to test his rooster. One of these men gibed at Orley, accusing him of cowardice, until he finally left in anger to fetch his rooster from home.

At four o'clock in the afternoon more than two dozen men were gathered in a circle. They had come from other houses being built in the new American subdivision near Clark Air Force Base. Their conversation was animated. The circle they formed was wide enough to allow Orley and Rodolfo to occupy a space in the center. Each held his rooster with two hands. Each was squatted on his heels in the dust. They were teasing the birds, pushing them toward each other and withdrawing them. The birds, with ruffled neck feathers, pecked angrily at one another whenever they were brought close enough to do so. Each tried to flap its wings, but was held tightly by its owner. Each attempted to strike outward with its spurs, but its legs were pinned by the strong fingers of the man holding it. Some of the men in the circle about them were shouting. There was much excited talk, cursing, laughter and, as all were construction workers and had been paid that afternoon, there were bets.

Several men started shouting to Orley and Rodolfo to begin. The money was placed. The birds were clearly ready. Were they afraid of the results? The crowd of men was growing impatient. It was Rodolfo who now showed hesitation. Orley's rooster, as red as its wild cousin, the Philippine jungle cock, was small like it too. But it showed much spirit. Its golden eyes flashed fire.

"Put them into the fight," came shouts from all sides. "Are you hesitating, Rodolfo? Wasn't it you who wanted this fight?" Several of the men shouted encouragement and profanity in English, for they came from other districts and did not speak the Pampangan dialect. English is also an excellent language for cursing.

The roosters were quickly fitted with their murderous blades and set loose, the two men scrambling backward out of the way and into the circle of onlookers. There was a hush. As much as a week's pay lay in some of the men's wagers.

The two roosters faced one another, necks extended and lowered close to the ground, neck feathers ruffled. But neither moved. They seemed to be sizing one another up. Suddenly the larger, white rooster flared, opening its wings, leaping into the air, and thrusting its spurs forward. The red rooster leapt back. A shout went up. "The red one is a boy. He is not a man yet. Take him home, Orley, and put him under his mother hen." Orley's face darkened with concern.

The roosters both leaped toward one another now and collided in the air. There was angry squawking as they hit in this manner two, three times, falling to the ground, pulling out feathers with their beaks. Then the red rooster began to falter. It seemed weak. It fell down. It did not rise to meet its opponent. But the white one leaped upon it nevertheless, pecking at the other, which lay prostrate in the sand. The red rooster panted heavily, and its eyes began to film. Rodolfo carefully removed his bird from the ring. Orley's rooster opened its beak, a dark circle of blood forming at its breast. It closed its eyes and lay still.

Though the fight was over, there was still much animation among the men. Money begrudgingly changed hands. Then the men went home. Orley and Rodolfo remained behind. Orley stood looking at his rooster, which he had not touched. Rodolfo, cradling his own on one arm with blood on both arms from the wounds on its legs, said softly, "Because I have done well today, I will not accept the money which you have wagered."

Orley looked at Rodolfo. He had a family to feed. He nodded, dropping his head in embarrassment. Rodolfo put a hand on Orley's strong shoulder. "An old man has seen many cockfights," he said.

Orley smiled grimly. "Yes," he repeated. "An old man has seen many cockfights. This a young man must learn." Orley picked up the dead rooster. It had no spirit now. It was a limp bundle of feathers. The blood had already dried, stiffening the feathers on its breast, and it had soaked into the ground as well. He kicked dirt over the spot where the blood was, spreading the soil evenly. Then the two men, who were from the same village, walked peaceably home.

In Possession of Oneself

She was worn out, tired of writing. She had written three novels in the last five years, and none of them had sold well. She had quarreled with her live-in boyfriend and he had moved out the week before. Strangely, that did not seem a tragedy. She'd almost forgotten how pleasant it was to be alone: the quiet, the time for reflection, no one's needs to answer to but her own.

She was falling into old patterns: long, luxuriating, hot baths in the morning, for instance. Perhaps that was why she wasn't writing. It was easier when you followed a set schedule and began work promptly at an early hour. Well, what did it matter? She still had enough income to get by. Marilyn fed the cat and went out.

"Good morning, Miss Hampton. The usual? Yes, well, you really should try something more substantial, dear. You're so thin. Put a little fat on them bones."

"I'm fine, Thelma." Marilyn was sitting at a small, glass and metal frame table on a weathered wooden deck. She was outdoors. Crossing her legs, she adjusted her skirt on her knees. She was thin but considered that an advantage at thirty-five. At a nearby table was an attractive man in what appeared to be his late twenties. Marilyn didn't recognize him. In adjusting her skirt she had considered drawing it up a little to show some leg. But she thought better of it. She really wasn't interested in another relationship.

"Here you are, Miss Hampton." Thelma set a cup on the glass table top and poured hot black coffee into it. "This should be hot enough to scald your tongue. No cream and sugar it is, isn't it, dear? And here is your breakfast." Thelma made a face as she took a small plate containing two sweet rolls off the brown plastic tray she had set on the table. She set the plate in front of Marilyn, then took up the tray and went back into the restaurant.

A few minutes later Thelma came out and wrote out a bill for the young man. He got up and went into the restaurant to pay as Thelma cleared his table. Then she went back into the restaurant, leaving Marilyn alone on the patio.

It was between eight and nine in the morning. The sun was up somewhere in a misty, somewhat gray sky. But the fog was clearing and Marilyn knew it would be a clear, sunny day. The thick evergreen forests of Western Washington bore down on her on either side, for the restaurant was on the outskirts of a small town on Puget Sound not far from Seattle.

The restaurant faced out over a small cove, or inlet, which at low tide became a mud flat receding out into the Sound. At such times the flat took on an unpleasant odor but the blue herons that fed there, standing rock still in shallow water or flying in and out on heavy wings with an occasional "gronk," were fascinating to watch. There were always at least one or two of them about, along with an intermittent raccoon venturing out from the green shoreline to dabble in some of the same pools of water left behind by the tide.

But the tide was high now and the water reached almost to the wooden deck which extended out over the flat on piles. Gulls were wheeling and crying in the inlet, alighting on a sand bar that remained above water. As the air continued to clear of mist and admit patches of blue and sunshine, Marilyn could see a ferry boat further out on the placid, gray blue waters of the Sound. It lumbered in white silence toward its regular destination.

"Miss Hampton." Thelma came briskly out of the restaurant. "It's Mr. Denison. On the phone."

Marilyn set down her coffee cup and let the hot liquid in her mouth drain carefully into her throat.

"Tell him I'm unable to come to the phone," she said. Thelma went back inside.

Marilyn finished her light breakfast as the sun dissipated the last of the fog. She could now feel the warmth of the sun. It figures Ted would call, she thought. She wondered why he had waited a week. She got up and went into the restaurant, not waiting for Thelma to bring the bill.

The restaurant was simple and roomy inside with brown Formica tables in Naugahyde booths lining the walls. In an adjoining room was the bar, from which a stale odor of beer always emanated.

"Going home to work?" Thelma asked from behind the cash register. "It's a beautiful morning, isn't it?"

"Yes it is." Marilyn didn't answer the first question. She paid her bill and went out the front of the restaurant to the gravel parking lot. The sun was almost white on the gray stones. Why, she thought, does Thelma always refer to me by my last name? I've known her for years.

The Wood Carver

He was retired but no one knew what from. Some supposed it was the military. This came from the fact that he kept his hair cropped short, was fairly trim in middle age, and had simply appeared one day in the neighborhood of Irondale eight miles south of the village of Port Townsend, Washington.

He cleared a dark stretch of spruce and hemlock forest next to a steep ravine and set a prefabricated house there. Surrounded by tall, looming trees he developed his passion, carving the local fauna of Olympic National Park, such as elk, deer, puma, otter and mountain beaver, from small blocks of red cedar wood.

These figures were crude at first but became intricate, expressive and beautiful with time. Perhaps as a carryover from his military days, he rubbed and rubbed the finished carvings with linseed oil until it brought out the natural warmth of the cedar wood and attained the satin finish of a well cared for rifle stock. The carvings were then transported once a month to be put out on consignment in a souvenir and crafts shop in the tourist and mill town of Port Angeles fifty miles west of Port Townsend.

He could be seen in his little, dented, blue, pickup truck, nodding but unspeaking and unsmiling as he drove five miles an hour along the dirt road that ran past other homestead lots cut from field and forest in the loose, irregular neighborhood of Irondale. Now and then, loading the bed of his truck with camping equipment, he would disappear into the national park for several days. When he reemerged it was with a sheaf of pencil sketches which would become the inspiration for new work.

One day, after he'd lived there for many years and was hardly ever observed to receive visitors, the neighborhood was set ablaze with speculation. A young woman, beautiful, slender, with long, shining, coal black hair and features as lovely and pale as Snow White's, took up residence in his home. Who could she be? The "tree man," a strange young fellow who had built a ramshackle home forty feet above ground by lashing four or five hemlocks together and laying plank and beam in between, provided an answer. He was a near neighbor to the wood carver and had gained his confidence. The young woman, he discovered, was the man's granddaughter.

Marilyn Forsyte did not carry the last name of her grandfather because she was his daughter's daughter. His name was Don Norton, well known to this day in the Pacific Northwest for the fine work he left behind. What the tree man also learned was that Mr. Norton had developed a heart condition. He was in need of surgery but refused it. Marilyn had come as an emissary of her mother to plead with his stubbornness. She was unsuccessful and ended up remaining with him for several years, the last years of his life.

When Mr. Norton died, Marilyn was not seen for two weeks. According to the tree man, she never left the house. But what she did there no one knew. The ambulance had come, had been unable to revive Mr. Norton after a particularly severe heart attack, and had taken him away. Marilyn had then followed the ambulance in her grandfather's little blue truck. Afterwards she had returned to the house where no one saw her again for the two weeks.

Apparently she did not attend her grandfather's funeral. He was buried in a small wooded cemetery beside a cliff overlooking a lonely stretch of beach and open bay in Port Townsend. Here the rolling gray wave crests, crying gulls and bobbing buoys under a dense, moisture laden sky are all that ever breaks the stillness.

Small sparrows, chickadee and warblers chitter softly as they flit from tree to tree in the cemetery, depending on the season. A simple flat headstone marks the grave where squirrels quietly search for nuts.

After the two weeks, Marilyn reappeared, driving the little blue truck ever so slowly down the dirt, homestead, field and forest studded road as her grandfather had done. She nodded to neighbors but rarely smiled and never spoke. So strikingly lovely were her features that men always stopped and watched as she went by. Two Labrador Retrievers always lay in the middle of the intersection of this and another dirt road that went on to meet the paved roadway just beyond, which ran the eight miles to Port Townsend. They never budged. She drove so slowly, they didn't feel a need to. So she maneuvered carefully around them, as her grandfather had done before her. She remained for six months, then disappeared.

The tree man knew she had gone back to California, from which she had come. But he never told anyone. A solitary figure himself, he continued his simple life in the tree house without benefit of water, sewage or electrical services. The crows, and sometimes raccoons, often raided his garbage pile, which he hauled out to the county landfill once a month.

Don Norton is now famous in the Northwest. His carvings still sell and resell for high prices. He has been represented by the exhibition and sale of several pieces in a New York gallery along Fifty-ninth Street, south of Central Park. Marilyn Forsyte, since married and with children of her own, is a legend in Irondale and Port Townsend, where these later facts about her are still unknown. She remains a symbol of untouched, perhaps untouchable, mystery and beauty. To the tree man she is a dream unrealized, truly felt, never really known.

A Pair of Hands

He was old, partially bald in the center of a cap of kinky gray hair, and he begged on the streets. He frequented Fairmount Park in the vicinity of the Philadelphia Art and Franklin Museums, where there were a fair number of tourists to be found, and he made daily rounds in the downtown business area around Arch Street. At rush hour and on cold nights he found his home in the underground station for the Speed Line train that went out to New Jersey. To many who made his sudden and often unexpected acquaintance, his most peculiar and annoying habit was the desire to shake hands with them—those who, in a furtive and embarrassed manner, paused for a moment to surrender a few coins.

"Thank ye, sir. I've been many days in need of a good meal and a … Well, thank you anyway, sir, and God bless you." The almsgiver would then beat a hasty retreat into a nearby crowd, or across the street, out of the park, or onto a train, depending upon the location of the encounter.

But the hands of the man were unforgettable. Whatever other nondescript feature may have appeared in the visage and physiognomy of this bony, hunchbacked, unkempt, craggy faced, black man of cold alleyways and drafty tunnels, those who paused long enough to look at them could not forget his hands. The hands, the hands. That was the feature. Even the bright, energetic, strangely alert, perhaps deep-seeing eyes of the man were dismissed from memory at the sight of those hands. Their skin was thick like leather; they were gnarled like Spanish ironwork. They were large and scarred, yet the fingers somehow slender, sensitive and delicate. The palms were fleshy and pink, though toughened like the fingers, which were also thickly calloused.

Here was a man who had obviously poured out the sweat of manual labor. Perhaps thousands of board feet of rough, fresh cut timber had slipped under the firm control of those fingers on the way to a circular saw blade at a yellow-pine pulp mill years ago in deep Louisiana or Mississippi. If so, those fingers looked as if they could even now pluck a finely articulated tune from a piano. In short, the man carried a history of long and varied life at his fingertips, and offered it to the world in the person of anyone who would shake his hand for a moment.

But few ever did.

One morning a young woman of twenty arrived in the tough city of "brotherly love" from some more congenial and comfortable suburb. At a little after eight, she had come early for a nine o'clock appointment. It was her first job interview outside of her home town. She was sweet in appearance, a bit over-bright, well scrubbed, perfumed and well dressed, with blue eyes the color of that morning's sunny sky, and soft brown hair cut to the contours of fashion.

"Mornin' Ma'am." Our man of the hands approached her at a street corner where she was waiting for a green light. She was standing there alone.

She glanced over at the man, then looked anxiously at the light. It was still red. The light for cross traffic persisted in being green, not having yet lazily lumbered over to the urgent task of turning yellow.

"Beautiful day, isn't it, Miss?" The man stopped beside her. He was smiling, stooped over. It seemed he couldn't stand upright. His clothing had the odor of much wear and fitful, sleepless nights.

The young woman's pulse quickened. Street people were dangerous, she'd heard. And black men were unpredictable.

The man looked at the young woman, who kept her gaze fastened on the opposite side of the street. In his expression she might have seen a flicker of curious tenderness. He understood, in a kind of bemused wonder, the extent of her fear.

Thirty seconds passed. The light for the moving traffic turned yellow. Amidst the crisp, rumbling sound of passing cars was a sudden pressing of brakes, a hum of impatient idling motors. The light turned red, and the adjacent light across the street turned green. It showed the figure of a person walking. The girl stepped hurriedly off the curb and into the street. The man watched her go, a thin smile on his lips. She disappeared into an office building half a block further on.

An hour and some twenty or thirty minutes passed. The young woman returned to the sidewalk from the building she'd entered. She hesitated for a moment, looking toward the corner where the street person had been. No one. Then, in obvious good spirits, she proceeded gaily toward the crossing.

On passing a tobacco and magazine stand not more than thirty feet into her walk, she saw the old man. It was in a moment of buoyancy at having been accepted for a clerical position she had wanted. She smiled generously at him.

"Good mornin', Miss." The man stepped forward and offered his hand. In a moment of confusion and unexpected panic the girl offered hers. The large rough hand gently held the soft, feminine hand, a clean slender thing with clear polished nails, a hand without a history, the hand of a mere girl. On this lovely, clear instrument was recorded nothing but the soft, pliable record of innocence.

The girl looked timidly into the man's eyes and attempted a smile. She glanced down again at his hand. It was a powerful yet articulate instrument, something about which she knew very little, though her father had big hands. The man's grip was firm but gentle and warm.

The man raised his left hand and joined it to his right, grasping the young woman's hand with both of his own. Then he released her. The girl hurried on. She had not even looked the man in the face after the first attempt, she had been so frightened. Why had she stopped at all? She didn't know. She had forgotten to give the man what he most likely wanted: money. But then he didn't ask. How strange that he had simply shaken her hand. The girl thought about this on the way home. She practically forgot to think at all about the exciting prospect of having landed a job on her first interview.

G. Lowell Tollefson

An Event Near Dupont Circle

She was cute. I'd always thought she was cute, ever since I first met her. But I don't know where she is now. A lot of years have passed. She had brown eyes, short brown hair, curves in all the right places, though not to the point of being top or bottom heavy. I think you know what I mean. She was the kind of girl who made you feel physical desire for her without really knowing her and then embarrassed about feeling that way at the same time. In my opinion, she would've made someone a good wife, if she could've been tamed. Maybe she finally was.

Three of us guys were living together in the same apartment in Washington, D.C. All of us were young Marines still in the service. It was 1966. We were in a civilian school, attending the Sanz School of Languages downtown, trying to learn Vietnamese. The Marine Corps and the Defense Language Institute had sent us there. So, for military personnel, we had a lot of freedom. Not that we were supposed to be renting an apartment. We were assigned bunks in a Naval Barracks in Anacostia, and had been expressly forbidden to live off base. But we were just using the apartment on weekends. It was near Dupont Circle, where New Hampshire, Connecticut and Massachusetts Avenues meet.

Dupont Circle was a hangout for Vietnam War protesters at a time when few people knew or cared what they were. They would gather there in the evenings with guitars and sing Joan Baez type folk songs. We used to go down there sometimes, Mack, Carl and I, and hang around listening to the music. The little park was pleasant and green. Bushes, trees and park benches on gently sloping ground. Lots of open grassy area. The girls were pretty. Naturally, we weren't wearing uniforms, though any fool would have recognized what we were by our haircuts.

It was Mack, a tall fellow with a big innocent smile and a tooth missing that somehow made him more attractive to women, who got to know her first. She was with one of those groups. Sylvia Parthening was her name. It turned out she lived in the same building we did, one floor above. The building was old and pink on the outside with big bay windows which extended into the sidewalk toward the street from the living rooms of the front apartments. It was only about two blocks from the circle, and was situated on a street corner. There were lots of buildings like it in Washington, and they were all uniformly ugly: big masonry dinosaurs lined up sadly on Washington's radial streets, waiting to be declared extinct and torn down by anyone who might care to lay the unfortunate to rest.

Sylvia and Mack became very close. They had a love affair. Carl and I would've liked to have been as lucky as Mack. But over time, a few months perhaps, things got kind of stormy between them. Mack had a tendency to be possessive and jealous, and she was an early progenitor of the flower child. He wanted to marry her, and she wanted to keep it friendly, whatever that means when you're already sleeping with someone. I don't think she was unfaithful to him, but her refusal to marry him made him think so.

It came to a head on a Saturday night. We had a few people over and were drinking too much and Carl was getting belligerent, as he always did under the influence of alcohol. Pretty soon all our guests left. It was just Carl and me and a living room full of empty beer cans. Even the furniture in that room was spare. The walls could've used a little fresh paint. Mack was up in Sylvia's apartment. They had been down at Dupont Circle, then went up to the apartment around eight in the evening.

At ten o'clock Carl was sitting in the corner of the sofa drunk. He knew he had ruined the party. He hadn't meant it to turn out that way. He just couldn't hold his liquor. Suddenly Mack comes in.

"Where's everybody?" Mack was always buoyant, even when he was feeling down, and I didn't realize at first that he was.

"Gone," Carl answered in a surly tone.

"Gone? Where to?" Mack looked at me with those big, blue, innocent eyes of his and the missing tooth.

"Carlos here scared them off." I was being sarcastic, but Carl didn't care.

"Oh. Well, it looks like Sylvia and I are about finished."

Carl was drawing something. He kept a sketch pad around and did a lot of that sort of thing. He was pretty good, in a cartoon character sort of way.

"What happened between you two?" I asked Mack.

"Nothing."

"Nothing? You just said it was all over."

"I didn't say it was all over." Mack opened a beer can and sat down on the opposite end of the sofa from Carl. The sofa had springs that were as inviting, comfortwise, as sitting on the bottom of a rocky stream in cold water. But it made out into a bed. "I said it was about to be all over."

"Oh." I had missed the fine point of distinction. I went over and looked out at the street through the bay window. The sofa was over against an adjacent wall. There was a little coffee table and one armchair, and there were no pictures on any of the walls, of course. The wooden framework of the bay window—it was divided into smaller panes and angled in three directions—was peeling paint.

The wood underneath wasn't particularly healthy either, being old and crumbly. Outside, the street was dark. There was one dull street light and no cars. I could hear a lot of excited talk, female laughter, and loud music in the apartment below us, which only pointed up the melancholy stillness presently prevailing in ours.

I turned around toward Mack. "Come on, buddy, what's Sylvia upset about?"

"I didn't say she was upset."

"Then what're you upset about?"

"I didn't say I was upset."

I looked at Mack in a kind of stupor. Maybe the beer was clouding my judgment. It wasn't any of my business anyway.

A weird little shaft of light lit up in me. It occurred to me that Sylvia might soon be free. I wondered if this thought had entered Carl's head. He was just finishing his sketch. He handed it over to Mack. Mack smiled and handed it to me. It was a picture of a Marine standing at attention with his rifle at shoulder arms, and holding a flower child girl around the waist with his other arm. She was wearing a mini-skirt (not one of those wagon train style, formless long dresses that were popular in the seventies), and she looked like she was high on something. They made an incongruous pair. I didn't think it was funny.

It turned out that what Mack was trying to tell us, but wouldn't say, was that Sylvia had suddenly decided to leave for California. There was no real explanation. Mack was too stunned to know what to think. None of us had expected it, but that kind of sudden departure must've been the reason for her unwillingness to accept stronger ties in the first place.

Flood

There are two kinds of rain in central Vietnam in the area around Da Nang and Hue. The first is the monsoon. It comes in a sudden downpour and disappears just as quickly. Overall at such times it's still the dry season. Everything is sunshine, heat, and white dust, dust that swirls so thickly on the roads you can only see the vehicle you are following if you are a few yards from it. But then the sky suddenly darkens and hammers down water by the bucket load. This only lasts about fifteen minutes, cutting deep gullies on any uneven ground. After that the sky clears and the world is sunshine, water sparkling on the ground and dripping. The green fields and jungle look as if they'd just been washed, and the local peasant farmers pay little attention to such rain, going on with their work as soon as it abates.

The second kind of rain is different. The sky is always cloud covered and gray, the temperature drops from the high nineties to the low seventies and the rain drizzles in an endless chilling spray. It goes on for months. The once dusty roads become sucking mud traps. Thick red mud. I once saw an amtrac, an amphibious tracked vehicle which is, after all, the size of a tank, with its whole bulk completely sunk into this mud! It was upside down with a big hole in the bottom. It had obviously hit a mine. But the point is that our vehicles could not get around much in this season. We were dependent on helicopters for just about everything: ammunition, evacuating wounded, sometimes even for food.

But the mail. Now that was critical, and we only lost out on that once, in a third kind of rain which I haven't mentioned.

It was a flood. Vietnam is practically nothing but rivers. The jungle grows out of them like moss on a stream bank. The rice fields catch them and there is always more. Brown, sluggish and not too healthy looking, they roll about over the countryside like lazy sunbathing crocodiles. Until the arrival of a typhoon.

One night a typhoon hit our firebase. I don't think the winds got over seventy miles an hour because they didn't tear our hooches down. They just slapped the canvas sides around and made us wet, miserable and cold. When it was over we slept like dead men. We didn't figure the Viet Cong would be around. In the morning there weren't any rivers. Our hill was sticking up out of a lake.

By afternoon we had some of the villagers up on the hill with us. Not many. Most of them didn't trust us and preferred to stay down in the valley where the water was neck deep. The few villagers who joined us were sick. We put them in a hooch and covered them with blankets to keep them warm. A corpsman attended them and a guard was posted outside. There was a young boy with malaria, an old man dying of tuberculosis and a few others.

No mail. A wooden bridge from a few miles upriver was on its way down to take out ours, which was already submerged under fast flowing water, but that was all. There wasn't any mail because the choppers had to bring us our food and ammunition, all of it.

The next day the water was down to waist level, and after that it began to clear off of some of the higher parts of the road. This meant some of the old men could stand on dry ground and cast their nets for shrimp.

Now here was a people hit by war and floods, and they rarely had enough to eat. So what is their response? They go fishing. They laugh and joke. The children often play with undetonated mortars they find that then go off, and the young women step on mines. There is weeping in the family, but life, laughter, moments of pleasure, street market haggling in the village center, still go on. These people work in their fields while we or the VC shell them accidentally or when trying to get at each other. That accounts for the hunger, since crops are hard to grow in a battlefield, but they keep on working. We shoot up their villages, shell and bomb them when we think there are Viet Cong in them. The VC too sometimes burn the hamlets and select uncooperative individuals to cut off their thumbs or assassinate them at night or even in the middle of the day. But they keep on going. What else can they do?

In Vietnam I have heard a kind of laughter which is clear and ringing like good crystal. I have never heard it anywhere else.

Knocked Up

They married when they were kids. He was eighteen and she was sixteen. She had become pregnant and, though an A student, was forced to drop out of high school. They are now in their early thirties. She is thirty-three and her oldest daughter, Brenda, is seventeen.

* * *

"Mom." Brenda knocks on the bathroom door. "Can I talk to you?"

"Now?"

"Yes, please. It's important."

Brenda sits down on the toilet lid next to the bathtub. Her mother, whose name is also Brenda, is stretched out in a tub of warm water holding a book. The room is small, like the rest of the house, hot and steamy.

"What're you reading, Mom?"

The elder Brenda turns the cover of the paperback book toward her daughter: *The Poetry of John Donne*. There is a grotesque picture of a woman, pale white, lying dead next to a skull.

"Oh. Dad thinks reading is a waste of time."

"Your dad thinks anything other than beer, pretzels and driving his big rig is a waste of time."

"It's steamy in here. Do you mind if I open the window?" Young Brenda leans over the tub and opens the window a crack.

"Brr." Her mother crosses her arms over her ample breasts.

Brenda looks at her mother. She has broadened a little in the hips and thighs and her belly is rounded. The dark pubic hair appears to move a little under the clear water, like eel grass Brenda has seen in an estuary along the Washington coast.

Brenda sits down again. Bright sunlight and the green of domestic foliage glare through the open space of the window. The smell of the outdoors freshens the tiny room. Sparrows and finches chirp. "It's a beautiful day, Mom."

"So it is, dear. Are your brother and sister up yet?"

"No … Mom, I'm pregnant."

The elder Brenda, struck speechless, sinks down to her shoulders in the water, folding her knees upward, and stares at her daughter. She closes her eyes. When words come to her, she says, "Oh, no, not again!"

After the kids leave for school, the elder Brenda busies herself. Dish washing, clothes washing, dusting, whatever. Tomorrow Dan will return, grumpy, dusty and sweaty from his cross-country haul. He will be furious when he finds out about their daughter, forgetting his own history. That's just like him, Brenda thinks. Seventeen years of marriage has put a good deal of distance between them.

That afternoon she brings her oldest daughter into the master bedroom, where pink curtains are the only touch of femininity allowed, and shuts the door. They sit down on a king-sized bed. It is the most expensive piece of furniture in the house. The bedspread on it is old. Brenda looks at her daughter. She is so slender and pretty. So bright. She just can't be pregnant.

"I've been thinking about you all day," she says. "You're not going to have an abortion, are you?"

"No, Mom. I wouldn't do that without you knowing. And I know the Church is against it."

"Well, the Pope never got pregnant at seventeen."

"I'm sorry, Mom."

"I know, sweetheart." She puts her hand on her daughter's. "I don't think you should tell your father just yet."

"But he's going to see it when I start showing."

"We've got some time. I called your Aunt Ellie this afternoon."

"Oh her."

"Brenda, listen to me. I went through this myself. You see what's become of me. I had a mind. I came from good people."

"Aunt Ellie's so hoity-toity."

"She loves you. She's always been fond of you. School's almost out. You can go to New York and stay with her till the baby's due. I want you to let her adopt the child."

"Mom, I haven't had time to think …"

"You listen to me, young lady. I've thought about it most of my life. You're not going to ruin your life the way mine was cut short. I want you to get an education. I want you to marry a man who can think, who can feel, who can …"

"Mom, Mark says he'll marry me."

"Oh, Lord!" Brenda feels panic rising within her. "No, no, no!"

"But I love him."

"You do not love him. You don't know what love is. Believe me, honey, I know. This is infatuation, passion. Warm kisses, a hard manliness between your legs. It makes your head swim. I've been there."

"No you haven't, Mom. You're not me. Mark is tender, sensitive. He cares about me."

"Do you really love him?"

"I … I'm beginning to feel …"

"Brenda. You listen to me. You're on the road to a lifetime of hell. I'm not going to let this happen."

* * *

The younger Brenda goes on to New York and gives birth to her child. Mark seems to have forgotten them. At least he has never asked about them. He does not even know if his child is a boy or a girl. Brenda's father, who of course knows now, hasn't shown much concern either, and is still driving trucks over long distances. Last year the Super Bowl pleased him with its results. Perhaps it will again this year.

The Kestrel and the Snare

John Marse was a critic in all things. A professor of English at various Eastern universities, he first made his public reputation in the production of magazine articles peppered with biting wit, later expanding his infamous activities to the lecture circuit. He moved about a lot because his caustic temper generally made him unwelcome in any one place after a few years. Writing on books, people, institutions and fashions, he seized with both tongue and pen upon whatever fell within the purveyance of his roving eye. It's not surprising then that he didn't marry until the age of forty-six. Who would have him, and whom would he have? But in that year he met his match.

Guinevere Marks was a young woman of something less than Arthurian grace. She had more in common with the bushy faced revolutionary whose surname her own name resembled. She was brilliant, studiously intellectual, implacable, determined. She spent long periods in libraries, dimming her vision beyond repair and painstakingly creating heavy, closely reasoned tomes which astounded her colleagues and confounded the world. She and John met at a combined colloquium for philosophers and literary critical theorists. It is said by those who knew them both that all nature was hushed on that day. Even the birds did not dare think of singing.

"I have read your articles, Dr. Marse," Guinevere said. The two of them were browsing through some newly published books at a table outside one of the lecture rooms.

"Have you indeed?"

"Yes. I consider them brittle, insipid."

"I—oh—well, the curvature of wit requires a well-rounded perspective, Miss ..." John stammered in surprise. Guinevere was in her late twenties.

"It is Dr. Marks," she interrupted, locking her dark eyed gaze upon him.

"Uhum, yes. Well ..." John began stroking his goatee. It was a manner he had when momentarily, though certainly rarely, stumped for an apt means of expression. He had not, after all, expected this frontal assault. It had an air of planning.

"Have you read my book on the *Epistemological Analysis of the Aesthetic Sensibility?*" Guinevere adjusted her glasses as she spoke, squinting at the elder and taller figure of the man. John might have observed the pleasant curvature of her breast against the tightened fabric of her blouse as she lifted her arm, but he would as soon have found pleasure in romancing a turtle.

"No, I don't believe I have. If you will excuse me, Dr. Marks ..."

"I am not through with you, sir."

"Pardon me?"

"I am not through with you." She smiled grimly. "I say I may not be through with you for quite some time, Dr. Marse." There was an inexplicable twinkle in her expression. She would surely crack the nut, for which task she had come fully prepared and sought him out. "For I believe we have much more in common than appearances would suggest."

"Oh no. I'm sure we don't. Ha ha. Would you believe I have only the most superficial acquaintance with a subject as arcane as epistemology? I would not dream of taking a moment's repose in one of its musty rooms, as I'm sure they must all be. Nor would I stroll in its shadowy corridors or breathe the crusty air of its moss clotted gardens." John was most pleasantly upon his way now toward making a new enemy. He felt refreshingly rectified, and regarded her with the satisfaction of a predator which has already hamstrung its mouse.

But then a terrible thing took place. At that moment, he saw with all the inviolate intensity of the sexual instinct (the curvature of her breast must have entered his mind after all) that this creature who stood before him was, in fact, a woman. What it was that made him suddenly aware of this, he wasn't sure. Never had a less promising candidate presented itself to the closely scrutinizing instrumentality of his critical mind.

In spite of her poor eyesight, she wasn't altogether a physical disappointment. But it wasn't this, he assured himself, which had seized upon the instinctive chords of his nature. It wasn't—well, he didn't know what it was. He sensed in her a vibration, a hunger beneath the heavy masonry of her scholarly facade. It aroused something similar in himself. Their eyes met with a kinder regard. He saw in those large, brown irises, beneath the lenses of her glasses, the wound which he had made, the forgiveness it had engendered (perhaps she saw through him and penetrated the soft gel beneath the cruel barbs), and he was sorry.

"I don't mean to be cruel," he said abruptly and dropped his gaze. It fell upon her breathing chest, her hips, and her flattened belly pleasantly contained within a tight skirt.

Guinevere smiled. "Why don't we go and have a cup of coffee," she suggested softly.

And they did.

Family Matters

He didn't want to write about the war. He had always avoided it. He was a good writer and had become fairly well known in literary circles as a novelist, if not rich. But he had always kept the war out of his pen. It was better that way.

Ralph Macklin did not, therefore, make his living by the pen. He was an English professor at Boise State University. He loved to ski at nearby Bogus Basin, and he occasionally hunted dove, quail and pheasant in the surrounding farm and sage brush desert country. His home was in a pleasant green neighborhood in the heart of the city of Boise, Idaho. This mixed middle and upper middle class community was known as the Bench. It overlooked from high ground the State Capitol Building and the broad lanes of Capitol Boulevard leading up to it, the boulevard being surrounded for half its length on either side by parks before passing into the downtown business district, beyond which lay the provincial yet august, and occasionally noisy, halls of government.

On a hot August afternoon, when the temperature was pushing well into the nineties and the dry air quivered with heat, Ralph had driven west of Boise. He was walking in a farmer's field with what had once been his father's old, over-and-under twelve gauge shotgun. Accompanying him was Tippet, a Brittany spaniel. Ralph was moving alongside a row of tall locust trees across a broad, green cow pasture, the grass underfoot cropped quite low everywhere by cattle except along the irrigation channels, one of which, running parallel to the trees, his dog was now working.

Ralph was presently, somewhat out of context, thinking about the poetry of John Donne, a subject he taught at the university.

A pheasant cock flushed suddenly, the green and gold bird exploding from the tall grass along the ditch, glittering in the sunlight and cackling loudly. Beating its stout wings, it sailed in a high arc toward the trees. As Ralph knew from past experience, this was a route pheasants frequently took from that field, hoping to land safely in another pasture on the other side. He quickly swung the shotgun through the bird's flight path and fired. In a few minutes, Tippet brought the pheasant to him.

"Good girl," he said, patting the dog's yellow and white spotted head and gently removing the limp carcass from her jaws. The dog licked her mouth, pulling her tongue in with the taste of blood on it. But she didn't seem to mind giving up the bird, and sat down calmly beside her master. "Good girl," Ralph repeated, pleased at the weight of his quarry.

At home he cleaned the bird, then left it in the kitchen for his wife to scald, pluck and prepare for the oven. For two adults and three half-grown children, it would provide slim pickings, but the wild meat was always a treat. Ralph spent the early evening correcting papers. He felt pure. The freshness of the outdoors was still in his clothes, and he had provided something for the table which was somehow deeply satisfying, clean, redolent of lean wilderness.

"Why is it," he thought, looking up from a student's paper, "that it makes me feel so good? This freshness and newness from being in a field." He didn't know. The sun had certainly been hot that afternoon. He told his wife and children so at the dinner table.

"You should wear a hat," Pamela said. Pam was his wife.

"I'm never out long enough to get sunstroke."

"All the same, it isn't good for you." She turned toward her son. "Michael, hold your fork right," she snapped.

Ralph looked at his twelve year old son, a stocky boy with hair in his eyes and an upturned lip his sisters interpreted as a perpetual sneer directed at them. The boy sat isolated halfway down the table between the two adults and opposite his two sisters by their mutual consent. The girls were fourteen and ten. These children had come singly in two year intervals until Ralph and Pam had decided three were enough. "Do as your mother says," Ralph reiterated.

Michael reluctantly turned the fork over, an expression of wonder spreading slowly across his bland features as a surprised recognition of the fork's undiscovered concavity dawned upon him. Ralph took his eyes off him.

"Missy, Tippet did well today." he said, addressing his oldest daughter, who had been the one to name the dog. Tippet was her pet, as well as his companion in the field.

Missy smiled. She was a pretty girl. Very quiet. Ralph loved her deeply. He had once offered to take her hunting with him, but she didn't want to see anything killed, as the sight of blood upset her. She has something of her mother's gentleness about her, Ralph thought. She was sensitive and bright.

He had read poetry to her since she was very small. The Romantics mostly: Byron, Shelley and Keats. Coleridge, Wordsworth or Bryant occasionally. This love of verse was something they shared between them. It made them close. Their special bond was recognized and more or less accepted by the other members of the family.

"Honey, we need to do something about the Plymouth. It keeps killing on me in the most awkward places." Pam was cleaning her mouth with a napkin, looking seriously across the table at her husband. Her voice broke his reverie. She gripped her napkin in one hand, her forearm now resting on the edge of the table as she continued looking at her husband, awaiting his reply. Her fingers were slender, her nails coated with clear polish. She worked weekdays in a downtown real estate office.

"It's the carburetion," Ralph said abruptly. "I tried to set the damn thing yesterday." He paused as though thinking about the problem. "I'll take the car down to the shop on Saturday," he added wearily.

"Daddy."

"Yes, Missy."

"You know that boy, Johnny Ferguson? He came by last Saturday, remember?"

"Yes." Ralph's face clouded.

"He wants to take me to a movie on Friday."

"He's too old."

"No he isn't, Daddy." Missy's eyes and lips were set.

Ralph turned to Pam.

"We've got to let go sometime," she said unhelpfully. She shrugged her shoulders and finished dabbing at her mouth with the napkin, leaving the decision up to Ralph.

"Missy's too young to be out on a date," he said lamely.

"I'll be home by ten. I promise."

"All right." It was against his better judgment.

Later, in the small room that served as a den or study, Ralph thought about Missy. He didn't want to let her start dating, so did that mean he was clinging to her? He glanced over the student paper he had just read, noting the remarks he had written in the margins. Then he put a grade at the bottom of the last page and wrote some more commentary beneath the grade.

Pam was in the bedroom getting ready for bed. She decided to wear the sheerest, shortest nightgown she had. It had been a hot, sticky day. For some reason, that often increased her libido. She got into bed. But lying quietly between the cool sheets did not assuage her need.

However, when Ralph finally came into the bedroom, she was asleep. He saw the nightgown and wondered if he should awaken her. He did so, and they made love, groaning and cooing with pleasure as a cool breeze blew across their naked bodies from the bedroom window.

Missy's date on Friday went smoothly, as far as Ralph could tell. She was home by ten as agreed. Still, he wasn't comfortable with the idea, and he wondered at Pam's seeming unconcern.

"Don't you think," he asked her when they were alone, "that Missy is a bit young yet for this sort of thing?"

Pam looked at him sharply with what he thought was an expression of defiance at his questioning of her judgment, or of disregard for his prudishness, but her eyes softened. "Yes," she said. "I *am* worried."

"Then why …?"

"Because," she turned to face him, "we have to show her trust." She unhooked her brassiere. Her heavy breasts fell out into the yellow light of the bedroom. She quickly pulled a nightgown over her head, concealing this subject of interest from her husband's eyes. She was tired tonight. It had been a long day at work. "She's old enough to find ways of getting into trouble without our knowing," she added.

"She's built like you," Ralph observed. "She looks mature for her age." Pam didn't answer. She was well aware of this fact and just as concerned as he was.

That night, lying awake in bed, Ralph felt unpleasantly disturbed by the thought of his daughter being with boys. He avoided the impulse to imagine what they might be doing. "It's not her as a person they want," he said aloud in the dark, defending himself for his concern about her. Pam was asleep.

* * *

During that summer Ralph had begun taking Michael out into the desert with a twenty-two rifle. The boy, being only recently introduced to firearms, was already becoming a good shot. He was in Little League as well and was developing into a fine ball player, which Ralph had never been himself.

They were now shooting at a target taped to the side of a cardboard box. He hadn't yet introduced his son to hunting. He felt pride in Michael's athletic ability, but the boy was a disappointingly indifferent scholar. This troubled Ralph a great deal because the life of the mind meant so much to him. He felt he and his son weren't as close as he would like. He sometimes even thought they might grow further apart. This was because he wanted the boy to be educated and thoughtful, but he didn't know how to impress the fact upon him.

"Dad," Michael asked, placing a carefully aimed shot, "Why don't you ever talk about the war?"

"It wasn't any good over there," Ralph said shortly. He didn't want to cultivate an interest in the military in his son, he told himself to excuse his unwillingness to talk about it. The whole thing irritated him.

"What wasn't good?" Michael persisted, ejecting an empty shell from the single shot, bolt action rifle. He closed the unloaded chamber and put the safety on.

"Nothing. Keep shooting. We need to finish up and get home. I've got work to do this evening," Ralph said, walking away. He picked up the box of ammunition that was lying nearby.

The boy did not ask any more questions. He finished off his shirt pocketful of rounds, and they packed up and left.

In the car Ralph said, "I want you to clean the rifle first thing when you get home."

They drove for awhile through gray-green sage brush country, the gnarled woody bushes growing thickly together and rolling endlessly over low, sandy hills like a shaggy mat of unkempt gray hair on the rounded shoulders of an old woman. They entered the city from the northeast, driving down Capitol Boulevard away from the downtown and the Capitol building, stopping in a park on their right near the end of the boulevard. The park was so new, its recently planted trees were still small, and its freshly-cut grass was short and dense like the turf of a golf course. In the intense heat, so little shaded by the young trees, the grass looked yellowish, almost brown. Ducks quacked and geese honked loudly beside the pond as Michael fed them scraps of bread.

Back in the car driving up onto the Bench, Michael said precociously, "Dad, I won't ever tell anybody if you want to talk about it some day."

Ralph put his hand on Michael's knee and silently gave it an affectionate squeeze.

* * *

Ralph was sitting upstairs in his office at Boise State University looking out over the Quad, a rectangular, grassy area surrounded and crisscrossed by sidewalks and flanked by academic buildings. He was between classes with an hour to spare, and students were crossing the Quad below him outside his window. They were headed in different directions, following their class schedules. One of them was wearing an olive-green military fatigue jacket. He was bearded, and slung over his shoulder on a military utility belt was a matching green, makeshift book bag, which had once been the knapsack portion of a field marching pack. Ralph suppressed a wryly bemused and somewhat irritated grin upon catching sight of him. This student, an undergraduate in his late thirties and a Vietnam veteran like himself, though somewhat younger, was in one of his classes. The student was a Marxist who could interpret the invention of ice cream as a capitalist conspiracy. He tended often to disrupt the normal process of interpreting literary works in class, though he did occasionally express original insights. Ralph would grant him that but no more.

Ralph was thinking of something else now, as he sat at his desk with his chin propped on a hand and elbow, looking out the half-opened window beside him. Pam had received results that morning from a biopsy and had been told she had been diagnosed with breast cancer. She had just called and was obviously upset. He had done his best to calm her but was stunned to numbness himself. That afternoon he had one more class which he wished he could get out of, but there was no one to replace him, and he didn't feel he should cancel it since his students were close to taking their semester exams.

By the time he did get home, he was surprised to find Pam in good spirits. They discussed it later that evening after the children went to bed. It turned out that Pam had been misinformed. She didn't have cancer but a sudden and alarming thickening of tissue in the lower part of her left breast, which suggested a high risk.

"Dr. Thornton thinks he should take it out," she said. "He won't have to remove the whole breast, but there will be some restructuring." When Ralph didn't answer, she added, "It could be a lot worse."

"I'd rather it didn't have to happen at all," he said.

Within a few weeks Pam entered the hospital and was out a few days later. In a month she went back for reconstructive surgery. They had not removed the nipple, so, with the exception of a small scar beneath her left breast, the restoration was almost as good as new.

There was an unexpected result though. Missy, who appeared to be taking events in stride, began to become morose, withdrawn. Her grades at school began to suffer.

Pam sat her down one afternoon, when no one else was home, and asked her directly, "Is it my operation that has you upset, honey?"

When Missy didn't answer but sat with her head hanging, Pam wrapped her arms around her. "It's okay, baby. Everything turned out fine."

"I know."

"Then what's wrong?"

"Nothing. It's just ..."

Pam understood. "Oh, sweetie," she said, rocking her daughter in her arms, "just because I had a problem doesn't mean you're going to have it too."

Missy looked into her mother's face with tears in her eyes. "I don't want to seem selfish," she said, wanting suddenly to smile in relief but fearing to show it.

Pam laughed. "It isn't selfish to be afraid," she said. "But you have nothing to worry about." She could only hope she was right.

* * *

Ralph was spending one of those pleasant evenings he loved to have with his oldest daughter. They were in her bedroom sitting on the edge of her bed reading poetry to each other. It was after dinner. Missy had just read aloud Shelley's poem, "Hymn to Intellectual Beauty."

"Many critics today don't give that poem sufficient credit," Ralph observed as Missy closed the book with her finger marking the page. Her eyes were misty with feeling. They were hazel colored like her mother's. In fact, she did look a lot like her mother. Ralph wanted to put his arm around her and pull her close to him. He had often done so in the past, Missy warmly laying her head with its light brown, silky hair on his shoulder or chest. It was very sweet. But now she was beginning to look a little too much like a grown woman for such things, Ralph had decided. A young and still in many ways childish woman, but a woman all the same.

"Why, Daddy? Why don't they?" Missy asked. She leaned over and put her head on his shoulder without prompting. He then put his arm around her. "I think it's beautiful," she said.

"So do I. But Mathew Arnold was one of the first to disparage Shelley. He once described him as a beautiful, ineffectual angel, beating his wings in a void."

"That's awful! Why did he say that?"

Ralph looked down into his daughter's face. He couldn't help but think how sweet she appeared with her girlishly soft, unblemished cheeks. "I don't know," he said. "He seemed to be of the opinion that Shelley's use of imagery was insufficiently concrete. Too abstract. Too far removed from life."

"Well, I don't know what that means, but I think it's a great poem."

"So do I, Missy. And you know why? I'm thinking he's talking here"—he tapped with his finger the book which Missy was still holding with the page marked—"about the way we can on certain occasions reach through ourselves to something more enduring …

and I believe ultimately more concrete in terms of our inner experience."

"You see things beautifully, Dad. You make me want to be a poet."

Ralph laughed with embarrassment and pleasure, hugged his daughter, and got up to leave the room. At the door he turned around, still smiling but looking serious, and said, "Being a poet in this world isn't easy."

"I know," Missy said.

When Ralph met the boyfriend, Johnny Ferguson, for the second time, he observed that the boy was at least reasonably intelligent. There was, he thought critically, a sufficient expanse of bare flesh between his eyebrows and hairline. The boy had sensitive eyes and seemed polite, gentle in his manner. This was a comfort. But Ralph thought, "He's still too old." Johnny was seventeen. Ralph recalled the fire that hung between his own legs at that age and the unrelenting sexual desire it produced.

* * *

Ralph finally took Michael with him one afternoon to shoot dove. As it was the first time they had gone after birds together, he had equipped his son with a four ten caliber shotgun. The recoil would be less surprising. They were in a marshy area in the desert twenty miles east of Boise along Interstate Eighty. The small marsh was rimmed with cattails and rushes. It sparkled with blackbirds and rasped with the harsh cry of an occasional magpie. Such areas harbor an abundance of wildlife, but it always amazed him that water should stand out against the open sky anywhere in such arid and otherwise barren country.

A flock of doves was moving about over the brush, appearing to skirt the top of it together like one connected sail, but in fact fluttering from bush to bush individually when more closely observed. Michael fired into the midst of them. He was out of range.

"Slow down, son," Ralph said.

"Sorry, Dad."

They hunted several hours that afternoon. Ralph, preoccupied with his son's shooting, only managed to wing two of the birds himself. One of them was wounded severely enough for Tippet to retrieve. The other was never found.

"This one bird'll make a damn small meal," Ralph said laughing, as they headed back to the car. Michael had failed to bag anything. Ralph observed that his expression was solemn, his shoulders rounded in defeat. "Don't worry, son," he said, rubbing the back of the boy's head. "This was your first day. And I kept you undergunned. It wasn't likely you would've gotten anything today. Maybe next time you should go ahead and try the twelve gauge. That'll take out a big enough chunk of sky for you."

"I can handle it," Michael said confidently. He began to brighten.

Ralph smiled. He was remembering the first time his father had let *him* fire a twelve gauge. He had not been prepared for the recoil, and it had knocked him to the ground. Musing upon this, he wondered at the way his father rarely spoke, never warning or preparing him for things. Unlike him, the man was inarticulate, a creature of few words, those often painful and labored when spoken on necessary occasions.

His father was not educated and, though in some ways brutal and taciturn, he had diligently seen to the manlier side of Ralph's development. The old boy, not quite sixty-five, had died unexpectedly three years ago from heart failure. Ralph thought about that. There were many things he had wondered about as a boy and in later years but had never had the courage to ask and had never been told. Well, he had long since decided he could not be so reserved and withholding with his own son. He never considered how much, under certain types of pressing circumstances, he truly resembled the old man.

* * *

Winter came, and the entire family went to Bogus Basin for skiing. There had been a fresh powdering the previous night. The brilliant white, nearly trackless snow on the slopes was almost blinding, the sun clear and yellow, the air cold. Coming down from the mountain after a day's exercise always left them feeling pleasantly tired. On this day, as on so many others, they pulled into their driveway in the dark. Michael got out and opened the front door of the house. Then they all climbed out of the car into the cold night air and quickly went in, leaving the skis strapped on top of the car.

Inside, Ralph lit a fire in the fireplace. As it flickered and smoked, then finally crackled with red flames, Pam went into the kitchen and made hot chocolate, bringing it out to everyone in steaming hot cups. They turned out the lights and sat in the living room in the dark. The neighbors' lights were on and could be seen across the street through the living room curtains.

Andrea, now eleven, had made her first downhill run and was feeling ecstatic in the silence. She had been so excited that day, that, by the time she had reached the bottom of the slope, she had wet her pants.

"Mom." Missy spoke out of the dark. "Do you suppose Lord Byron was a skier?"

"I don't know, honey."

"He was lame and could swim very well," Ralph said.

"That's what I mean, Daddy. A person can do almost anything, if she or he really wants too."

Andrea was still silently glowing in her triumph on the slopes that afternoon.

* * *

In the summer Missy had a new boyfriend. Then by the fall she was back with Johnny—now John—Ferguson. Missy was fifteen and a half and was being allowed to stay out until eleven. Johnny was a senior in high school. He and Missy seemed to be getting serious, but Ralph had developed more trust in his daughter's judgment. She had broken up with Johnny in the summer because, as she put it, "Things were getting uncomfortable."

Missy and her father still shared a love of poetry. She was also reading a lot of fiction, much of it of literary quality. This pleased Ralph, though he tried not to influence his daughter beyond the poetry. He didn't want to interfere in her choice of a future career. But if she should chose to major in English in college, he knew he couldn't help but be delighted.

Ralph saw literature as more than a vocation. He felt that in an age devoid of sacred oracles and prophets, or at least the recognition of such men or women, great writers were among the principal guardians of inner truth. It was they alone in a purely secular civilization who could yet reveal the truths of the spirit. Well, they and other artists, like serious composers and painters.

He didn't know anything about the latter, but literature was life to him. It affirmed the dignity of refined imagination, and, within that, the whole glittering experience of simply being alive. Life without imagination is life without a soul, he would say to himself.

Long ago, nearly twenty years ago in the war, he had formed a resolution. It was not one he thought about, but something which solidified within him. He would live as though every moment of life was a celebration of its beauty, no matter how difficult its unreasonable moments might be. For Missy or any of his children—but Missy seemed the most likely—to carry on this conviction couldn't help but please him. Though he would never force it on her. She had her own destiny to unfold. A young plant had to shape itself in sun and wind, just as she must find the special nature of her soul on her own.

* * *

Michael, nearly fourteen now, had become an excellent field sportsman. He frequently accompanied his father to desert and farm and often returned with more game than Ralph did. But Michael was still something of an indifferent student in school, though he did keep his grades at a respectable level. He was good at most sports, and the outdoors was the all in all to him at present. Ralph figured he would settle into the quieter, more reflective aspects of personal development in due time. At least he hoped so.

One afternoon, coming back from a good birding with his son, Ralph suddenly turned to him inside the car and said, "I will tell you now what I have been unwilling to say about the war." But then he thought better of it and stated lamely that war is not pleasant.

When Michael pressed him for details, he grew irritable. "We'll talk about it further later on, son," he was forced to explain. It was not much of an explanation, to be sure.

Bewildered and hurt, Michael finished the trip home in silence. When they got there, he unloaded the car without saying a word and went into the house ahead of his father.

A few minutes later Pam came out and approached her husband.

"Honey, why did you tell Michael you would talk about the war and then leave him hanging?"

"I realized it might interest him too much."

"Might interest him! You've kept him in suspense for years. Why?"

"Pam, I want to talk to him about it, but I'm afraid to."

"What are you afraid of? Is there something you haven't told me?"

"No. It's just …"

"I thought you said you were simply trying to protect him from becoming too interested."

"I was."

"Well?"

"Well … nothing. I don't know what. I can't explain it."

Pam looked at her husband incredulously. Ralph went into the house.

After dinner Ralph picked up a volume of Milton's shorter poems and entered Missy's room without knocking. Missy was partially undressed.

"I'm sorry," he said in surprise. "I didn't think."

Missy covered herself. "That's okay, Dad," she said. She knew something was troubling her father.

Ralph sat down on the side of her bed with the book. Missy sat down beside him. Ralph opened the book without any explanation and read the sonnet on Milton's blindness.

"That's beautiful, Dad," Missy said quietly when he finished. She had heard the poem before.

"Sometimes we don't understand why things happen, and we can only stand and wait," he said.

"What things, Daddy?"

Ralph looked at his daughter. He had an odd far-away expression on his face, as though he were looking at something she didn't see. It frightened her a little, she couldn't have said why. "Things within ourselves," he said.

"In the war?" she asked.

"Yes."

"Did you … did you do something …?"

"No, honey, nothing like that." Ralph smiled. "I was just thinking," he said. "I better let you finish getting ready for bed." He got up and left the room.

He could not have explained it to his daughter, his son, or even his wife. He could not explain it to himself. It was stuck deep in his soul, a living thing, yet dormant, like a seed formed within an apple, a seed that would probably never bear visible fruit.

Thanksgiving Day

The peacocks were out early, giving their hysterical cries. The turkeys were gathered in their pen, pecking the ground or observing the open sky with profound and steadfast wonderment. The sky was neither blue nor gray, but something in-between. The air was still: a November frost. The evergreen trees, in the forest surrounding the farm clearing, were motionless and, without a wind, unable to shiver. An axe lay on an old stump, ready for use.

Inside the log house, bathed in the heat and smoke of an old wood furnace, Marilou was preparing herself for the ritual sacrifice. She was at the yellow, Formica topped kitchen counter, eating a hearty breakfast of ham and eggs seasoned with intense conversation, most of which she manufactured herself. Her mother, the recipient of the majority of these remarks, was stationed at the stove, for there were other members of the family to be fed.

"I don't know if I'm going to like doing this," Marilou said, her mouth full of ham. She flooded the ham with orange juice, sending it partially chewed into her stomach. "I meanph, wha'f he tries to jump'ff the stump?"

"Would you please repeat that, dear. I didn't get a word of it."

"Mmm." After the juice, "Sorry, Mom. I shouldn't talk with my mouth full."

"Well, my dear, I'm afraid that would be like asking those peacocks out there not to yowl like back fence cats." She smiled at her daughter as she set a fresh plate of ham on the table.

"They do sound awful, don't they? Why does Dad keep them?"

"I really don't know. I believe he has the idea that I think they're beautiful."

"Do you?" Marilou's mouth was full of eggs. She was able nevertheless to talk around the corners of her food, as her mouth had long since been worked into a considerable plasticity of expression.

"I suppose sometimes I do," her mother answered wistfully, back at the stove.

The front door banged, and Marilou's father and two younger sisters came in. The youngest, seven years of age, was a man of few words like her father. The other one rivaled Marilou in loquacious intensity, the principal difference being that most of her conversation consisted of cutting remarks made to her older sister, who was older than her by only two years. Marilou was seventeen.

"Well, Marilou, are you ready to do your duty?" her father asked as he trod heavily into the kitchen in his unpolished, black leather boots and hung his coat on a peg in the adjoining mud room.

"If it doesn't try to get away."

"Get away? Why, where's it going to go, Marilou? It loves you after all the tender loving care you've given it, raising it."

"Please, Dad. This is hard enough."

"Hard? There's nothing to it."

Marilou got up from the table, wiped her mouth with her napkin, crossed the living room and went out the front door. On the way out, she said, "I'd better get to it if I'm going to do it."

"Don't chicken out and cut off your own hand," her sister called after her.

"Hush!" her mother said. "Don't go putting terrible thoughts into her head. Your sister is having a hard enough time with this."

"With what?" Marilou's father asked, raising his voice to a high pitch. "I do it every day. Just one quick …"

"Never mind, Fred." Marilou's mother set a plate heaped with scrambled eggs and ham in front of him. With a flurry of knife and fork movements, Fred set about reducing the steaming pile. His youngest daughter, who was sitting on a high stool beside him at the counter, was served next. She covered everything with five ounces of syrup. The front door banged shut.

Out in the yard, over by the mud room, Marilou stood in front of the stump with the axe lying on it. The stump was soggy from years of northern Pacific coast weather. "God!" she said, pulling her shoulders together and rubbing her upper arms with her hands. "It's cold out here!" She had a warm coat on, but her breath did steam. There was still frost on the ground.

Over near the turkey pen, Marilou found her intended victim, which she had carefully mothered all summer long. It was fat and mottled brown like all of its fellow inmates. "Here, turkey, turkey," she said, opening the wire gate. "Come to mama." She was not a sentimental person, and Turkey was its name. However, the bird did come over to her as she tossed some pebbles on the ground, pretending they were grain. And this did tweak Marilou's heart. "Dumb bird," she said, as she grabbed the trusting creature around its body, pinning its wings to its sides. It squawked, and the other turkeys in the pen scattered. It turned its head and looked stupidly at her, as she pushed the gate closed with her shoulder and walked away with it, its feet dangling beneath its body.

Marilou knew this was a test of her courage and an inevitable result of her decision to raise the family's Thanksgiving meal herself. She was not a sentimental girl, but she had never done this before. She had seen her father do it many times.

Lying on its back on the stump, its greenish gray legs held firmly in Marilou's left hand, its neck stretched out in guileless submission, the bird seemed awfully willing to give up the only life it had. Well, she had brought it into the world, so to speak, by caring for it. Now she would take what she had given. She wondered if this was the kind of mother she would be to her children.

Whack! Marilou's right arm brought the axe down squarely on the bird's neck. She rolled the body off to the left, and the head fell to the ground on the right. It looked up at her in a moment of remaining consciousness.

The Staircase of Loretto

She was young, darkly pretty and a Twentieth Century anomaly. What made her different was the quality of her mind. Her formal education had ended with the twelfth grade in high school. But within a certain area of special interest she was deeply and widely informed. For she had read Thomas à Kempis, Archbishop Fénelon, Meister Eckhart, Saint Thérèse de Lisieux, Saint Theresa of Avila, Madame Guyon, the anonymous *Cloud of Unknowing* and other mystical works. She had even taught herself Renaissance Spanish so she could appreciate the poetry of Saint John of the Cross in its original language and meter. Her love for both the Spanish mystical poetic tradition and the English metaphysical poets was almost unbounded. She read them over and over, aloud and in silent meditation.

Now it is true she was of Hispanic background, which accounts in some measure for her mastery of Spanish. It was still spoken by her parents, herself and her brothers and sisters in their home when she was a girl. But the conversations carried on in this manner were of a less than fluent nature. These homely dialogues were interspersed with many English words or English neologisms rudely inducted into the peninsular purity of the Castilian tongue. More often than not their talk simply broke into full English, which was more comfortable for them all. After all, American English had been the language of work, school and play in New Mexico for well over a hundred years.

Eva Fuentes was very slender in her teens, dark eyed, small boned, with straight black hair to her shoulders. Her skin was of a brown olive complexion, her features refined. She was passionate, her mouth sensual, and she was profoundly religious, even in the outward forms. What made her an anomaly in her time was both the depth of her exposure (for she did much of her reading when young) in an area of knowledge currently considered to be out of use, and her extraordinary lack of learning or interest in most other things. She was a creature of what now seems a darker, more otherworldly age, a period of mendicant friars and transported nuns.

Eva's parents—her mother especially—feared these developments in their daughter when they began to notice them in her early teens. Though devout Roman Catholics, they did not understand. There was a terrible passionate intensity to their daughter's long periods of prayer and meditation, when she would shut herself up in her room. It was as though the overpowering drives of puberty in this warm, reflective nature were somehow turning inward.

"My dear girl," her mother would often exclaim in those days, as she happened upon her daughter in the hallway, when the latter was still in a dreamy, self-enclosed state of mind, "it isn't healthy to be so much involved in these things. You have to live in the world."

"But I do, Mother. I just want to be a good Catholic."

"There can be too much even of that, my dear. You must come out of your shell."

"I'm not in a shell."

"Listen, last week I went to see Father Reuben."

"Father Reuben. What for? You didn't go to see him about me, did you?"

"Yes, I did. I'm sorry, dear. But I'm worried. Your father says it's an adolescent thing. That it'll pass. I don't know. Every day you seem to …"

"What did Father Reuben say?"

"Don't be angry with me, daughter. I'm only trying to understand."

"Mother, what did Father Reuben say?"

"Well, nothing really. He seems to think it's natural for a deeply sensitive nature like yours to go through a period of intense devotion. I told him of your love for animals and plants, your tenderness toward all wild things, how you could observe a sunrise or sunset fixed to one spot for hours without speaking. I explained to him the way you refuse to fight with your brothers and sisters, and that they have come to regard you as strange and even behave almost as if you weren't in the house."

Eva sat down in a chair, her hands folded in her lap. Her mother stood over her, tears in her eyes.

"Do you know what he said? He said, 'Leave her in the hands of our Lord. She is one who has been touched by the Blessed Virgin.' Now what can that possibly mean?" Mrs. Fuentes' voice rose with a tone of irritation. She appeared about to wring her hands.

Her daughter sat before her looking at her own hands folded in her lap. A soft smile played about her full lips. When her mother said nothing more but remained standing anxiously before her, she looked up at her with gentle compassion. "It'll be all right, Mother," she said. "Please trust me." She lowered her head, then raised it again, meeting her mother's eyes. "I'll find my way," she said in an almost inaudible whisper.

Eva Fuentes did find her way, but it was not as her mother had hoped. Eva didn't become a nun as her mother had assumed she would. Though she never went out with any boys in her teens, she seemed to fear her own nature and considered herself unworthy of taking vows. Instead, she went into the mission fields of her church as a lay person. She worked in many places and left behind her everywhere a sense of her goodness.

Something of her passion was also felt. Her love for all things. Men secretly desired her. Women were a little afraid. She seemed to infuse those about her with an intensity of quiet longing, which would quite literally disturb and shake them into uneasiness within. She worked hard, spoke, ate and slept with a sincerity of expression, thought and demeanor that is not usually devoted to such mundane acts. It was as if life were a prayer. It was also as if, in some indefinable way, existence itself were being made love to.

Eva died during a period of famine and revolution in Africa. She was murdered, caught in a crossfire of ethnic hostilities. When her body was sent home, her mother remarked that her life had been like the miraculous staircase in the Chapel of Loretto in Santa Fe. The polished, wooden staircase is said to have been built by a mysterious carpenter who fitted and formed it into a perfectly symmetrical, rising spiral without the use of any nails.

At the top of that staircase, in the darkened choir loft, is a large, stained glass window, its particles of transparent color joined in an uneven circular composite, like the petals of a flower. Through it the light of ordinary day is first broken into subtle hues, then mingled with shadow, as if to interfuse the interior of the chapel with another world.

Cold War

Dave was a fighter pilot. Flying was his passion, and the Air Force was his career. Mary had always accepted that—worried, but accepted it.

Northern Japan was a forbidding, cold, isolated place. It was eight minutes bomber flying time from Russian installations off the coast of Siberia. In the middle of winter the skies were gray, the winds howled and roared, and the snow piled up to your waist or shoulders in a matter of hours, drifting over cars and houses, burying them. The roads froze into ruts of ice that lasted for weeks before a thaw, sending vehicle after vehicle sliding off them in the same places.

But it was a Monday around noon in early winter now, so the ground was still dry and clear, hard with the cold, a cold that was rarely sub-zero but chillingly damp. The first snow of the year had begun to fall in large dry flakes. Mary glanced out the living room window. She was concerned about her daughter Melissa. A junior in high school, Melissa was not due home for several hours. That was long enough for the snow, if it should turn into a blizzard, to pile up and drift. An Air Force staff car was pulling up at the end of the front walkway. Mary saw a young lieutenant get out and head toward her front door. Suddenly she knew.

At three o'clock Mary sat down in the living room. One lamp was lit. The front door slammed.

"Hi, Mom."

Melissa came into the living room and tossed her books and notebook onto a chair. She was tall, slender, and had nut brown hair that fell a couple inches short of her shoulders.

"Mom, Charlene says we're going. Isn't it wonderful? We're the smallest school with a band and one of the best. Mom …"

"Melissa, sit down for a minute, honey, please."

"Mother, you look like you've been crying. Is something wrong? Has something happened? Is Dad …" Melissa screamed.

There were demonstrations in Tokyo and Yokohama at that time concerning America's nuclear role. They had been going on since early May, off and on throughout the year. The Japanese police used powerful water hoses to control the crowds, who sometimes got out of hand. The police were used to these things and were well prepared in handling them. Still, precautions were in order.

Colonel Nichols' widow and daughter were escorted aboard a small Air Force transport plane which carried them from the little fighter base at Misawa, Japan to the big U.S. Air Force headquarters at Tachikawa Air Force Base near Tokyo. They were then driven by staff car to Tokyo International Airport. Captain Barker, the man accompanying them, wore civilian clothes. In the airport he kept his distance, minding his own business, but he was always nearby. Finally the two women boarded their airliner and were lifted into the night winter sky.

Mary and Melissa had been in Japan for a year. Colonel Nichols had preceded them to Misawa by six months, and they had had about six months left before they would have returned stateside at the end of a normal tour of duty.

Melissa, sitting by the aircraft window on the right aisle side, watched the lights of the most densely populated part of Japan recede into the distance beneath her as the plane banked out over the ocean. She felt a heaviness. They would never return. Her father's body had already been flown stateside the day after the crash. In fact, it hadn't been but a few days since he'd frozen to death in the cold waters off Northern Japan. When his fighter plane malfunctioned upon takeoff, he had parachuted into the sea. Rescuers, though always at the ready, could not reach him as quickly by helicopter as those waters could freeze him.

Once aloft, Mary unfastened her safety belt and leaned back in her seat. The Air Force would take care of packing and shipping her household goods, which had been hurriedly left behind. Meanwhile, she had a daughter to take care of, but what would she ever do? She glanced down at her knees where her skirt had slipped up over them. Her slender legs were crossed at the ankles and tucked beneath the passenger seat in front of her. In her late thirties, auburn haired and still very attractive, she could easily remarry. She pulled her skirt down over her knees. No! The thought had merely flitted through her mind, but she felt as if she were being unfaithful to her husband. She would find work. She had never done so in the past, having met and married the Colonel, then a lieutenant, in her senior year at college, where she'd majored in one of the liberal arts. But she would find a way now.

The Colonel was given full military honors. A veteran of the Korean War, he was interred at Arlington National Cemetery near Washington, D.C. His body had been brought to the gravesite by a horse-drawn caisson. Mary and her daughter stood quietly as the military casket team secured the flag over the casket, which they had placed near the freshly dug grave. These six men in Air Force uniform then stood at attention as the chaplain spoke. This was followed by the firing of a rifle volley and the playing of taps. Tears ran down Melissa's cheeks as the flag was prepared for presentation to her mother. The air was cold and dry. The leaves were gone from the trees in the cemetery. A wind picked up.

Melissa could not help saying, "It's so cold down there!"

Her mother put her arm around her shoulder and pulled her close.

"Oh, Daddy, Daddy!"

In the eye of one of the airmen, a staff sergeant, the one who had played taps, was a tear, which broke loose and ran down his cheek as he stood at attention, bugle lowered to his side.

Part Two

Viet Cong Ambush

They hit Larry in the stomach. The bullet went into his side and there was a lot of bleeding. We were crossing between two rice fields on a dike, going carefully, watching for trip wires, when that first shot was fired. It struck Larry and we all went down in the cold paddy water and mud ooze to form a defensive perimeter around him. After that you could see the bullets hit the water in front and to one side of us and you could hear the faint whistle when they were close overhead. We waited for mortars, searching the tree line for movement.

"Get a compress on him! Stop this bleeding!"

The corpsman crawled up and John, our squad leader, moved aside to give him room. He rolled onto his back, his rifle in his hand above the sloppy water. There was a leech on his bare forearm and he brushed it off leaving a tiny trickle of blood.

"They're over there to the right," he said, looking over his shoulder at the tree line. "We need more cover. O'Connor, Johnson, Delaney, over on the right!" he shouted.

The three whose names he'd called started directing bursts of automatic and semi-automatic fire toward the right side of the tree line. The rest of us got up, myself and another guy supporting Larry under each arm, and scrambled for the patch of brush jungle that was only about fifty feet behind us. Larry was getting weak, unsteady on his legs, and weighed a ton, it felt like. He wasn't a big guy but we were trying to run in muck and water.

When we got into the brush, which was so thick you could hardly crawl into it, we spread out in a line and started firing at the Viet Cong. You couldn't see much, even in broad daylight, but we had a clear idea of where they were now. Our base of fire let O'Connor, Johnson and Delaney get back to us. Larry was still our only casualty.

"Mathews," John shouted, "get a round in there. Damn it, what's taking so long?"

I could see Lance Corporal Mathews fooling with his grenade launcher but I don't know what the problem was. He got two rounds off and the second one seemed to do the job. The shooting stopped, except for a couple shots fired from our side.

When the last shot was fired, John scrambled over to have a look at Larry. I was lying beside Larry, one hand on the compress bandage, trying to slow the bleeding. Larry was almost unconscious.

"Hey, what are you doing?"

The guy who'd helped me haul Larry into the brush had his canteen out. I guess he'd been planning to give him some water.

John knocked it out of his hand as he came up and shouted, "Idiot!"

John and Larry were good friends. Larry was my fire team leader, the first fire team. He would take over the squad if something happened to John, that is if he hadn't been wounded himself.

Larry was real woozy. He smiled at John and just kind of rolled his eyes and grimaced. We didn't have a radio.

"The lieutenant should have heard us," John said.

"We going over there?" I meant after the VC to see what we'd done to them, if anything.

"No, we got Larry to worry about. Take McDonald and find O'Connor and go get the lieutenant. Tell him we need a chopper."

When the three of us got out of the brush we saw a patrol approaching us about a hundred and fifty yards out and realized it was with the lieutenant. McDonald and O'Connor went to tell them about the medevac and I went back to John, Larry and the other guys. Larry was out, white as a sheet.

"Is he breathing?" I asked, almost in a whisper.

"Barely." The corpsman was attending him, doing what I'd been doing with the compress. He'd given him morphine but Larry hadn't really made an issue of the pain. John was sitting a little ways off, his knees drawn up, his rifle in his lap and his face in his hands. When I went over to him, he said, "We'd better check it out."

On the way over to the other tree line, we heard the helicopter. It came down in the middle of the rice paddy. The two guys we'd left behind with Larry ran out to the chopper and then ran back to the brush with another guy and a stretcher. Because they went for the stretcher and didn't just bring Larry out, we knew he was dead.

Stevie Harris

Dawn came early. ZuZiga, the rooster, was scandalized by the sudden appearance of the sun. It rose up over the Philippine Sierra Madre mountains and popped into a suddenly blue sky. ZuZiga flapped up onto one of the gray, cinder block walls of the five foot high yard fence and belted out a tune. It rattled up his long, gray mottled throat in a scratchy tone. ZuZiga tried again. He screeched. It sounded as though someone were strangling him. Then to his left, from the same fence, came the clear song of the big, red rooster, master of innumerable hens. ZuZiga, the youthful and untried, modestly hopped down.

One day on central Luzon Island is not unlike any other, except for the two seasons, wet and dry. This was the dry season, hot and sunny. When day arrives in such a place, it is instantly noon and remains so till dark.

Stevie Harris, a boy of ten—if such boys have ages—was awakened by the red rooster. He thought he had heard something awful but was not certain, coming so freshly from a dream. His mother and sister were already in the kitchen, smelling of perfume or some other objectionable substance, and dressed. They were going into Clark Air Force Base to do some shopping at the Base Exchange.

"Stevie, Marsha and I are going onto the base for the morning," his mother said as he wandered into the kitchen. "You be good and mind Laurie—for once."

"Yes, Mom. But my name isn't Stevie. It's Steve. Remember?"

"Well, yes dear. Steve then. You mind Laurie, son. Maybe we'll pick something up for you at the BX."

"I don't want anything."

"Good. Then we won't get you anything," Marsha said. She stuck her tongue out through a mass of twelve year old freckles.

"Hush," their mother said. "Must you two argue over everything?" Stevie left the room muttering something about his sister being a marshmallow with measles, or maybe rabies too.

By the time Stevie was dressed and had lazily eaten breakfast, daydreaming over what he would do for the day, his mother and sister had gone. The six foot, ironwork gate had clattered shut. The family car had rattled down the potholed dirt road of the American housing area, leaving a cloud of dust. Bernie, the female family dog, who was in heat, was still barking at her tormentors. Three large, panting males with erections sat outside the front gate.

Stevie went out the back door. Laurie, a slender Filipino girl of nineteen, was doing the family wash on a metal washboard. Unwilling to use a machine, she squatted on her heels beside a wide concrete basin near the door, the water tap extending from the side of the house turned on and running, soap suds reaching up to her elbows.

"Good morning, Stevie. Ow!"

Stevie had pulled one of her pigtails.

"Why you always do that? I'm going to tell your mother."

"She won't do anything."

"I'm going to tell your father."

"No you won't."

"Go away, Stevie. Don't bother me anymore."

Stevie looked down at the large metal container which held his collection of leopard frog tadpoles. It was sitting on one side of the basin. A number of the tadpoles, swimming in the murky brown water of the container, had developed into frogs and were gathered on a large, now slippery green, rock he had placed in the center, above the water line. Quite a few had already escaped into the yard and were being fought over by a flock of hens.

"They make a mess," Laurie observed.

Stevie was aghast. He had not expected such a bloody exodus for his frogs. But there was nothing he could do about it. He wondered if the bullfrog tadpoles which he kept in a glass jar in his bedroom—along with a mynah bird, some small green parrots, and the usual gecko lizards that lived on the house ceiling, chirping day and night, eating bugs which gathered evenings by the lights, and leaving white eggs to hatch in the sun on the window sills—he wondered if these big bullfrog tadpoles, the size of marbles, which had already formed back legs, would be a problem. They had cost him considerable effort in collecting them, as he had had to slip unauthorized into a neighboring, flooded rice paddy to do it. He'd gotten leeches on his legs, but they had been easy to brush off. Ugh!

In the side yard, which was the main, open, grassy area of the property, he found the rest of his chickens. They were gathered mostly amongst the rows of cool, wide stemmed, waxy leaved water plants close to the cinder block walls that enclosed the yard. Here the soil was damp, and they squatted in it, fanning cool, loose dirt over their bodies with their wings. They were panting, saliva dripping from their beaks. Already it was hot. For this reason, Stevie knew they did most of their morning feeding in the pre-dawn, when he could sometimes hear their soft, muffled clucking outside his bedroom windows.

There were hens under the shady leaves of those succulent plants, and little brown and yellow chicks peeped in and out among the green stems. White ducks were also there in the nearest channel where fresh water ran off from Laurie's wash basin. Some of them had ducklings. Stevie caught one of the adults, took it outside the yard and walked a block down the yellow sand road. Then he threw the duck into the air, releasing it. It swooped low, gracefully over the empty field between the corner of the road and the house. Its wings made a whispering sound, clean like scissors working.

Back in the yard Stevie surprised Laurie washing something she didn't want him to see. They were small strips of white cloth with brown stains on them.

"What's that?" he asked.

"You go on. You should not always be bothering me. Ow!"

Stevie pulled her pigtail and ran into the open side yard.

Laurie muttered, finishing what she was doing. But there was a smile at the corners of her lips. She thought of young Stevie as a meddlesome little brother, whom she both loved and abhorred.

Stevie spent several hours hunting the smooth skinned, green and tan striped skink lizards that hid in the open spaces between and within the cinder blocks of the yard wall. He speared several with the rubber band gun he had made, which fired needles mounted on slivers of bamboo. The lizards crawled away wounded into the crevices.

When Marsha and his mother returned, he was out in a nearby field. There were goats and water buffalo feeding there, and his dog began chasing the buffaloes around in a circle. But she was soon distracted by a squadron of suitors which had followed her to the edge of the field. She and the largest of them now stood back to back, stuck to one another on the nearby dirt road.

Stevie crept slowly through the tall grass, red and yellow winged grasshoppers flying off in all directions. A rice bird made a clicking chirp, but he did not recognize the breed of the bird he was pursuing. Yellow and brown, it rose high on fluttering wings, hovered, then fell back into the tall grass, each time a little further away. It took three or four attempts before Stevie finally hit it with a stone from his slingshot and brought it down, still alive, for his collection. Not that any of these birds, being insect eaters, survived for more than a day or two in the cage he had built for them in his yard.

Where Intellect Has Its Home

She had ears chiseled like fine porcelain. This was true of all her features. Her nose, cheek bones, hands, wrists, ankles, feet, everything was of the utmost delicacy in proportion and refinement. Though lovely to look upon, shapely, green eyed, taffy colored hair in a short close-set cut that set off her face and the tiny gold earrings she frequently wore, she never suggested sex at first sight to even the most lascivious male.

There was one flaw: she had a mind, an intellect so strong she terrified her admirers upon close contact. It seemed she couldn't keep it hidden, though she tried, and it cost her many moments of anguish and sudden regret. I'm too honest, she would tell herself after some disappointing encounter with an interesting young man. I always end up saying what I think, and they don't know how to answer intelligently. Why do boys, why do men always think they have to be mentally superior? Who gave them that right? Oh, how I wish I knew how to hide it!

Joanna Marie Davis didn't hide it. Quiet, unprepossessing, she nevertheless made A's in all her high school classes, joined the chess club, beat all the boys, smiled shyly and never achieved popularity, in spite of her unsurpassed loveliness.

In college Joanna majored in physics. It came easily, for she loved theory. She was careful, meticulous in the performance of experiments, but she was principally a systematic thinker who wished to apply her great powers of mind to the resolution of the most abstruse problems in empirical science. Her professors admired her, her fellow students envied her. To escape the latter difficulty, she left college at the end of four years and taught high school for two. It was unbearable. She went on to graduate school.

After attaining her doctorate, she entered government research in particle physics at Los Alamos, New Mexico. She found the work mentally constricting, though she learned a great deal. After four and a half years she accepted an assistant professorship at the University of New Mexico.

Now she was in charge. What a surprise to her students when this diminutive woman entered the classroom for the first time at the beginning of each semester! Every new male student fell immediately romantically and protectively in love with the pretty little porcelain doll, now in her early thirties. She felt as if she were made of glass. She had to be careful how she sat, how she bent over, how she dressed, how she moved. They were all ravenously hungry young men, with probing eyes that reached out to her like burning tongues. But then they would discover the dark, gaping maw of her intellect, and her authority was coldly established. Coldly because they could not conceive, or at least maintain, their initial passion for a little woman with such big mental teeth.

Seven years at the University brought Joanna tenure and an associate professorship. However she did not attract support for the university from the business community through any kind of research. And this was not to her advantage. But she was known as an excellent teacher. Her students revered her—from a distance— for she saw clearly into the depths of any problem and explained things well. She was patient and tireless in her effort to communicate both the rudiments and the arcane depths of her beloved chosen field of knowledge. She was so fluent in the subject she still terrified even her most experienced students, but they learned much from her and were strengthened by contact with her mind.

She had also published a number of important papers. She hoped to systematically reunify physics by giving it a stronger mathematical and conceptual bridge over the broken terrain of particle theory. She was becoming widely known and respected in the international physics community.

"Darren," she once said to a colleague and male friend one quiet afternoon in the physics department graduate student and faculty lounge, "I think I've begun to see a way clear on this problem."

"Joanna, if you do, you'll be the greatest scientist since Einstein and do much to strengthen the integrity of his work and lifelong conviction. He always insisted that God didn't throw dice."

"I don't know what God does, Darren. I really don't. I wouldn't venture to guess. But I do know that the human mind will always be uncomfortable with anything suggesting contradiction or inconsistency. Maybe the universe is governed by chance, but the human mind can't conceive it. Our paradigms must not reflect it. The human spirit won't tolerate it. We are only fooling ourselves if we ignore this."

Joanna and Darren were sitting in straight-backed gray metal chairs at opposite corners of a small bare wooden table at one end of the lounge. In the excitement of thought Joanna crossed her legs. Darren observed the unspeakable loveliness of those slender limbs and then cleared his mind. He was married.

Crossing her legs brought a warmth and sent a sweet feeling throughout Joanna's body. It was a sort of self embrace and had certain physical results. These were, of course, unknown to Darren and not really present to her own consciousness at this moment.

"I think it's a matter of psychological or philosophical perspective," Joanna continued, feeling secure in herself. "What I mean, Darren, is ..." She took a sip of her coffee. It was very hot, having been freshly brewed in the carafe on the counter by the sink on the opposite end of the room. Darren sipped his too, listening.

"What I mean is we have to make some kind of definite distinction between two separate paths of theoretical inheritance in classical physics: the wave and particle modes of looking at the behavior of matter and energy. At the subatomic level, what were two different perspectives, as in Huygens' and Newton's conflicting theories of light, become imperceptibly intermixed. The question is one of how we should conceive of matter and energy in themselves. Do we look at point mass or at a spatially extended mode of representing these phenomena? Do we, for instance, conceive of gravity as extended from a point in space or as an expression of the space-time continuum itself, to be described in the latter terms, not extended through space but as an integral component of space and time? Is space-time some kind of irreducible structure or just a part of our perceptual apparatus?" Joanna was excited, flushed, intent on communicating something to her friend yet lost within herself. She was enveloped in the warmth of her own physical, emotional and intellectual being.

Darren looked at Joanna. She was radiant, suffused with thought. She leaned forward, unconsciously uncrossing and recrossing her legs. She seemed almost seraphic to him, caught up as she was in the grip of ideas that were the very substance of life to her.

A Summer Idyl

Twelve year old Sarah Munchausen was not like other girls. She dreamed and lived in an unformed cloud of bright and variegated emotion. Other girls in her seventh grade class were already wearing bras and putting on lipstick. In fact, she knew of one girl who had secretly confided to her that she was having sex with her fourteen year old boyfriend. It was not that Sarah wasn't interested in boys. She thought about them often and tried to imagine being touched by one in an intimate way. Meditating on such things she would fall asleep at night with her pillow wound tightly in her arms.

But Sarah was sensitive, intelligent, perceptive, while the boys she knew were often rough, uncaring. At least this was true of the ones she was well enough acquainted with to carry on a few words of unfulfilling conversation. Her best friend, Marta, had once told her that you had to go along with them, ignore their crudeness, if you wanted their attention. They were just too inexperienced to know better. Sarah couldn't bear the thought of what this might entail. And she didn't like being an object of amusement, to be teased in an unkind spirit at one moment and treated like a glove to be worn and thrown off at another.

One thing Sarah did feel close to, and which gave her much solace, was nature. The neat, green rows of corn that her dad planted every spring, working the big draft horse and plow in his suspenders and yellow straw hat, told her of the rich providence of God. Of course, this sentiment was repeated in her father's strong voice, echoing in the big kitchen of the white farmhouse at every meal. But Sarah truly believed it.

She saw it in the robins of the meadows and bluebirds along country roads and at the forest edge, their cheerful song. She felt it in the sparrows that gathered uproariously about the golden cracked corn in the chicken feed bin near the barn when the heavy wooden lid to it was left open. She even saw it in the swooping and diving, amidst hackles of cawing, when flocks of crows descended over her father's deep fields. "Thieves," neighbor Schoenberg called them, but Sarah's father passed no judgment on the things which God made.

Southeastern Pennsylvania between Lancaster and York is known to many as Amish country, but Sarah's family was of a more liberal Mennonite persuasion. They could've farmed in good conscience with modern machinery but chose the simple method of their conservative neighbors, since they were able to live modestly and make it pay.

Passing through a cornfield one afternoon—a neighbor's, not her father's—Sarah came to a small wood lot in a gentle ravine. It was a familiar place, which she often visited. She slipped down the bank between large, old oak and hickory and came to a clear, shallow, softly moving stream, which was still narrow, erupting from a nearby spring. Birds sang in the trees. Scarlet and summer tanagers flashed their greenish yellow and bright red plumage among the green leaves. Jays rasped. A flowering dogwood stood alone, small compared to the towering oak and hickory around it, but glorious in its display of solitary, large, four petaled, white flowers. A warm breeze stirred the leaves of the tallest trees.

Sarah sat down on a rock near the stream bank. The rock was large and gray with moss growing near its base. She plunged her bare feet into the cold water of the stream, being quick about it for the sake of courage, and winced as she drew the ample folds of her long skirt up to her knees. Brr! She felt a coolness under her dress and a thrilling shudder went through her. Then she withdrew her feet from the water, placing them on the damp earth. Gripping some small plants between her toes, she closed her eyes.

Opening her eyes she saw a small crayfish and tried to reach for it, but it disappeared under a rock, and she almost slipped off the one she was sitting on. She giggled with happiness. The water curled like glass over golden brown pebbles, bending the light and catching sparkling bits of it in a sudden array of color to be sent on down its flow. Clear ripples eddied about and slipped downstream as well.

Sarah closed her eyes once more and felt the cold dampness of her feet, now pressing her toes into the soft earth, where it was relatively warm. There was no one here. It seemed as if the earth itself were a lover. Was that wrong? She opened her eyes with a start, then closed them again.

Sarah let her mind drift, mixing into it the sweet languor of her limbs and green freshness of plants, water and earth.

"Sarah." She heard a voice far out in her reverie, as though in the midst of a dream, softer than a butterfly's flight, and she knew she had imagined it, or at least she thought she had.

"Sarah, I love you," she warmly felt, rather than heard, the voice say, and she wanted to let go of herself, her body and mind. But that would've meant slipping off the rock. Vaguely, in a distant part of her consciousness, outside the self-imposed perimeter of pleasant feeling, she became aware of a sting of forest floor litter on the palms of her hands. But she didn't open her eyes.

"I will never leave you," the voice said, and Sarah sensed, passing from head to toe, something that seemed to take bodily possession of her. Then she opened her eyes suddenly and sat up on the rock. Her heart beat in her chest, her breathing was faster than normal. Her senses were acute. She could hear the smallest twig rub against another high in the treetops overhead, and she picked up the soft weesee weesee of a warbler concealed above her upon the trunk of one of those trees.

On her way home, walking barefoot, as she had come, beside a cornfield, purple tasseled but not yet bearing the ripened grain, Sarah felt wonderfully happy. The warm sun on her hands and feet was like the gentle touch of a reassuring presence.

Runaway

Two American boys, one fourteen, the other fifteen, huddled against the predawn chill of Subic Bay in the Philippine Islands west of Manila. A thin spray flew over the bow of the navy launch that held them and two American sailors.

"Here. Use these." One of the sailors stepped into the semi-sheltered portion of the boat. It was open toward the front. He tossed blankets to both of the boys. Each boy wrapped one around his shoulders and pulled it together over his arms and chest. The sailor stepped back out into the blowing mist. He had a dark blue wool, navy peacoat on.

"Sure would like to have one of those," the older boy said, pointing toward the sailor's coat, which extended well below his waist and could be turned up at the collar for warmth. The boy was tall and thin, sallow of complexion and pockmarked on his cheeks.

"Sure," the other one said. He lowered his head and hunched over in the cold, knitting his brows against it and sniffing through pale, slender nostrils. "What do you think they're going to do with us?"

"It's starting to get light."

"Huh?"

"I'm going outside." The older boy got up and stepped out of the cabin area. "Cold," he said in the open air and darkness. The spray was wet and stung his cheeks, numbing his jaw and thickening his tongue, making it difficult for him to speak.

"It'll warm up," the sailor who'd given them the blankets said.

The boy was wearing the gray wool blanket he'd been given. "You taking us to Subic Naval Base?" he asked. The two boys had spent the night under a sort of house arrest at Cubi Point Naval Station near the end of the peninsula forming the western limit of Subic Bay. They had been picked up by the U.S. Navy shore patrol in the town of Olongapo the evening before. There had been plenty of bars, muddy back streets, and at least one sailor with his head split open by a prostitute's spike heeled shoe in that town.

"Yes," the sailor answered. "What were you figuring on doing in Olongapo anyway?" There was a grin on his face.

The boy felt foolish. He dropped his eyes and looked out over the black water of the bay. The boat was traveling between twenty and thirty knots, creating a wake which was white against the dark salt swell. The wake cut away from either side of the boat at a forty-five degree angle. The rising sun, not yet visible, was now beginning to turn the black water blue some distance to the west of them.

"Nothing," the boy answered.

"Trying to find work?"

"We went down to the shipyard in Manila, but they weren't hiring." The boy thought of a huge, red brick colored, iron hulled ship, where the men spoke English with an accent, and of another ship where they didn't speak any English at all.

"You were wasting your time," the sailor said. He was fooling with something in the front of the boat.

Ahead of them the shore was clearly visible in the rapidly increasing, early morning light. The water was getting bluer and the sun was up over the mountains of the Bataan Peninsula in the East. Immediately, it began to feel warmer. The boy's spirits rose, but the younger one remained in the sheltered part of the boat, where it was still dark and the sun didn't penetrate.

"They wouldn't have hired anyone so young," the sailor continued. "And there was an all-points bulletin out on the two of you, anyway. They probably knew about it. At least, we knew you'd been there. We're going to send you back to Clark Air Force Base today."

"I thought so," the boy said. He headed back toward the cabin area but turned around again to look at the sailor. "Thanks for the use of the blanket," he shouted over the noise of the boat.

"Sure, kid." The sailor grinned. "Any time."

As he stepped back into the sheltered area, the older boy observed the other sailor, who was in the stern of the small vessel. He was steering it toward its moorings.

"I've got an idea," the older boy whispered when he sat down next to his friend.

"What?" The younger boy was still shivering, hunched over inside his blanket. He was tired of this adventure.

"We make a break for it."

"How? You think they're just going to let us walk away?" Though the younger boy was also of a slender build like his companion and about the same height, his clear, fair complexion and look of inexperience made him appear to be several years younger.

"No, listen …"

The sun was fully up in a blue sky. It was a bright yellow sun. Brackish green, oily water lapped the brown piles of the pier on their left, where the navy launch had come to rest. The piles were slippery and black at the water line. The sailor wearing the peacoat was on the pier securing the boat's rope to a small wooden capstan.

The other sailor had quieted the motor and was now instructing the boys to get out of the boat. The boat rocked in the pulsing water. The water smelled like salt and seaweed. But it was not quite the sewer they had seen in the busy shipyard in Manila Harbor. The boys left their blankets in the cabin area and went ashore.

The two sailors were still busy with the boat, taking equipment out of it. The boys stood on solid ground talking to each other in whispers. Near them, to their right as they faced the launch, was what appeared to be housing, a row of houses with low three and four foot cinder block walls or fences around each of them. The sun was warm and the land smelled green. They were standing in a grassy area. The boys' spirits were very high.

"Hey!" One of the sailors looked up. "Where're you going?"

"Damn!" the other sailor cursed and set a metal box he was carrying down with a bang on the wooden pier. "Shit, they got away!"

In the distance, the two boys could be seen vaulting a third, then a fourth fence. They disappeared around a house.

A week later the two boys, completely out of money and now a burden to a Filipino friend who was housing and feeding them, turned themselves in by calling home. They were in the resort city of Baguio, a hundred sixty miles north of Manila in the cool, evergreen forested mountains of west central Luzon.

At First Light

Bob Martin had a degree in horticultural science and had worked as a federal county agent for a number of years. He had been assigned to districts in several eastern States and had been instrumental in eradicating a particularly virulent strain of fungus that attacked the leaves, blossoms and nascent fruit of peach and almond trees. He was not involved in original research on the disease, but the procedures, based on that research, which he helped put into practice out in the field, saved crops and nursery stock in South Carolina, New Jersey and States as far away as California and Texas.

Mary Martin, his wife, was also a horticulturist, specializing in floriculture. It was she who was principally responsible for their decision to start a business of their own. They settled in Alabama, Mary's home State, on thirty acres near the town of Madison between Huntsville and Decatur.

Four years into the establishment of their nursery business, when it looked as if they might begin to realize a return on their investment and effort, a tornado destroyed most of what they had. Mary was despondent and wept intermittently for three days. Bob observed laconically that the climate was unfit for human settlement and went fishing on a murky brown tributary of the Tennessee River.

They rebuilt their business, prospered, prayed other tornadoes in subsequent years onto other parcels of land, and raised three children. Both Bob and Mary put on weight over time. This was natural. Since they raised much of their own produce, cultivating it to a peak of fruitfulness and flavor, they enjoyed eating it, supplementing their diet with an abundance of cakes and pastries. They were country folk at heart and wore their educations as one wears an old tee-shirt in a hot climate like Alabama's: for comfort, not show. Nevertheless, they saw to it that all three of their children grew to be large, rosy cheeked, and recipients of college degrees.

One evening—which will not go down in history as a momentous event, but which was indicative of the day to day progression of their lives—Bob and Mary were sitting out on the front porch of their second or third generation farmhouse (no one was sure how old the house really was), looking out over their property. The sun was setting on the Tennessee River, below Wheeler Dam. Thinking about the river as he looked out over the greenhouse buildings and green fields under a red sky, Bob said, "Fishing'll be good tomorrow."

Mary, rocking beside him and moving a piece of gray chipped paint on the wood porch floor with the toe of her shoe, remarked, "Place needs work, Bob."

Bob looked at the floor, then over the fields. "Red sun means rain maybe in the morning. I could slip out early and catch a couple largemouth."

"Last time you brought home black bass you cut your hand up on its fins trying to get the hook out of one of them." Mary looked wistfully at her husband and moved the paint chip back over to the bare spot it had left on the floor.

"Could troll the bottom of the river for catfish. Saw some gar the other morning. About the same size, all lined up in the water facing the bank of a little stream. Strange fellows, gar. Lined up side by side like arrows. Nasty looking fish!"

"Did you hear what I said, Bob?"

"Yeah, I know. It isn't just the porch, Mary. The whole house needs painting."

"Well?"

"Did you ever chip paint off old, swollen wood like this, when the paint's all buckled like barnacles on a steamer? It's murder. And it's going to take me more than one day, I can tell you."

Mary sighed. It was a deep sigh of the heavy chested. "Why if I didn't know you, Bob, I'd think you'd gotten lazy," she said. "It's a good thing Robert's home taking over the business."

"He and Suzy," Bob said. "What do you think? Think it'll last?"

"She misses the northern city life, but she's settling down."

"Yeah. It takes getting used to. Sure I'm lazy, Mary. Haven't we earned it? The business is good. We worked hard and made it that way. Remember that twister in sixty-eight?"

Mary was looking out over the property. The air was growing darker. She didn't answer.

Bob's mind returned to the river. "Cut my hand on that largemouth because of a snapping turtle. Big fellow. Came near to the bank floating just under the water. Like a big rock, only floating. There were some red sliders sunning themselves on a felled tree. Suddenly that old boy, or girl I should probably say, rose up out of the water and climbed up the bank. Those little turtles were gone. Not a red slider anywhere. She must've been looking for a nesting site."

Complete darkness fell. The night was heavy with fireflies. They drifted in and about with noiseless flight. Crickets, spring peepers and other frogs began to chorus.

"Bob."

"Yes."

"I think you're right."

"What about, honey?"

"About letting the painting go. We could hire a contractor in to do it."

"Hire a … what … a contractor? No, Mary, we couldn't do that." Bob rose up in his chair and looked at his wife. He couldn't see the mischief in her eyes.

"Why not, honey?"

"Well, we just couldn't." Bob sat back in his chair in the dark. A cricket chirred from somewhere on the porch. The frog chorus seemed to thicken. The night was humid. Though the sky immediately above them was clear and starry, clouds were beginning to obscure the moon.

Mary rocked softly on the old boards of the porch. In the human silence it was understood that the scraping of old paint would begin at first light.

In a Small Park

In a small park near Washington Square in Manhattan, an old man sat upon a wood and wrought-iron bench which was backed by some form of mountain laurel or rhododendron. The bush was not in flower but was a deep green. It was the fall of the year, warm without being hot, the air lighter than in the summer. There were tall deciduous trees in the park—oak, ash and so forth—providing shade. The space itself, not larger than a building lot, was flanked by small office buildings. The park was enclosed by a seven foot tall, black wrought-iron fence, the gate to which had been left open. It was through this private gate that the old man had taken it upon himself to enter at about the noon hour. For it was hot in the busy streets of New York, even in this quieter section of Manhattan, and the park was dark, shady and cool.

Three young women entered the park shortly thereafter, sack lunches in hand. They had spilled out of the office building which blocked sunlight from the park on the south side, the park belonging to that building. The young women settled together upon a bench near the old man before they noticed him.

"Oh!" one of the women, a pixie little blond with an upturned nose, small mouth and full lips, exclaimed aloud, adding in a near whisper, "Maybe we better move."

The other two studied their shabbily clothed neighbor, who was sitting not more than fifteen feet away on the gradual curve of a circular path. He was obviously a street denizen of some sort.

"He shouldn't be in here," the tall one observed loudly. She was big boned and of a rugged, forceful demeanor.

"It's not our concern," a very thin, sandy haired, gray-eyed girl remarked. She unfolded cling wrap from a soft, white sandwich and began to eat the sandwich with small bites and delicately poised fingers.

The blond followed suit, taking out her lunch. It consisted principally of a thick, submarine style sandwich in a bun covered with sesame seeds. It was loaded with cold meats, pickles, lettuce and mayonnaise, which it fairly oozed, and was of rather large proportions for such small hands.

The old man, having heard the remark of the burly one, had glanced over at the three women. Awakened from his reverie, he was astounded by the flowing bulk and richness of the submarine sandwich. It had dripped a pickle on the ground, exuding mayonnaise. He involuntarily wet his lips.

"I'm not staying here," the tall woman said and removed herself to a more distant bench. But, as her companions did not budge, she soon returned. The old man eventually looked away and fell into another reverie. He appeared to be having a discussion with someone, though no one was about.

There was much talk and laughter between the pixie blond and the thin, gray-eyed girl. They were two of a kind. Both were animated over some young man who shared work space with them, and they giggled over recounted adventures at the office water cooler and over other such encounters they either imagined or had actually experienced. The other woman sat moodily masticating her lunch. She had a tight grip on the bun she was devouring, and it was clear it had neither a prayer of escape nor hope of survival.

Just then a wondrous thing happened. The young man, who had been the subject of so much verbal attention, entered the park and took up his station on the bench with the old man. He looked over at the women, nodded (nearly producing a universal swoon), and took out his lunch. Curly dark haired, slender but deep chested in white shirt and tie, he was of a composition fortuitously designed to produce disturbing sensations in the heart and abdomen of the opposite sex.

The women pretended to ignore him, laughing a little louder now and staring at him, as best they could, through the backs and sides of their heads. They crossed their pretty legs, allowing air and dappled sunshine to ventilate their knees. They flung their hair. They were delightful, each of them privately thought.

The tall woman, however, had a distinct advantage, for she was seated at such an angle to the other bench as to be able to more comfortably, if unobtrusively, observe the young man. She saw that the old man, who was shaggily bearded and gray-eyed like her thin, wispy companion of the fluffy white sandwich, stole occasional glances at the young man and his lunch. These were longing looks seized with tired, bloodshot eyes.

The old man's need did not escape the younger one. He reached into his brown paper sack and pulled out a large, red apple, offering it to the older man. The street denizen was startled, and his wizened features showed surprise, but he accepted with thanks.

This man's surprise could not match that of the tall woman. She dropped the remainder of her cold cross bun on the ground. It rolled forward. Pigeons, swarming like army ants, fell upon it. Her mouth hung open, baring teeth and tongue. The other two women looked around to see what could have affected her so.

A reverent hush fell over the three women. The old man was eagerly spinning the core of the apple between his gnarled, unwashed fingers, hungrily biting off the remaining chips of edible flesh. The young man folded his lunch sack into unceremonious creases, arose from the bench, and strode out of the park, dropping the crumpled brown bag into a trash receptacle as he went. He didn't appear to notice the women watching him leave.

But that didn't matter, really. The next encounter at the water cooler was destined to be a sacred event. As a subsequent topic of discussion, it would probably crowd out most productive work activity for the next several days.

Life in the Field

Ham and eggs. A C rations Ham and Eggs is the caviar of foxhole life. It comes in a little olive green can a couple inches high and about two inches across. You open it with a tiny can opener half the size of a quarter. The opener folds up for convenience and several of them come in a case full of C ration boxed meals. The cans are in the boxes. Some of the others contain fruit like pears or peaches, bars of chocolate and hard crackers that are built to last. But it's the main meal, like ham and eggs, that is a hallucinatory experience. It comes out of the can in a single slippery glob, like oiled Spam, that keeps the round shape of the container. The ham and eggs are perfectly blended and indistinguishable. The meals can be heated in the can with little dry pellets that burn clean and hot. But why bother?

Bathing in Vietnam was a kind of exhibition of naked male bodies. We went down the hill from our firebase in the sunlit evenings, stripped off our grimy, smelly jungle utility clothes and stood in a line in front of a thin horizontal pipe. The pipe extended from a little fiberglass water gathering pool that was set up beside the muddy brown river. Water the consistency of syrup was pumped out of the river, purified in the pool, and shot through the pipe, which had little holes all along its length. The water squirted out the holes and onto the line of naked men. The water was cold. The evening a little cooler than the day, but not much. It felt good. We scrubbed the dust and stickiness from our arms, legs, faces, groins and armpits. I don't know what the young women and girls thought in the village on the opposite bank of the river. If they noticed, they were discreet.

We retreated back up the hill and inside the perimeter wire after the bath, as the sun began to go down. The nights were generally muggy. We globbed on mosquito repellent. Some of us slept on cots, others in foxholes on the perimeter. In this way we began preparing ourselves for the next day's bath even before the next day started.

In the morning we went down with five gallon GI cans to get more water and lugged them back up the hill. There we washed our faces and shaved out of our steel helmets. We also washed our clothes with that water and a scrub brush. This meant throwing away underwear, since it was just something more to wash.

A Marine's best friends are his suede jungle boots. They are not originally suede but black leather. But it's a mark of not being in the rear echelon somewhere to possess them. I wore mine proudly and carefully cultivated their worn out look. A hole or two in the canvas tops was especially nice.

I'm describing this because these conditions weren't really unpleasant. It was a matter of living simply. I have never lived any better, though I've lived more indulgently.

On the other hand the war deprived the Vietnamese peasants of many of the basics of life. There weren't any fat Marines, but there weren't any weak ones either. The Vietnamese, with their farming methods disturbed, often had little to eat. We were clean. Their children were often covered with sores. I can give a couple examples.

Once we discovered a baby in a nearby village, whose parents had been killed by American artillery. The aunt and uncle were supposedly taking care of it. But they had little food and couldn't spare any. The baby was less than a year old and was only small bones with muscle wrapped around them like dry cords. It had glazed eyes, when open at all, that looked like a dull blue gray mucous. We took it away, but it died the following day, too weak even to cry.

We sometimes supplied medical help to this same village. We would send a corpsman, and I went along as an interpreter. We set up under a tin roof extending like an awning from an old French colonial building. The people lined up, including many children.

"Toi bi hao." I'm sick.

We gave them mostly placebos. Fake shots and worthless pills. But we did take care of wounds. And there were often plenty of them from the previous night's fighting, which usually somehow centered itself in the middle of the village.

One woman came to us carrying a small boy in her arms who had fly infested sores all over his head. Yellow puss and black knots of flies. It made you sick. We told her to go wash the kid in the river. She panicked and refused, not understanding that we would use antiseptics immediately afterwards. So we did it ourselves.

One more example. We had a doctor with us one day. A woman eight months pregnant arrived and wanted to be examined to see that all was well with the fetus.

"I'm not that kind of doctor! Tell her!" the doctor ordered me in a panic.

She insisted. I smiled. The corpsman kept a straight face. The doctor, a Navy lieutenant, was his boss.

In the end the doctor took the woman into the building and did whatever he had to.

Good and Evil

He had spent twenty years as a Naval chaplain, had served aboard ship and been with Marines in Vietnam. Upon retirement he had come to the Diocese of the Rio Grande. There, as a priest at the Episcopal Church of Saint John in Silver City, New Mexico, he had served a broader community extending southward toward Lordsburg and Deming. This was hot country, as hot as Vietnam, though not as humid. There were many Mexicans in the vicinity, for they came up from the border to find work in construction or as domestics. Father Charles Desmoines, therefore, endeavored to learn Spanish.

The majority of Father Desmoines' parish work was with people of an English speaking background, as most Hispanics in the region were Roman Catholic. Nevertheless, he hired a young Mexican woman to teach him her native language two nights a week. He became quite proficient.

At age fifty-six he left the priesthood. He could not have said why. To have described it as a crisis in faith would have been an oversimplification. For, in hazarding Viet Cong ambushes in Vietnam, he had long ago questioned and affirmed his belief in a personal god. No, it was not that. Nor was it a loss of commitment toward presenting the sacrament of the Holy Eucharist to hungry souls. This priestly function continued to hold meaning for him.

He had never liked funerals, of course. Attending the wounded and dying at some lonely fire base in the midst of vacant miles of jungle and rice paddy had been simpler and easier than officiating at services for the dead at home. The pomp and ceremony of a church and graveyard burial had always left him with a sense of inadequate expression. He mouthed, along with the prescribed rite, what were generally considered to be the proper words on such occasions. But, compared to the few words needed to comfort those who were at war, these comments had been difficult to make.

His concern for correctness of form—and an accompanying general sense of being ill at ease with it—had eventually led him into serious questions concerning the Nicene Creed. Such a doctrine as the Trinitarian nature of God, maintained in juxtaposition with a one substance postulate, was far from convincing to his mind. Nevertheless, every Sunday that same creed was repeated by him or any other Episcopal clergyman, and at every funeral its fundamental tenets were reaffirmed.

But was it true? Were the conclusions of the Council of Nicaea in 325 and other such resolutions of doctrinal dispute over the long and sometimes troubled history of the Church really an expression of what we know to be true within ourselves, in our deepest contemplative nature? Or were they merely formulas designed to clear a way through the clotted ice floes of history?

It was the simple faith of several Mexican friends he had found which had led to this problem. They did not believe in God so much from a knowledge of creeds and doctrines, as from a simple engagement with life. And mixed in with the orthodox in their minds and hearts was much that was pre-Columbian in origin. Was there a spiritual truth that could be apprehended by anyone anywhere? Was this expressive of some sort of indwelling universal need that ran deeper than any doctrine?

Well, he didn't know. And then Christine, his beloved wife of nearly thirty years, had passed away. An unexpected and ravenous form of leukemia had taken her in less than six months. His children were grown and gone. So, like Saint Paul, he retreated into the wilderness to reorganize his faith. The year he left the priesthood at the age of fifty-six he took a summer job as a fire lookout for the U.S. Forest Service in the Gila wilderness north of Silver City.

Gazing out over green mountains from the high position of his lookout station, he could now see in the undulating oneness of an ocean of craggy forest what the essential question was. It asked, what is the nature of spirit and how does it differ from that which appears to materially surround us? From a resolution of this problem, he thought, might come a better understanding of such philosophical conundrums as the nature of the incarnation, redemption and sin.

Most importantly perhaps, it could resolve what he frequently found to be a source of personal embarrassment: the awkwardly simplistic, anthropomorphic kinds of perceptions many Christians seemed to harbor in their notions of the divine. For this had always been both a moral and intellectual trial for him. It had left him feeling quite empty, even dishonest, when he had given what he felt were inadequate explanations to the grieving—employing the too literal, earth-bound terms of common religious discourse.

But how else would he have explained, in their great moment of anguish, the future domicile of their departed loved ones? On the other hand, was heaven really even a place, as we might conceive it? Well, at least no one had asked him about the eternal habitation of their dog. He smiled. Rumors of such questions had been whispered in his ear more than once by indulgent colleagues.

The summer he chose to work for the Forest Service turned out to be an especially hot and dry one, even for southern New Mexico. Crisp underbrush, which had accumulated heavily in some places, crackled underfoot, and on adjacent mountainsides thickets of

Gambel's oak had become withered and brown under an unrelenting sun.

Up near the lookout station chipmunks were busy as ever inside the dark, damp trails of fir and aspen shrouded forest. But below them was this parched, crackling tinderbox of dried oak and Ponderosa Pine.

In these lower forests, the gentle tassel-eared squirrels with their long, black tufted ears and white streaked tails would soon discover the fall crop of acorns to be unseasonably thin. They would thus find themselves thrust into an early dependence for sustenance on the bark of the yellow pines they lived in, and there could be a threat of fire awaiting them as well.

It was perhaps midway into summer when he spotted the first plume of smoke in a draw between two mountains. The smoke curled upward over the nearest ridge like a single, pale gray feather against a clear blue sky. It was ten o'clock on a Tuesday morning. There shouldn't be many campers.

Charles looked at the large map which was mounted on an easel before him. Then he took out several smaller ones to fix details of the canyon. He could find no campsites within it. His log showed no indication of backpackers in that area either. He got a precise compass reading and used the phone to notify the ranger station. Shortly, the hum of a spotter plane could be heard overhead. He listened for their transmissions on the two-way radio.

Though he had trouble making it out at times because of radio static he couldn't seem to squelch, the talk between the pilot and the ranger station indicated a hot, red, burning patch on the back side of the ridge facing him. The smoke was thickening. He could see nothing else but that. A light wind somewhere between five and ten knots was blowing from a northeasterly direction along the canyon.

* * *

Once in Vietnam while conducting a Protestant service on a hilltop (he alternated with a Catholic priest in giving these services every other Sunday morning), he had witnessed a bloody, if small, firefight a quarter mile down the dirt road that led away from the platoon position where he was located. The countryside along that road was mostly jungle, open rice paddies and corn fields being less common than in other areas.

Four Marines in a truck—two in front and two in the bed of it— had been ambushed from dense brush alongside the road. The truck, following the blast of the mine explosion which had gotten his attention, was overturned and burning, billowing black smoke. He could clearly distinguish what he was certain was the body of one dead or seriously wounded Marine lying in the middle of the road.

It was impossible for the Marines on the hill to call in artillery support, due to the closeness of the fighting. So a squad-sized ground reaction force was sent out from this temporary fire base where he was presently conducting his service in the pleasant morning sunshine. But when they got there and drove off the Viet Cong, killing several of them without taking any casualties, they found two of the young Marines already dead and one seriously wounded. All this while he had watched from the safety of that hilltop.

Perhaps the strangest circumstance that morning, and on several other subsequent occasions like it, was in the demeanor of the Marines he was conducting the service for: those in the platoon who had not gone out with the reaction force. Some of them

*watched the little drama unfold with mild curiosity. Others were
more interested in the service.*

* * *

Charles wondered how young boys like those, many of them in
their teens, could learn so quickly to take in stride the horrible
events of war, and to do it with such matter-of-fact resignation.

Sitting now on a different hilltop in New Mexico, he was calmly
witnessing another such drama. This one was not the work of men,
he hoped. But he knew there had been no lightning strikes. It was a
cloudless, summer day. And spontaneous combustion was, at best,
a far-fetched probability. Far-fetched but not impossible, of course.

The spotter plane returned to its airfield. For twenty minutes the
fire burned on alone, impervious to the interests of men. Charles
did his best to observe and calculate the direction and volume of
the smoke. Then he saw flames on the ridge. The smoke, which
had become a pillar, was blackening as it thickened.

The phone rang. An advance ground crew was being lifted in by
helicopter. Others would soon follow along the main road in trucks.
He was to get on the radio and stay there. If any seed fires broke
out on adjacent ridges or hillsides, he must immediately notify the
people on the ground. Some of them would be working in the
ravine between his observation point and the burning ridge. Others
would be on the hillside below the main fire, which was burning
behind the ridge.

"By the way, Charles," the man on the phone said. "If you want
to put in a good word with the man upstairs, we wouldn't object.
The weather people are telling us the winds are going to pick up
this afternoon. Oh, and one more thing. There may be someone
down in that valley. On the other side of the ridge. As I said, we've

got a crew going in there to try to stop the fire from jumping the ravine. But we can't get any heavy equipment in. It's too far from the road. They'll have to build the fire line by hand. Maybe they'll spot the campers, a young man and woman."

Not long after Charles hung up the phone, a helicopter flew in and placed a small crew near the southwest end of the burning ridge. Within ten minutes he could hear diesel engines laboring out of sight below him. Those are the trucks on the main road, bringing the crews and heavy equipment in as far as they can, he thought. By this time two thirds of the ridge was aflame, and the entire back side of it was billowing black smoke.

In the early afternoon the wind suddenly picked up, and Charles spotted a thin gray plume rising from the far southwest end of the burning ridge, behind the air-lifted crew, and another faintly sifting upward into the clear blue sky from the top of the ridge beyond. A light plane was dropping chemical retardant into the wall of flame on the back side of the burning ridge. A running description of the frantic efforts of the crew that was in the ravine behind the ridge was coming over the radio. Charles added what he could observe about the two new seed fires. He heard someone say they had found the couple who'd been camping in the ravine. They were led out of the fire danger. He wondered if they were in any way responsible for the fire.

By evening the wind shifted, reversing direction and causing the fires to burn into themselves creating natural firebreaks on one side. Within a few hours after darkness had fallen the fires were under control, burning out their fury only in designated areas. No one had been hurt, including the air-lifted crew that had appeared to be trapped on the ridge.

It was near ten o'clock, twelve hours after he had spotted the first plume of smoke. In the darkness of the night, through the glass walls of his lookout station, Charles could see burning embers and a few small flames isolated in a forest of ash. He could still hear sounds of heavy equipment in the ravine below him. Other than this, it was eerily still. The departure of evil, he reflected, is as sudden and unapologetic as its arrival.

But, what is evil? he thought. Is it a material event wrought by either nature or man? Or is it nothing more than the sorry state of our finite minds pining miserably over an adverse outcome of circumstances we would as soon have work out in our favor?

Well, what is good, for that matter? What we want? No, there is a good, as they say in the East, which is beyond good and evil. It is the universal underpinning of all things, which have their purpose in it. Our problem lies in recognizing this true good. Yet we do sometimes, if only for a moment. And often we don't.

Charles pondered this as he watched the glowing embers and isolated, dying flames, some of the red coals winking and going out in the darkness. Those that remained defined the ridge line as though it hung in empty black space unsupported by its mountain of earth. He could make out the features of that mountain terrain in the moonlight. But only faintly.

The good, he decided in a sudden access of insight, is a sense of oneness derived from a perception of the unity of our own consciousness. We recognize this oneness when we pull ourselves apart from the worldly content of our minds. That is, we find it when we lose our attachment to small cares and egotistical drives. These are what separate us from our larger selves, from one another, and from the underlying universal harmony in all things. For what appears to make us finite, vulnerable, and fearful of each other is the act of looking within the borders of our own minds and discovering ourselves existing there as objects crowded among other objects, jostling for space and importance in that space. This illusion is what we think of as the world.

The idea gave him an enormous sense of comfort. He decided he had finally discovered the immaterial nature of the soul in a form he could accept. Not that he could have described it further than this or given it a specific place in the cosmos. It was, after all, a negative concept—a description of what the soul wasn't rather than what it was. But the surrounding night sky did now seem somehow larger. Its finite boundaries had been removed. It was large enough to encompass everything. As large as pure consciousness itself. Big enough to make a raging fire seem like a small moment of forgotten passion. Big enough to include Christine somewhere in a place of happiness and well-being.

Was this heaven? Perhaps. But he wasn't going to assert that it resembled life on earth in some sort of second image, ghostly way. Whatever it was, it might be felt, but not understood, and he would leave it at that.

Somewhere in the night a coyote howled. It was a series of yips rather than the majestic, drawn out bugling of a wolf. But it was no less wild. It quickened Charles' senses. For it had come in to him on a cool breeze through the lookout station door he had left open to get some air.

Now take coyotes with their mammal blood warmth and craving for other flesh. Are they good? They kill, causing pain. They are an example of nature red in tooth and claw, snarling in every vein and tearing at the throat and sinews of the living. But they also play with one another and show affection. Like people, who kill to eat, or just kill, or even destroy with their words. People, who can think as well, weigh their actions, cling desperately to a sexual moment, or risk all for a friend.

"Bah!" Charles got up. That damned ridge had mesmerized him. He shut the door, unfolded his cot, and laid his blankets out on it. In a few minutes he was asleep.

At seven o'clock in the morning he was awakened by the sound of an engine laboring on the steep road approaching the lookout station from the valley below. A Ford van pulled up beside the station and stopped. It was driven by the technician who monitored the electrical equipment in the radio relay compound located next to him. The equipment inside this compound was housed in a small, rectangular, ten foot by eight foot, cinder block building with a narrow metal tower extending above it.

"You ain't up yet?" the technician asked jovially, getting out of the van as Charles came bleary-eyed down the wrought-iron steps of the lookout station. Charles was hanging on to the iron rail with one hand, rubbing his eyes and face with the other, still a little unsure of his footing. The technician was a stocky, middle-aged man with a paunch and a somewhat wind-burned face. His meaty, ruddy face may well have been the result of too much good food and drink, or just high blood pressure, rather than any wind. But he was an outdoorsman, an avid hunter. He had retired from the Navy, and this experience, which the two men held in common, had forged a casual bond of friendship between them.

"I overslept," Charles said, smiling sheepishly.

"That was some fire yesterday," the technician said. His name was Ralph.

"No one got hurt," Charles answered. He was now standing at the bottom of the steps, feeling a little more awake than he had a moment before. "We can be thankful for that."

Ralph, who was gazing at the burnt top of the neighboring ridge, looked curiously at his educated friend. He knew Charles had been a chaplain. "I seen em worse," he said. He paused, glancing back over at the ridge. "You spose God had a hand in it? He can deal a mighty strange one sometimes."

"I don't know," Charles said. "They say fires are good for reseeding the forest, clearing the underbrush and getting rid of harmful insects and disease."

"Maybe." Ralph cleared his throat and spat. This always made Charles flinch a little in his stomach. "But it ain't too sweet for the animals. You think? I mean, they don't all get away."

"No, I suppose they don't," Charles said.

After Ralph had gone, Charles continued to think on the matter and had to concede he still didn't really understand the nature of evil. Well, evil understood as pain anyway.

The good in Christ might be a transcendent good of some sort. But, since the idea of a vengeful god was unacceptable to him, how this mild, universal good could explain a whole raft of other enigmas, like sin, suffering and redemption, he still didn't know. And just how was an honest person to ignore this problem of not knowing? Well, he didn't have the slightest clue.

That was the problem: all this thinking seemed to do nothing but take him around in circles. Maybe, he thought, I shouldn't think about it at all. But, of course, one would have to be dead to do that.

Inner Resources

"I build houses," he said.

"I know that, Mr. Graves." The bank loan officer pushed back his thinning black hair and leaned on the arm of his chair. It was a comfortable Naugahyde office chair with padded arms. He regarded his client through small, round lensed, wire glasses, observing him with a mixture of amusement and sadness. Or perhaps it was pity.

"You know I already have several spec houses built and they're waiting for buyers. Things are a little slow now, but they'll pick up." Ted Graves was in his middle thirties, a blond, sun bronzed, muscular man who kept his hair cropped short in a military fashion. The bank officer was East Indian, of about the same age, slight of build and soft-spoken with a light British accent.

"I'm sorry. We cannot expand your loans any further, Mr. Graves."

"But my credit is good."

"You must sell something."

"I will. I always have. Look, remember last summer. And even last winter. I have always met my obligations."

"But you have extended yourself in a tightening market. Interest is up. The bank ..."

"Yes, I know. The bank can get better returns with less risk in other markets."

"I never said that. I am only doing my job." The loan officer leaned forward. "Sell a house, Ted," he almost whispered. "Sell at least one house. Then come back. I can do nothing at this time."

"I'll find another source."

"No one can help you in this market, Mr. Graves. Not with as much money as you have tied up in unsold properties. You don't have any fluid assets as long as those houses don't sell."

"What am I supposed to do? We have to eat. And I owe others who depend on me for work and contracts."

"I am very sorry, Mr. Graves. Truly sorry."

Out in the parking lot, Ted Graves opened the door of his pickup truck. It made a loud groaning noise, the sound of tired metal, then squeaked as he slammed it shut. The truck smelled of grease, sweat, nails and lime. It turned over several times before starting. He drove over the hot sun glare of nearly white concrete in the bank parking lot, then out into the street traffic.

At the building site Ted got out of his truck and slammed the door. He leaned one hand on the rough, chipped paint of the door and wiped the sweat from his forehead. Sweat ran from the blond hair under his arms into the body of his sleeveless shirt. Several men were laying tiles on the roof of the house he stood before. He had contracted out for the roofers. They weren't part of his crew. He wondered how he'd pay them. Two other men were removing a glass sliding door from a flatbed truck, gently lifting it up over the hooks along the outer rim of the flatbed.

"Morning Ted." One of the men glanced over in his direction and smiled. The two men went into the house with the door. It would be installed in the living room, facing out over the patio. Ted followed the two men into the house and stood in the middle of the living room. The men set the glass door down, leaning it against the wall. Ted was looking at the stone fireplace. One of the men walked over to him.

"It's looking good, Ted," the man said. "The roofers'll be out of here this afternoon. Then we can lay the concrete apron in front of the garage."

Ted looked at the young man addressing him. "Good," he said.

"Any luck?" the young man asked quietly.

"No."

They both stood in silence looking at the fireplace.

"It's a good house, Ted. We do good work."

"Sure."

"They're all good houses."

"I should've stuck to building fireplaces and installing inserts."

"Maybe we should go back to putting in those inserts till the market picks up."

"How, Mike? I'm stretched out to the limit."

"I know." Quietly, then, "Let's you, me and Don here knock off for the day, Ted. We can let the roofers do their thing, then come back in the morning to finish up."

"We have to get that apron poured."

"It can wait."

"All right."

The three men drove out of the city of Boise in Ted's pickup truck. They had left the building site in the subdivision west of Boise and stopped by Ted's house on the east side of town. Marta wasn't home. She worked as a paralegal. Their two children were at school. Ted, his brother Mike, and their friend Don picked up three fishing poles at the house and then stopped at a convenience store for a case of beer. They drove a little more than an hour up into the Boise National Forest.

Along the banks of the river the men could smell the evergreen needles and feel the crunch of them underfoot. Most of them were dried and brown, last year's crop. Or from the years before. The three men fished in silence, separated from each other by twenty or thirty yards. There was no one else around. The men were fishing from the bank, casting bright silver spinners through the sunlight into the fast moving water. The water was cold, clear and whitecapped. They could feel the pressure of it turning and pulling among the big rocks. The spray of white foam coming off the rocks felt pleasant and cool on their bare arms and cheeks. The smaller smooth gray and brown stones lying in the river bed seemed almost, by refraction, to be just below the surface. The men were fishing for trout. The sky was bright and cloudless overhead. There was a slight breeze which could be heard among the tall evergreens.

Ted was working his red and white bobber downstream. It was glistening wet in the sunlight. As the water carried it, he kept the fishing line taut and maneuvered the silver spinner among the rocks. He wanted to stay near the quiet, shaded pools by the opposite bank without snagging his line because he knew the trout would be resting in those pools, under the cool, overhanging evergreen branches in the rich, oxygenated water. He was concentrating, sipping his beer, which he stooped and set on the ground near where he stood. By some means, which he did not understand but which he had experienced at a few such moments in the past, his mind and heart became limpid, translucent, swelling and relaxing with strength and quiet like the river. Out of a dark, voiceless pool in his consciousness came the knowledge that things would somehow work out. He didn't know how, but things would be fine. The beer was also having its effect, easing the tension he had felt.

Ambiguities

The commuter train from Philadelphia to Harrisburg paused at one of its innumerable stops in the outlying Philadelphia suburbs in southeastern Pennsylvania. The stop was a small covered platform beside the tracks. Several people got off. One person got on. Lavinia looked at the houses lying beyond. Though in a small town, they looked like farmhouses. Most were covered with wood siding. A few were brick. Some were in better condition than others. All had been there since the town's original founding as a small farming community. Several more stops and the train was out into open country. Green fields with occasional farmhouses and woodlots slipped past the train windows.

Lavinia had grown up in the Amish and Mennonite farming center of Lancaster, a town of sixty thousand. Though only at a distance of sixty miles from Philadelphia on the commuter route upon which she was presently traveling, Lavinia hadn't been home in five years. She closed her eyes. The train rocked from side to side as it sped along.

* * *

Fireflies in the dark on her grandparents' farm west of York, Pennsylvania. They have often spent weekends there, as it is only an hour's drive from Lancaster. Fireflies in a clear glass jar.
"Look, Grandma, look what I've got."
"They're very pretty, darling. Did you catch them yourself?"
"Yes, Grandma. And see, there goes one now. It's lighting up!"

"Yes, I see. Isn't it wonderful!"

"How do they do it?"

"Well, I don't know, honey. Maybe your grandfather can explain."

"Where is he?" Lavinia is breathless with wonder. The night summer air is warm. The smell of mown hay is sweet. The iridescent green of Japanese beetles bright in full sunlight is fresh in her memory, and the hot, sandy brown, hazy, afternoon hum of cicadas is still buzzing in her ears. "Where is he, Grandma? I want to know."

"I know how they do it," says a small, important voice behind Lavinia.

Lavinia turns around. It's her sister Alicia, older by one year.

"No you don't."

"Yes I do. It's some kind of chemical reaction."

"No it isn't. It's magic. I know it's magic."

* * *

Lavinia opened her eyes. The train rocking, the fields green. There were some Amish in a field with their huge brown draft horse. The horse was plowing a small strip of unsown ground. The field next to it was already high in corn. The corn had not yet tasseled but the stalks were healthy and broad leafed. The soil the plow was turning over came up a rich golden brown. A small cloud of dust trailed behind the plow along with two men in straw hats, apparently father and son. Lavinia turned her head from the window and closed her eyes again.

Martin had been her boyfriend for more than a year. They had talked of getting married some day. Lavinia was sure she loved Martin. More than anything. Martin loved her too. He was always telling her he did. She felt his strong warm hands inside her bra, removing her panties. She felt his strength. She didn't care.

* * *

"I'm going to tell Mother what you're doing."

"If you do, Alicia, I'll kill you."

"No you won't."

"I will."

"I could have Martin for myself if I wanted him."

"You could not!"

"Sure I could. You've seen the way he looks at me." Alicia, slender and blond, stands in front of the mirror admiring herself. She is in her underwear. She runs her long fingered hands along both hips then onto her stomach. "See, no stomach," she says snidely, turning sideways to the mirror.

Lavinia, who is fuller figured and self-conscious about it, turns away in anger. She goes into the bathroom.

* * *

"Next stop Lancaster." The conductor passed through the aisle and entered another car. Lavinia quickly pulled her few belongings together and prepared to leave the train. Her heart suddenly seemed to be racing. "It's ridiculous," she thought.

* * *

Lavinia arrives at a party late, accompanied by a friend. Someone's parents are out of town and their house is being used. It's a nice big house. The lights are turned low. The living room is almost dark. Music is playing softly, a voice singing something about the new age that is coming. A gravelly voice and a twangy guitar. In the dim light Lavinia can see several couples. One couple is in an armchair, and the boy has the girl's blouse unbuttoned. She is resisting him.

Lavinia hears a groan and what sounds like soft sobbing. In a corner on the floor, she recognizes her sister's blond hair, very mussed, her clothing in disarray.

"Oh no!" Lavinia almost shrieks. The boy with Alicia is Martin. Lavinia turns and flees from the house. She runs in the cool night air under the street lamps, tears dampening her cheeks.

* * *

The train having stopped, many people had gotten off. This was a major unloading point. Outside Lavinia walked the distance home through north Lancaster. She knew Martin and her sister and their five and a half year old son were living with her parents in their two story home on West James Street in the northwest corner of town. She was in no hurry to get there. They didn't know at what hour to expect her anyway. The streets were old and familiar, full of memories of her childhood. It would have been a pleasant walk some other time.

Having married Alicia right out of high school, Martin had a problem holding jobs. Lavinia thought about that. Perhaps she was lucky things had turned out the way they did. She wondered how she would greet Alicia. Had Martin ever thought of her, of the way things might have been? Certainly that was irrelevant now, she reminded herself. It was Mom and Dad's twenty-fifth wedding anniversary. That was what was important.

She came up to the house, ascended the concrete steps to the porch and rang the doorbell. Her blouse was unbuttoned casually almost to her brassiere in warm, summer lightness. She was wearing a short, bright, yellow and green patterned cotton skirt, a little wrinkled from the trip, no nylons on her lightly tanned legs, and a pair of sandals. She liked the way she looked: casual, a little carefree, even sexy. The door opened. She hoped she wouldn't lose her voice.

Family Relations

Charles Sumter did not live in the South. He would have told you so forthright—for he was a Pennsylvanian, born and bred—had he been inclined to offer opinions to just anyone. But he generally kept them to himself. However, when questioned, it was clear that he had never been to South Carolina, didn't know anyone there or in any neighboring State, would just as soon never have heard of Fort Sumter, and would probably have fought on the side of the North, had he been around and asked to do so during the late Civil War.

Charles' wife, Ann, did not share these sympathies, for she was from the rolling hill country of Tennessee. What had ever possessed her to venture, as a young woman, into the bone-chilling North, she was never sure. She had attended Temple University in Philadelphia for a short time, where she met Charles, who spent a few months at the same university. Perhaps that northern sojourn of her youth was the real source of her downfall.

Today their daughter, Lolita, and her husband were coming for a visit. Yes. Lolita. That had been Charles' idea. A favorite aunt of his was named Lolita. He had even gone so far as to change the name on the birth certificate from the more dignified Sarah. This was while Ann had been too weak from delivering her child to defend its honor. What a name! And to make matters worse, Charles called her Lolly most of the time. Still does.

Lolita and her husband pulled into the driveway at four-thirty on a Wednesday afternoon. They were there for a four day visit. Ann came out of the house and embraced her daughter. Charles got up from his lawn chair on the porch and shook hands with Timothy. The two women went into the house. Timothy sat down in a lawn chair next to Charles'. Charles returned to his.

"So what's this noise I've been hearing about you turning down that offer at Blue Mountain?" Timothy asked. His tone of voice was confident and cocky, the attitude of a son-in-law who feels he's doing well by his wife, perhaps better than her parents had done.

"They offered me management of the place. It's a swanky club, but I couldn't go in for it."

"Why not, Charley?"

"Too many shady financial goings on and other illegal nonsense. I didn't like the Saturday night entertainment. It was bordering on breaking the law."

"Topless women?"

"Pretty near."

"Well, it packs 'em in, doesn't it?"

"I suppose so."

"Aw, Charley, you should've done it. The salary was almost double what you're getting now."

"No was my final word. No amount of pay could change my mind." Charles picked up his drink from the concrete floor of the porch beside his chair. The porch was really the carport, but the car, a huge old Mercury that smoked from its tail pipe and rattled a bit, had never ventured to enter it.

Timothy contemplated his father-in-law for several minutes. He had always considered Charles to be something of a fool. "Too many ideas," was the way he generally put it when discussing the matter with his wife. "The man has no ordinary common sense." What he meant was that Charles had always let his ideals get in the way of his own and his family's well-being. Charles was in many ways a proud man. But in Timothy's opinion a man had no right to be proud when he hadn't done the best he could to put food on the table.

"We always had enough," Lolita had said.

But Timothy knew from other things she had told him that that wasn't true. And besides, the acne scars Lolita had on her face were proof enough for him that they hadn't eaten right.

"I think I'll go in and get a drink," Timothy said to Charles, when he had completed these reflections.

Charles was looking out over the neighbor's lawn. A robin was hunting for worms and a squirrel had come out of the woods that ran behind both houses. He nodded. His mood being mystical and somewhat mellowed with alcohol, there was a delicate white bloom of dogwood in his heart, and he had no doubt Timothy knew where to find his whisky decanter anyway.

Timothy went into the house. He engaged in a short conversation with the women. They were ecstatic over the news. Had he told Charles? Well, no, he hadn't, as a matter of fact. But he would in due course.

Lolita wanted very much to tell her father herself. But Timothy's bearing was one of clear judgment. He would find the appropriate circumstances under which to deliver the news.

Ann, in her personal excitement and the enjoyment of sharing women's gossip with her daughter, simply hadn't thought of telling her husband anything. They didn't exchange many views. Charles left for work very early every morning six days a week and came home early each afternoon. They both ate when individually hungry and rarely sat down together for meals. Late afternoons and evenings, Charles puttered in his garden or sat on the porch with his drink. What he thought about, Lord only knew.

Timothy came out and sat down with his freshly poured drink. "So you're going to continue work out at Carlisle?" he asked.

"Yep."

"That's a long drive from Harrisburg. I mean, to run a cafeteria in a small college for low pay. Still think you should've taken them up on their offer at the club."

"Didn't suit me."

"No, I suppose not." Timothy noticed that Charles was still watching the squirrel, now in the neighbor's front yard. "Must've buried a nut out there somewhere," he observed.

"Could be."

Timothy took a long pull on his drink, letting himself relax in the lawn chair, settling back and crossing his legs, neatly arranging the crease in his slacks over his knee, and setting the drink on the ground. Charles was in a white undershirt, his arms hairy to the shoulder, his shoulders heavy from the daily sampling of food.

"Lolita's going to have a baby in the fall."

"Lolly?" Charles nearly started out of his chair, a big smile creasing his round face. "My little Lolly having a baby?"

"Yeah. One and the same."

Charles sat back, a pleased smile still on his face, picked up his glass and emptied it, setting the empty glass down again. He looked out over the neighbor's lawn. This was indeed a matter for considerable thought.

Late in the evening and several drinks later, he came in from the outdoors, its swarm of fireflies and busy chirring of crickets. He brought the cool night air in with him. Timothy was asleep in an armchair with a newspaper in his lap. Lolita was on the sofa, conversing quietly with her mother upon some feminine matter. She got up on seeing her father come in. He gave her a big bear hug and went off to bed without saying a word.

Old and New Life

"Look it up," she had said. Her ten year old son had wanted to know the meaning of the word *perambulate*, which he had encountered in a book beyond his years, and she had not been inclined to tell him. "If you find it out for yourself, you won't forget it," she had made a point of adding.

He thought of this now, leaning his head against the hard metal strip running down the center of the window on the Trailways bus. It seemed like only yesterday: twenty-two years ago and six years after the death of his father. Yet the memory of it was still fresh. It had come to represent the way his mother had sought to awaken curiosity in him and the important virtue of discovering things for himself.

Maybe she was too successful, he thought. Maybe I should've been more responsible and less searching. The rattling of the bus and the banging of the window against his head were giving him a headache. He shifted his head back into his seat. It was the middle of the night and the bus was on a lonely Nevada highway. He fell asleep.

In the morning he awoke as the bus slowed upon pulling into a small restaurant. The young, slightly stocky but shapely woman sitting in the aisle side seat next to him was still asleep. He nudged her.

"We're stopping for breakfast," he said.

"Oh. Thank you." The young woman, who had been sitting with her head slumped awkwardly to one side, awoke, adjusted her short cropped, sand blond hair and straightened her blouse. The bus stopped. A very thin woman brushed suddenly past her in the aisle, carrying an infant and followed by two small children. The thin woman looked frazzled, a worried expression on her face and her hair in disarray. She seemed to be in a hurry, and she was trailed by the odor of a full diaper. The young woman in the seat rolled her eyes and looked at Jeff, the man next to her. He smiled without speaking.

Jeff and this young woman, who was between eighteen and twenty, had become fairly well acquainted on the bus and were now breakfasting together. The restaurant was a small diner. They were seated at a table, as opposed to sitting at the counter, and they had already been served. The room was noisy, full of patrons from the bus. There was a clanking of silverware against plates and the sizzle and greasy odor of eggs, ham, bacon and sausage frying on the big black open grill behind the counter where a crowd of people was sitting. Outside, the early morning sun glared through the plate glass window, which was streaked, dusty and sorely in need of a washing. The main street of the dusty town was deserted.

"We must already be in Idaho," Jeff said, transferring grape jelly from a small white paper packet onto his toast. He performed this delicate operation with a table knife and almost dropped the jelly on the table.

"Really?" Tamara looked up. Tamara was the young woman's name. "How do you know?" She had a pleasant, teasing look in her hazel eyes.

"I just heard someone say something about our having only recently crossed the Oregon line."

"Maybe we just left Nevada." Tamara grinned.

"We're in Idaho. We'll be in Boise inside an hour once we leave here."

"Is that where your mother …? I mean …"

"Yes. The funeral's tomorrow."

"I'm sorry."

Jeff looked at Tamara. She had already offered him condolences on the bus. She had even touched his hand in sympathy. That's how well acquainted they'd become. "I'm used to it," he said. "Or resigned to it. She'd been sick for some time. My sister was taking care of her."

Tamara concentrated on her meal. They hadn't been in the restaurant twenty minutes and already a number of people were outside, preparing to reboard the bus. Jeff watched the first ones get on. He felt his chest tighten. This wasn't going to be easy. In less than an hour he'd be in Boise. His sister would be waiting.

"Your sister will be waiting for you, won't she?" Tamara asked. She was finishing her orange juice and preparing to get up from the table.

"Yes."

Tamara looked at Jeff as if studying him. She paused, then went ahead and said what she was thinking. "You two don't get along very well, do you? I'm sorry," she quickly added.

"No. No, that's alright. We don't. She's a lot older than I am. We were too far apart in age to be close, and she feels I never did enough for our mother. She thinks I deliberately left it all on her."

"Did you?" Tamara had the boldness of youth, and her question was as innocent as the naked curiosity that put it forth.

"In some ways. I left home and moved away. My sister was already married and had four kids. When our mother started getting sick, she was close enough to take on the responsibility for her care. Then Mother's illness lingered on for four years. I've never made much money doing what I'm doing, painting pictures that rarely sell, so I haven't been any help that way either."

They both got up from the table and hurried out to get on the bus. They were the last two people to climb on board. It was already growing warm outdoors and the air conditioner was on inside the bus. Tamara sat down immediately, then got back up to let Jeff into his seat. "Brr," she said embracing both her bare shoulders. "It's cold in here!" She was wearing denim cut-off shorts and a sleeveless blouse made of thin cotton. She sat down again.

Jeff looked at her as she sat down. Her legs were not tanned. Her thighs were especially white, and that somehow made her shorts seem even shorter and more close-fitting. He watched out the window as the bus pulled away from the rest stop and left the town for the open road. The air was already growing warm enough to cause the sunlight to quiver in liquid planes above the gray green sagebrush of the desert. Jeff knew that if he could have seen in front of the bus—he and Tamara were seated near the rear of it—he would have noticed tiny mirages on the road ahead, resembling pools of water.

"It's going to be a scorcher today," he observed.

Tamara didn't answer. She was resting in the seat with her eyes closed, breathing softly in the full bloom of young womanhood. Tamara was on her way home for summer vacation from a small college in southern California. Her destination was Twin Falls, Idaho, a hundred and thirty miles southeast of Boise.

I wonder what she thinks of me, he thought, looking at her. I probably shouldn't have told her so much about myself. Well, it doesn't matter.

He turned and looked through the window at the road. A heavy sense of the emotional complexities that lay ahead came over him. He thought of his sister, his mother. The road sped along beneath the bus, as if it were in a hurry to get away from the bus and push it forward to its destination.

Infantry Training Regiment

They called him Mickey because he was Irish. Irish and Scottish. Never mind that he was several generations American. Of course, his ears stuck out a little too. Especially so on the close-cropped head of a Marine recruit. So there may have been some reference to Mickey Mouse. His name was McFarlan.

The other guy's name was Quincy Jones. Just Private Jones to the men of Delta Company. They were all privates, with a few privates first class.

It was late Friday afternoon at the Marine Infantry Training Regiment in Camp Pendleton, California. Delta Company was about to go on its first liberty in three and a half months. Three months of boot camp and two weeks now at the regiment. But before anyone could leave, differences had to be settled.

The men of Delta Company formed a tight circle about McFarlan and Jones. Wearing boxing gloves the two men circled each other. They wore dusty combat boots and green, or olive drab, utility trousers, also covered with dust and the caked white dirt of the Southern California rolling hill and dry thorn bush country, but were bare chested. The slanting sun shone on them from the west, blinding whichever one was facing it. Nearby a horde of yellow jackets was buzzing about some ripening garbage in a GI can next to the end of a wood and screen hut that housed some of these men.

"Come on, Mickey, hit him."

"Tighten it up, Jones. You're running away."

The two men continued to circle amidst calls from the crowd. The troop leader in charge of Delta Company that afternoon stood back from the crowd and watched. Jones struck first, planting his glove in McFarlan's face. McFarlan staggered back and blocked a second blow.

"Way to go, Jonesy. Hit him!"

"Come on, McFarlan. Don't let him run you down."

McFarlan was circling wide now.

"Don't be chicken, man."

Jones pushed in on McFarlan, pressing him in on the circle of men. Someone gave McFarlan a shove from behind and he stumbled into Jones. Surprised, Jones stepped back, then hit McFarlan in the stomach.

"Come on, man, didn't your mother ever teach you how to fight?" The crowd was disgusted. There was swearing. McFarlan had fallen back, partly doubled over from the blow to his stomach, and had taken a wild swing at Jones. He made a lucky connect. Jones was not hurt but was stunned by the fact that he had even been hit. The sun was in his eyes. There was dust in the sweat of his lean, muscular arms. The sunlight showed up the dust as dull patches in the shining sweat. The circle had tightened about the two men so they could hardly maneuver.

The men of Delta Company all smelled of the day's sweat from running, crawling in dirt under barbed obstacles, firing weapons. Several had torn trousers and cuts and bruises from crawling over sharp rocks on the Infiltration Course. All were tired but excited about the prospect of getting a little freedom that weekend.

"Get back!" the troop leader shouted. The circle widened. "Let's get this over with, girls," he said to the two men in the middle.

McFarlan took advantage of the lucky blow and moment's delay to catch his breath. Then he charged into Jones, hitting him again in the face and the chest. They clenched, trying to pummel each other.

"Hey, you're not in there to make love."

"Come on, let's have a fight. A real fight."

"What is this—a dance?"

"Mabel, would you care to join me out on the ballroom floor? It's a slow number."

Everyone was shouting, laughing, cursing. McFarlan, a freckle-faced, tall young man, seemed to have gotten new spirit. Jones was bleeding from the nose and mouth and seemed stunned. McFarlan hit him again and again, standing over his shorter opponent.

"All right, that's it." The troop leader moved into the circle, which divided for him. McFarlan and Jones both dropped their fists with evident relief, though McFarlan seemed for a moment to be reluctant to do so. They pulled off their gloves, went into the crowd and handed them to the next pair of pugilists.

It seems Jones had had some sort of a grudge and had hit McFarlan in the back with his rifle butt during the rushed and confused scramble to come out and get into formation in front of their huts at five o'clock that morning. But the fight seemed to settle it. After a few more fights and a long standing in line alphabetically by last name for mandatory head shaves, the men of Delta Company were released on liberty for two days. Most went into Los Angeles or to the town of Oceanside to wander the beach.

Monday morning found them out in the field again on the Infiltration Course. They were doing the low crawl in circular sand pits, going around and around in circles. There were several troop leaders present. One of them, a corporal in starched, neat utility uniform and well shined boots, was stomping on McFarlan's head. His boot came down repeatedly on McFarlan's helmet, shoving it into the sand. "When I say 'low crawl' I want to see a groove. You understand? I want that helmet cutting a groove in the sand."

That night in the pitch dark, Jones and McFarlan were together behind the infrared scope. Jones looked through the scope and tried to make out the figures of troops. What he saw was a confused red field of vision with whiter areas. "It's kind of hard to see," he said. "I can't make out anything definite."

"Yeah, I guess you get used to it," McFarlan said sympathetically.

Later on, panting for breath, resting beside a narrow dirt trail in the dark with his head bent over, almost ready to throw up, Jones turned to McFarlan and said, "Sorry about the rifle blow. What happened was really my own fault."

"That's alright. Sorry I got you thrown down that stairwell in Combat Town last week. I didn't have time to get out of the way before Corporal Drammand got to you. Guess you won't forget to yell 'fire in the hole' next time you toss a practice grenade down a stairwell." McFarlan and Jones both smiled, showing white teeth out of dirty, indistinguishable faces in the dark.

"Shut up down there!" someone whispered harshly. It was a troop leader. "You want to get everyone on this patrol killed? Enemy's got ears." The night air felt damp and cool, and in the distance heavy streaks of tracers could be seen coming from troops who were night firing their weapons on line.

Marine Sniper

Nguyen Van Sung was working in our battalion command post mess hall when I arrived in Vietnam. He was quiet, friendly, middle-aged, overpolite. But then most Vietnamese are, until they get fired up over something. We knew he was getting threats from the Viet Cong, that they were collecting taxes in his village and he was refusing to pay them. He never made a fuss about his problems, just showed up one day without his left thumb. The Viet Cong had cut it off.

His hand was wrapped up in a dirty white piece of cloth covered with dried blood. The thumb was cut off clean between the two joints. You could see the white end of bone and the now dried and clotted blood and muscle. It must've bled like a fountain for awhile. We cleaned and dressed the wound at our aid station and then he went back to work as if nothing had happened. His work in the mess hall involved heavy lifting.

Amid the hot, steamy, greasy smells of the mess hall I watched him one afternoon as he went about his work. It was about three days after he lost his thumb, and he was scrubbing out with soap and boiling water some of the big GI cans that we slopped our food scraps into and washed our trays in. His bandage was soaked. He was outside in the hot sun with another white rag tied around his head to keep the sweat off his face, and there was a short line at the door as some stragglers were going in to get some lunch. They were part of a convoy of Marines that had just brought in some supplies for us.

"Hey, Sung," one of them shouted. "What'd you do with the food that was in the can?"

"I bet it's inside being fixed for us now."

Several of them laughed, the young black Marine who'd made the last remark laughing loudest. I'd never seen this new driver before. Sung smiled, crinkling up the long lines in his face, and went on about his work.

"He doesn't understand," the black Marine said.

"Sure he does. Sung, you got boom boom?"

"Oh, many boom boom!" Sung looked up at the Marines with a big grin on his face. One tooth was missing and some of the others around it were black. "Many pretty boom boom. Pretty good."

"How much, man?"

Sung laughed. It was a standard joke between him and the rest of us. Sung was no pimp, and as far as I know his village had no whores. He was just a hard worker.

That night we were mortared. Just for the hell of it, I guess. There wasn't any follow-up assault. Just a few random bullets fired at our hilltop position from across the river. We lost only one guy. The black Marine. That's why I mentioned him. He was new in country and inexperienced. The mortars came in at two o'clock in the morning, and he had stopped to put on his pants. A piece of shrapnel went through the canvas side of his hooch and into his chest. Must've struck the heart, because he died instantly.

The Colonel was furious. This was the same village Sung was having tax trouble in. It was supposed to be friendly, a secured hamlet. The next day Colonel Williams called Sung into his hooch and had a long talk with him.

About a week and a half later we had a sniper, another young black Marine, imported from regiment.

That night I had sergeant of the guard, and this sniper, John Collins, was positioned on top of a bunker on our perimeter facing the village across the river. He was armed with an M-14 rifle with a scope mounted on it. It was one of those starlight scopes that use concentrated starlight to help you see in the dark.

Because I was sergeant of the guard, I learned a few things. I knew the tax collectors were supposed to visit the village around 1:00 a.m. They were very punctual. They got there at exactly one. Just walked in along the village street, three of them. The night was cool and smelled of the river that moved like a black shadow below, and there was one dog barking. Otherwise it was real quiet. A baby started crying but was hushed. Two villagers came out into the street to meet the tax collectors. The street was a narrow dirt road, huts and small, French built masonry buildings on either side. The five of them stood close together in the middle of the street conversing. I know all this because I was looking through the scope at the time. It gave a pale green, dusklike appearance to things but you could see clearly.

"They just came in," I said handing the rifle to John.

Corporal Collins placed the butt of the rifle securely in his right shoulder. He shifted his long slender arms and narrow shoulders, pivoting the rifle slowly on its bipod.

"See them?"

He didn't answer. His face tensed as he put the scope to his eye and his cheek bone against the rifle stock. He was lying down on top of the sandbag bunker. There was a light breeze and plenty of stars.

"Don't chase the bull," another Marine with us remarked.

"Shut up," I said.

John's face relaxed as we watched the smooth, gradual squeeze of his trigger finger. I could barely see the figures in the village without the scope. Apparently one of them started back toward a hut. That's the one who died.

Sung died too. About a week later. Some Viet Cong came into the village one night, dragged him out into the street and shot him through the head.

The White Gibbons

Melanie Thurgood had chosen photography as a career. She had traveled widely and experienced things only men were accustomed to experiencing before her time. She was thin, lithe, small, dishwater blond and somewhat leathery in appearance from long exposure to sun and wind. But she had had a good figure in her young womanhood, and beneath sun bleached eyebrows in a tan face was a pair of piercing blue eyes that never lost their clear comprehending vision.

"You are no longer pretty," she said to herself one morning, standing in front of her full length mirror. She was naked, fresh from her bath, and her hair hung long and damp behind her shoulders. She cupped her hands under her breasts and lifted them. Where has my youth gone? she thought.

Melanie had developed a masculine toughness of demeanor but men still liked her.

"Oh, Melanie, I need to see you." Jim Rothko, a magazine article writer on nature topics and an old friend, called out to her from the rich mahogany bar in the lounge of the foreign press club in Manila. He came over to her table. "I've arranged for a guide. Two, in fact." Pulling out a chair, he sat down, setting his half-consumed whisky sour on the table. Then he picked it up again, wiped the moisture off the table and the bottom of his glass with his hand, and set it back down. "Experienced trackers. They'll take us in tomorrow."

"Good. Thanks, Jim. They know what we're looking for?" A waiter placed a Tom Collins in front of her. "Thank you."

"Yes. One of them says he made a sighting just a few weeks ago."

"Dr. Marks told me there should be three or four white ones in the group."

"It's rare enough to see one." Jim was obviously excited.

"You've seen stranger things than that, Jim."

"Ha ha. Do you remember the cold night we spent in the monsoon when we couldn't find our way out of that miserable, rain-soaked swamp in Malaysia? Remember that?"

Melanie was embarrassed.

"I'm sorry, Melanie. Forget it."

The Filipino guides were familiar with the Subic Bay jungle country. Melanie and Jim traveled light, though Melanie did engage one extra man as a porter to help in transporting her photographic equipment. They were taken to the base of a mountain by truck. From there they had to hack their way into the jungle with bolos, or Filipino machetes, through dense bamboo thickets. This was the kind of bamboo with razor hairs along the stems that left stinging cuts all over their arms and legs as they passed through it in the light clothing necessitated by the humidity and heat of the tropics. It was similar in effect to the shoulder high, wide bladed grass they also passed through in a clearing. That lacerated them too, and their salty sweat got into the cuts and burned.

Melanie nevertheless advanced aggressively against the brush, following the first tracker, widening the trail with her bolo, and this in spite of having photographic equipment slung about her body and a light bedroll and rucksack on her back. Jim, having grown portly since the memorable incident in Malaysia many years before, followed some distance behind, where he panted in the heavy heat, sweating profusely, cursing the salt in his cuts and the branches in his face.

They camped the first night on a high plateau above the clouds. Having originally settled at nightfall into their individual bedrolls, they were awakened in the middle of the night by a chilling cold. The clouds, which had been situated well below them during the day, had ascended the dark, steep mountain slopes after sundown and now enveloped them. They got up, thoroughly chilled and wet, first Melanie then Jim, and joined the three Filipinos who were squatted around a blazing fire.

"Cold!" Melanie said, crouching and extending her hands toward the flames. "Brr."

"The fire soon make you warm," the first guide said.

"Man it's cold!" Jim said as he came up to the fire. "What happened?"

"Clouds rise," the tracker said.

"Tomorrow," the second tracker said, "we go into the valley." He pointed toward the steep slope on the side opposite to the way they had come up. "It will be easier. Trees do not grow toward the sun but straight out the side of the mountain and farther apart."

"That's strange," Jim said.

"This a strange mountain," the guide said. "People who live here are even stranger." He looked at Jim and smiled. The guides and the porter had already developed a profound respect for Melanie. "The American woman has much strength and courage," they had observed. But for Jim they reserved silence.

Melanie and Jim eventually returned to their bedrolls and slept. Jim was restless. He remembered that night so long ago in Malaysia. His love affair with Melanie had been short lived, though they had remained good friends.

At first light there were whistles in the valley and along the mountain slope they were descending. They never saw anything but knew they were being observed. They took a long, winding route to the valley floor, as the slope itself was almost vertical. In the valley they spent a full day and a half in a clearing of very large mango trees. It was dark and spacious in this clearing beneath the dense canopy formed by the huge trees. The second guide assured them the gibbons they were after often fed in this very spot while the mangos were ripe, large and golden among the dark green leaves of the trees.

They saw nothing the afternoon they arrived, but on the morning of the second day they were awakened by a tremendous ruckus. Black gibbons were in the canopy above them, shrieking and leaping from branch to branch. Several wild pigs had wandered into the clearing and the gibbons, already there feeding, had ganged up on them from above, pelting them with ripe mangos. Melanie grabbed her equipment, which was already set up, and got a number of good shots, including several of the three white gibbons they observed with the troop, or family group.

The gibbons left after the fracas, and Melanie sat exhausted on the ground, surrounded by mangos that had fallen from the trees and those that the gibbons had thrown. She picked up a mango and began to laugh, tears filling her eyes and rolling down her cheeks. It was so wonderful to be alive! She couldn't imagine doing anything else.

The Seminar

Dr. Douglas Norman entered the classroom and took his seat at the head of a long brown wooden table. He was there to conduct a small graduate seminar in philosophy on the subject of Aristotle's *Nicomachean Ethics* and the *Politics*. There were nine students.

"Good morning," Dr. Norman said with his head lowered as he spoke, absorbed in getting his Greek language copy of Aristotle's works out of his briefcase and setting it on the table in front of him. He opened the book and, moving his lips silently, carefully tracing the sentences with his right index finger, found his place. "We had before us yesterday the problem of acrasia, or weakness of will. I want to quote here something from another of Aristotle's works, the *De Anima*, which I believe will help to elucidate our problem."

The nine students, six men and three women, sat in rapt silence as he read the passage from Aristotle's treatise on the soul. The essence of this passage was an attempt to answer the question: How is an object perceived?

"Doug, I don't see the relevance," Sally said when the professor had finished reading. "What's that got to do with our problem?"

Professor Norman looked at her over his glasses. Her familiar tone of address did not lessen his amusement. He smiled. "Yes, John."

The young man sitting next to Sally suggested that perhaps the passage bore some relevance to the manner in which we formulate a problem in our consciousness, about which we must then make a decision.

Sally, an attractive blond in her mid twenties who dressed in such a way as to be noticeably good to look at and who only wore glasses in the classroom, turned red in the face.

"Yes," Dr. Norman said, "the problem of will leads us to the nature of consciousness." He brushed back a dark hank of hair that hung over his forehead and almost touched his bushy eyebrows, which had more gray in them than the hair. The incessant beeping of a delivery truck backing up somewhere on campus could be heard through an open window. A robin also sang in the green campus foliage outside, and crows cawed from some more distant point. "But what is consciousness? It would appear the good doctor" (He meant Aristotle) "would make little distinction between the organ of perception, or consciousness, and the image which it perceives. What does he say here? He says the perceiving organ assumes the form of the thing perceived. Notice he does not say it contains an image of the perceived object, but that it takes its form."

"Well, I don't see how this relates to will," Sally said, recovering herself. "Or to a problem confronting the will, which may not be an object."

"Will is part of consciousness," John pointed out. He was a lank, thin man in his thirties who spoke nervously, creating an air of anxious concern. "We are conscious beings. If our conscious awareness takes the form of the thing perceived, then the movement of will must be inextricably bound up in our awareness of the thing itself. Or of a problem, if that is what is focused upon in the conscious mind for the purpose of making a decision."

"That doesn't make any sense," Sally said, turning red again. And knowing that she was embarrassed, she felt irritated at herself for being so. "I know myself as something separate from whatever I make a decision about. I hold the image I'm deciding about in my mind as an object of contemplation." She gesticulated with her hands, drawing the object out of her forehead and holding it figuratively in front of her. The entire class laughed, including Dr. Norman. Sally fell silent, crimson.

"Sally, I'm not denying that we can make this distinction. You're absolutely right." Professor Norman paused to allow his soothing confirmation to sink in. He glanced over his glasses at the young woman who was regathering herself. Then he got up, walked over to the window through which the irritating beeping noise could still be heard, and shut it with a thump. "There," he said, rubbing his hands together with a look of satisfaction, as if he had vanquished a dragon, "I've made a decision." The entire class burst into uncontrollable laughter.

Dr. Norman sat down. Everyone was in a much more relaxed mood. He looked at the nine faces, mostly young, a few older. "We don't have to settle this issue today," he said. "This controversy has been raging for over two thousand years. It would perhaps not be unreasonably modest of us," he continued—there was a mischievous twinkle in his eyes—"to assume the problem will not be resolved this afternoon."

"No, that's for sure," someone said.

"On the other hand," Professor Norman added, "we shouldn't shortchange ourselves. Maybe we'll find a solution."

"Oh, God!" Sally said.

Dr. Norman smiled. "I want you to consider something, all of you. If consciousness can be more than our field of focused attention, if it can include semiconscious as well as unconscious urges, impulses and memories, then there may be a great deal in the mix in the way we either perceive an object or focus upon a problem."

"As if we'd wrapped ourselves around it," Sally said, looking bright.

"More or less."

"Then much of the real deliberation going into a decision, even if not wholly conscious or thought out, is already weighed before the rational process of deciding even begins," John added. "The logic of our subsequent thought processes may even end up contradicting the unseen role played by our own unrecognized inclinations which are bound up in our perception of the object or problem. We might then act in contradiction to what would appear to have been the result of a conscious decision. It would look like weakness of will."

The bell rang. Students gathered up their possessions. Sally, John and several others, crowded in a huddle about Professor Norman, squeezed out the door with him in the full heat of a continued discussion.

The Book

As a historian he loved the research, research he did anyway in the course of preparation for classroom presentation. He could relay the dry facts and seemingly moldering thoughts of a dead past in a manner that kept his students on the edge of their seats. His interest was the history of ideas. His specialty, the development of mysticism in Spain and southern France out of the medieval scholastic philosophical tradition as reiterated and modified during the Renaissance by such philosopher theologians as Francisco Suarez.

He submitted occasional articles to the various scholarly journals and he had read papers at numerous colloquiums. He was widely respected by his colleagues, but unknown to the world because he had never written a full length book. He was, at forty-six, in his own estimation, a failure.

He had also never married, never wanted to sacrifice his freedom for domestic chains, lest the inspiration for that great book that would secure him to literary immortality suddenly come upon him and he be too busy with milk bottles, mop pails, garden spades and taking out the garbage to notice. This was his general condition the morning he met a new colleague in the college faculty lounge.

"Bill. Bill Richman come over here. I want you to meet someone. Someone new. Bonnie, this is Bill Richman. Bill, this is Bonnie Richmond. Ha ha. You could almost be married your names are so close. I thought you'd find it interesting."

"Yes. Thank you, Don. Hello Bonnie." Bill felt the heat in his neck and cheeks and knew he had colored significantly. Bonnie also seemed embarrassed. He shook her small white hand, looking into the large brown wells of her eyes. They were eyes that pulled you in softly, eyes that were immediately intimate, though the rest of Bonnie's manner was held in reserve. Her chestnut brown hair was soft, full, a little too long at the shoulders for a college professor.

At the coffee house for a light lunch several days later they sat looking at each other across a small table. They were alone.

"I've read some of your papers," Bonnie said. "Your friends … Well, Don, as a matter of fact," (the one who had introduced them) "tells me you're working on a book." She looked at Bill over the rim of her cup, setting it down as she spoke."

"I … Well, I … Look, Bonnie, you know Don by now. He's full of air."

Bonnie smiled. "Well, you should write a book. I've read enough of your work to know you have a good one in you."

"I never seem to have the time."

"You have too much time. You need a wife to organize things, to give you a sense of routine and security." Bonnie suddenly turned a deep red. "What I mean is. Uh … I'm not trying to pry into your personal life. Please excuse me for being so abrupt." Bonnie dropped her eyes to her coffee cup, picking it up and setting it back down. She glanced at Bill. He sat wordless, staring at her.

In a matter of weeks they were married. Bonnie's slip of the tongue had opened a window for Bill. A gentle, warming breeze had blown through it. He smelled the scent of green meadows he hadn't known were there. Bill was a big, hairy, awkward sort of man. He had no idea how he had ever pulled it off, or why after years of comfortable bachelorhood, but he was now a domestic man, a boar in a corn field, he thought, clumsily stumbling this way and that, trampling the lovely green stalks.

Bonnie saw it differently. Here was the man she'd been truly looking for. Much older than herself. But the instant recognition had shown that first day in her eyes. She received him into her heart and the moist warm passion of her love, melting herself into the powerful thrust of his gathered strength and need.

Things began to happen. First of all Bonnie became pregnant, joyously, intensely fulfillingly fruitful. Bill seemed to be as happy as she was. They bought a small house near the college. There was a flower garden by the front picket fence and several in the back yard. Bill worked them faithfully, helping Bonnie, turning the soil, planting, weeding. To colleagues paying occasional visits and knowing Bill for many years, it was all a miracle. Don certainly thought so.

"I can't believe it, Bill," he proclaimed one afternoon, sitting on a lawn chair in the Richmans' back yard, holding a drink. "You a gardener? You a married man? Whatever happened to the old bachelor who was going to devote his life to the single task of producing the one great book he never got around to writing?"

"I don't know, Don," Bill answered from where he was on his knees working the soil by the side fence.

"Now you are actually doing it, and with a kid on the way. How is the book coming anyway?"

Bill came over near Don and leaned with one hand against the yellow clapboard side of the house. In his other hand was a green garden spade, caked with moist, brown earth.

"I feel so much more free now," he said. "I know it doesn't make sense. You want to know something strange, Don?" He crouched down beside his friend, speaking in a low voice. He stuck the garden spade into the grass with one hand and leaned on it.

"Sure," Don said. He took a drink from his glass, then inclined his ear, leaning to one side of the lawn chair. He was always interested in a new revelation.

"I used to believe ... Got it from Hemingway I think. Ridiculous, I know, but I really believed it."

"Believed what, man? Come on. Don't leave me in suspense."

"Well, I thought ... I mean I was convinced that ..." Don was craning his neck. Bill continued, "that if you weren't careful you'd lose it all in the marriage bed."

"All what?"

"The book, of course. What else?"

Don withdrew himself back into the lawn chair and looked at his friend. He took another drink.

Bill was crouched beside him with a simple sincere expression on his face.

The Scent of a Rose

She had given a good deal of consideration to her personal morals. She had burned for men. She had felt indifferent to them. She had even once felt unnaturally close to a woman but had failed to act upon it. She did not regret this but only wondered at times what might've become of her had she followed her inclinations. The woman she had not expressed her feelings toward had been her best friend, but since then they had drifted apart.

It was a number of years ago, and Allison Sorensen was now in her early forties. She was a striking woman in her way, having inherited the physical traits of her naturalized-American, Swedish-born father. She was tall with straight blond hair that fell to just below her shoulders. The bone structure of her face was prominent, but overall her bones were not large. Somewhat thin and modestly proportioned, she could not have been said to be beautiful. Yet she certainly was attractive, and there was a kind of raw, natural energy, a physical projection of truth, an intolerance for nonsense and guile, that emanated from her. Her somewhat masculine mannerisms and the husky range of her voice reinforced the impression.

Allison had never married. She was too independent, too free-spirited to come under the domination of another person. Her large, creative intelligence surpassed that of most men she had known. It seemed the more intelligent ones were afraid of her; the others, perhaps as a result of a similar reaction, needed to possess her in a smothering way. So she had had many boyfriends, discarding them when they became too oppressive.

Allison had been brought up a good Lutheran, and her sexual life had been, to say the least, less than upright in her own opinion. But to sacrifice who she was—never! On the other hand, her needs were too strong for denial. Thus her ongoing dilemma. The choice she could never finally make was between two extreme, unpleasant options: one of submission, and the other a kind of physical and emotional starvation. She vacillated unhappily in the middle.

Allison had a boyfriend at present. He was a stockbroker and worked in lower Manhattan. She lived in a cozy second floor condominium on the Upper East Side, and he lived nearby. That was how they met. The first floor of her building had a pleasant lobby and sitting room, and the building owners also employed a doorman. These owners, of course, were Allison and her fellow condominiumites. Allison taught art history at City College and freelanced part-time as an art consultant for several of the galleries located on Fifty-ninth Street.

The boyfriend's name was Todd Johnston. She occasionally called him Toddy for fun. "Let's have a toddy," she would say. This was, of course, always in the privacy of his or her apartment and usually followed several drinks.

She and Todd had been together for about six months. They had had a lot of fun. But Todd was interested in something more permanent. So was she, to tell the truth, if it could've been done without sacrifice of personal sovereignty. One evening at dinner in a small restaurant which they frequented, and which was not far from her apartment, Todd said point-blank—and rather awkwardly in the middle of the meal—"Will you marry me?"

Allison dropped her eyes to the table.

Todd waited. He knew he shouldn't have popped the question.

Allison looked up. "I'm not sure," she said.

"Not sure! We're sleeping together. What's there to be unsure about?" When Allison merely looked at him sadly with her blue eyes without responding, he said, "Okay, okay. I shouldn't have asked. I don't want to ruin a good thing."

They finished their meal in silence. But inside Allison's head there was no peace. It was like a legislative assembly hall: argument and counterargument. Wouldn't it be nice to join the morally at peace? She did enjoy being with Todd—in almost every way. But marriage meant gradual submission. She was sure of it. She'd seen it too many times among her friends. And she'd enjoyed her own personal freedom for too long.

Also, she had to admit to herself, with a species of cold and unpleasant recognition, that she enjoyed keeping a man emotionally hungry. It was almost cruel. But the thought of a full surrender of her heart—something more than her body—produced a vague sense of revulsion in her. She didn't know why.

What about kids? She'd long ago discarded that notion. It wasn't for her. Was she an unnatural woman? Was she immoral? She did believe in God, and she had no desire to hurt anyone. Not really. Though, of course, she couldn't be responsible for other people's emotional expectations. As for God, well he would just have to understand. After all, he was the one who had made her the way she was.

That night Todd had insisted on their going to his apartment. They almost always went to hers, which she preferred. When they made love, she didn't let on there wasn't any feeling in it for her. She just couldn't let go and relax. The question of marital surrender kept bothering her. It set up an adversary emotion in her mind.

In the morning Allison got up and went home to her apartment before Todd woke up. There, putting on her makeup for the day—a light application, since she didn't doll up for her students—she thought about her dilemma.

"I'm an old maid," she told herself. She was talking to the person in the mirror and wanted to frighten her a little. Just a little. "I could grow old and die alone with no one to mourn me." She looked at the lines under her eyes. "Soon no one will be interested," she said.

But it didn't matter. The image in the mirror only looked back with mild curiosity. After twenty years of adult life, she already knew the score.

Allison put her morning in at City College, and then, having no afternoon classes to teach that session, went on down to one of the galleries on Fifty-ninth street.

"Allison, I want to show you something," Meg, the gallery owner, said when she came in the street door.

They went into a small room which was separated from the main display gallery by an open doorway, and there on the wall was a strangely familiar painting. Allison recognized the style and signature. It was that of her old friend, whom she hadn't seen in fifteen years and for whom she'd had such confused and tender feelings.

* * *

Meg arranged for Allison to become reacquainted with her old friend. Miniver Peechi—yes, this really was her name—was a tiny, porcelain doll of a woman. Everything about her was petite: her ears, her narrow, china plate transparent nostrils, her slender, almost sparrow-boned ankles and wrists. She was a little over five five but looked smaller, with glistening black hair cut off square above the shoulders and banged straight across her forehead. Her dark brown eyes seemed to pull you into their depths. Her mouth was a fragile rose petal in a lily white face. Even her voice was preternaturally small and quiet, her manners precise yet unassuming. All in all, there was something of a concentrated sensuousness about this woman, like the nectar of a flower reduced to a tiny drop of French essence. Though both women were reserved, they were, as observed by a third party, in a temperamental relationship of male to female.

This was the way it had been years ago and the way it was now in the cozy little restaurant where they met near Eighth Avenue and Forty-seventh Street in midtown Manhattan. They had a small table with a clean white cloth in a semiprivate, semi-dark alcove next to an interior brick wall. It was picturesque. They needed the candle on the table to provide sufficient light. It threw shadows on the wall.

"Minnie, I can't believe it after all these years. How little you've changed," Allison said, leaning toward her old friend, her hands clasped under her chin, her elbows on the table. The waiter came with their lunch. Allison leaned back in her chair.

As the waiter placed the hot metal and wood platters of veal cutlets on the table—they were having a hearty lunch several days after Allison's discovery of Minnie's presence in the city—both women looked him over from head to toe. He was a handsome young man in his twenties.

The waiter seemed embarrassed.

"Don't mind us," Allison said to him, suddenly a little embarrassed herself. "At our age we can only fantasize."

The young man's face turned red. Minnie tittered behind a napkin.

After the waiter left, the two women continued their conversation, gingerly testing the first bites of their food for hotness.

"Handsome, isn't he?" Allison said, a steaming piece of meat hovering in the air on a fork just out of reach of her sensitive tongue.

Minnie smiled.

"You haven't married either, have you?" Allison commented.

"No. Been too busy," Minnie said, biting off a piece of garlic bread with her two perfectly aligned rows of small front teeth. She did this carefully in such a way as to intimate, to anyone who might be so callous as to scrutinize her in this animal function, that no crumbs would find their way onto forbidden surfaces. Her sensitive lips folded themselves over the bit-off piece as though an exotic flower were closing its soft petals for the night. She cupped a hand under her chin.

"The painting is beautiful," Allison observed. "Have you been selling?"

"Enough to get by," Minnie said, her eyes smiling.

"It's a tough business, but I love it," Allison added.

"Teaching is a little more secure."

"But you're doing okay?"

"Yes."

"Just like old times," Allison mused. She was turning the candle in its crystal holder on the table. She looked up at her friend. "I'm thinking of finally settling down maybe."

"You?" Minnie tittered. Her dark eyes flashed sweetly, a little mischievously.

"Yes, me. What about it? You think I'm too old?" Allison was suppressing a smile. Her blue eyes were full of a familiar energy.

"No." Minnie looked down, negotiating a cut of meat, taking her time at it.

Allison studied her. Then she said by way of further experiment, "My boyfriend wants me to marry him."

"Is he handsome?" Minnie looked up, putting a bright face on the conversation.

"Yes. He's a stockbroker. He's good at everything."

Minnie smiled.

The two women looked at each other transfixed. Deep blue eyes looked intimately into deep brown ones, and the brown ones looked back. All the old affection was there.

"Well," Allison said, breaking her gaze. She felt somehow shaken and, at the same time, uplifted. The two women finished their meals in silence, each in her own world.

After they left the restaurant, they took a cab up to Fifty-ninth Street and spent some time at the gallery with Meg.

Meg was a little older, a woman in her late fifties, married with grown children and grandchildren. She had known Allison for six years, and, though theirs was primarily a business relationship, it had ripened into friendship.

"I made the Parelli purchase," she said. The three women were sitting at a small table in one corner of the main room of the gallery. It was shortly after lunchtime, and no one else was in the shop.

"Good. I like his brushwork," Allison said. "I think there's something there. He's still young. Did you sell the Ronstadts? There are two of them in the shop," Allison added, looking at Minnie.

"No," Meg said. "Not yet. I think I have them reasonably priced though. And I've generated some interest. There's a bank ..." The bell above the door tinkled. A customer came in. It was a woman.

She proceeded slowly along one wall, looking at the works mounted there.

The three women at the table looked at each other. "You know what," Meg said, rising to her feet. "I think you two good friends meeting again after all this time calls for some kind of a celebration. What say we get together this evening after I close the gallery and go down to Harold's for a little of the pink, bubbly stuff?"

"I would love to," Allison said. "But I promised Todd …"

"Well, some other time then." Meg went over to the customer.

Allison and Minnie left the shop, said good-by outside the door, and went in separate directions along the street.

* * *

That night in Todd's arms, Allison was beginning to become quite concerned. This problem lately of little or no arousal was growing ever more insistent. She didn't understand it. Todd was handsome, a fine lover. He looked damned good in the buff. But something inside her wouldn't click. Her emotions were disengaged. Fortunately, until she figured this problem out, she could always claim a climax during the moment when Todd was preoccupied with his own ejaculation. But it was altogether unpleasant. It wasn't the way it should be or had been until recently.

Todd seemed to sense a problem. He lay beside her afterward and said into the dark, "You're not enjoying it."

"Yes I am."

"Do you still love me?"

"Yes."

"Well, let's get up and watch some TV."

"Now?"

"Sure. There's a good movie on late. Besides, I'm feeling restless."

Well, I'm not, Allison thought, lying in bed alone after Todd left the room. She placed a hand on a breast and touched herself between the legs, feeling arousal. "Strange!" she said out loud and got up and threw on a robe. Probably some darned old war movie he wants to watch, she said to herself as she did so.

Sure enough, it was a war movie. World War Two. About a bunch of desperate, down-in-the-dirt guys on some canal that was an island in the Pacific Ocean. She gathered that much from Todd's brief commentary when she asked him what it was about. But she couldn't have cared less. If he liked war so much, why didn't he go to one? There's bound to be one available somewhere, she thought.

No, she just didn't understand men sometimes. Their lack of tenderness and sensitive awareness. The smell of a rose, the beauty of a painting was of infinitely more worth than dying like a pig shot to death in a mud wallow.

She didn't realize that men thought their bravery, real or imagined, appealed to a woman. She couldn't have cared less about it. If things got desperate enough that one must die like a pig shot in a wallow, the world wouldn't be worth living in anyway.

Allison sighed. She was lying on Todd's shoulder with one of his arms around her. They were on the couch facing the TV. The room was dark, except for a light in the kitchen.

"What's the matter?" Todd asked, glancing over at her.

"Nothing."

He became reabsorbed in the movie. A handful of Marines were down in a bunker being bombed by Japanese planes. They looked very uncomfortable.

Allison lifted Todd's inert arm and got up, letting the arm drop to his side. He didn't even glance over at her. Events on the screen were too absorbing. But as Allison walked away, he said, "Honey, could you refill my glass?"

"Sure." She picked it up off the coffee table and went into the kitchen.

Allison brought the refilled glass back out to Todd and returned to the kitchen. She thought she ought to go to bed, but now she was restless. She felt empty. She made herself a pot of tea and sat down at the small kitchen table, warming her hands with the cup. When she lifted the cup to drink out of it, her long blond hair almost got into it. She irritably flipped the hair over her shoulder with her free hand.

"What's the matter with me?" she said. She hoped Todd hadn't heard her. No problem there. He was oblivious. She smiled. "Maybe it's because he asked me to marry him. At some level I must be resenting it, and it's making me cold."

She tried to reason with herself in this way. But now she really was tired. She went to the bedroom and got into bed. They were in her apartment that night. Almost immediately she fell asleep.

The next day in the classroom, she suddenly announced to her students, and to her own surprise, that Murillo was the greatest of all Spanish painters. The class looked at her in dumb silence. Murillo's reputation, according to modern sensibility, was somewhat reduced by his reputed tendency toward sentimentality. She didn't try to explain herself further to the class. She had no explanation. No idea why she'd made the statement she had.

In the afternoon, she went to see Meg and confessed her faux pas of the morning. Meg didn't see any problem with it, but then she wasn't a scholar. Her interests were purely contemporary, never far from the tinkle of money.

They were sitting at the little table in the corner. Minnie walked in, hauling a canvas in a large carrying case. She took it out and set it on the table before the two women. "I promised you I'd bring it today," she said to Meg. "I'm as good as my word." Her eyes twinkled with the charm of her excitement. Her entire manner was that of one who had just executed a brisk walk in cold air. But it was warm outside.

"Yes. My lord, yes!" Meg leapt up and took the canvas joyfully. She went over and hung it on the wall next to the other canvas Minnie had painted. They looked good there together. Meg had moved the other canvas out into the main room that very morning in anticipation of the arrival of the second. "Now we'll make a sale," she said beaming at her smaller companion.

Minnie was standing next to her. She glanced back at her friend, who was still at the table. Allison had tears in her eyes.

"Oh! Are you all right?" Minnie went over to her quickly. Allison couldn't seem to stop the flow of tears. Wiping them away repeatedly, she kept sniffing, forcing a smile.

"I'm fine," she said. "I don't know what's the matter." Her lips trembled as she spoke, her voice thick with moisture. She got up clumsily, knocking over her chair.

Minnie held her as she wept in her arms, sobbing heavily, hardly able to sustain her own weight. Minnie thought her heart would break, seeing her friend like this.

Meg simply stood by and let her cry herself out. She had absolutely no idea what to do.

* * *

Descending on foot down spiraling concrete steps beneath a sidewalk and tall buildings, Minnie was headed toward the Fifty-ninth Street subway platform when she suddenly stopped. The damp tunnels always stank of urine. She thought, "Oh, I can't do this!" A high-pitched screeching of train car wheels on metal tracks came from below. "God, it sounds awful!" She wasn't in any mood for a pushing, suffocating crowd anyway. So she turned around and climbed back up into daylight and fresh air. Walking to the corner of Fifth Avenue, she crossed over to Central Park.

There were a couple of streetside bookstalls there, and she paused to browse in the afternoon sun. Ducks were swimming, feeding and happily chasing one another in the pond behind the bookstalls. The sun was very warm. People were out in it all along Fifth Avenue, walking hurriedly or leisurely up and down the broad sidewalks, or standing idly around the bookstalls, browsing. A horse carriage clip-clopped nearby along Fifty-ninth Street, looking for tourists. New York was today the massive village it probably always had been.

Minnie was very much aware of the nature of her own inclinations. Much more so than Allison was. She knew she had strong emotional feelings toward her friend and that underlying them was a sexual attraction. For, unlike Allison, she had never courted the affections of men. That had been settled long ago in her adolescence.

But why, she mused to herself now with irritation and frustration, didn't I let Allison know how I felt fifteen years ago. Minnie knew, when she thought about it, that she had been afraid, had been unsure of what her friend's response would be to any such gesture, hint or suggestion. Just as she was almost equally unsure now. But the sudden outburst of weeping this afternoon. What was that about? Her heartbeat quickened a little. Was Allison experiencing the same feelings she had long ago recognized in herself? That would explain a lot of things. But if she, Minnie, was confused about this … if she made a clumsy move …

Oh! She couldn't bear the thought of her dear friend, whom she loved so much, looking upon her with sudden horror at the unexpected revelation. No, anything but that!

Yet … how long could she endure this, suppress such an overwhelming passion? God having thrown them together once again … yes *God*, damn it! Could even he despise feelings so pure, even if they weren't in accord with animal procreative function?

Yes, she knew it was wrong. It was so confusing. She'd wrestled with it most of her life. She couldn't change who she was. But that didn't give her the right to turn someone else in her direction. But then—what if Allison just didn't realize who she really was? She was beginning to believe that was the case.

Minnie had been holding the same book for ten minutes. The vender inside the bookstall was looking at her. To tell the truth, she hadn't yet even read the title. Looking up into the vender's inquiring eyes, she was suddenly embarrassed. "I'll take this one," she said, reaching into her purse. It only cost a dollar.

She went into the park and sat down on a bench in front of the pond. There were low bushes behind and to either side of the bench. Mice were running about in this greenery, sticking their heads out now and then investigating the greater world with their dark beady eyes and little ears, possibly specifically trying to have a look at her. She didn't notice them. A male mallard was chasing another in the water in front of her. Both were squawking loudly.

There's animal instinct for you! Minnie thought with a wry smile. Aggression and possessiveness. Don't the men of this world ever have a tender moment?

She knew she was being unfair. But it made her feel better to believe for an interval, however short that interval might be, that she was right.

A man walked past her bench and looked her over with interest. She smiled at him. He smiled back and went on. She really didn't mind being admired by them. It reminded her that, in outward terms at least, she was on competitive terms with any other woman. She wasn't a freak.

But all of her tender feelings were toward women. Never men. The only man she had ever loved was her father, and he had been killed in an accident when she was twelve. That had closed a chapter on something. She wasn't sure why.

Allison. How lovely she was! So sweet and good! In all the past years no one else had ever meant quite as much to Minnie.

She got up and walked towards home. Home was a modest apartment on the Upper West Side. She thought of Allison's blue eyes. So full of life! Her straight blond hair and somewhat bony shoulders. She was so vulnerable. Truly she was, in spite of her strong manner. Hadn't those precious tears proven it today? It nearly broke Minnie's heart again to think of it.

* * *

Allison had taken a cab back to her condominium. As the taxi nudged its way through a stream of pedestrians crossing the street at the corner of Fifth Avenue and then began an easier trip toward the Upper East Side of Manhattan, she glanced over at the park, her eyes passing along the bookstalls. But Minnie hadn't yet emerged from the subway station on Fifty-ninth Street, so she didn't see her.

Allison's face was red from crying. She hadn't the least idea what had caused her to suddenly burst into tears like that. So convulsively too. Going over it, she remembered feeling joy at the quality of Minnie's work, at the exhilaration of triumph in what her friend had achieved as an artist. Joy and then … well, then an anvil fell over in her chest. A dam burst. All the frustration and worry with Todd, all the loneliness she had inexplicably but truly felt over the years. It was suddenly clear, and it all came down, crushing her into tears, like a flower coldly pressed into its essence for the making and sale of a commercial perfume. This clarity of feeling was new and foreign to her. As yet, she could not assimilate it.

Allison sat in the back of the cab with her legs crossed, the hem of her skirt above her knees. The driver saw those slender knees in his rear view mirror. It nearly caused an accident.

When she got out of the cab, her skirt flipped up as she set one leg on the sidewalk. Any man worth his salt, having seen this, would've suffered cardiac arrest on the spot.

* * *

At home Allison made herself some tea. Todd was still at work. He wouldn't be by until later in the evening anyway.

Allison had taken off her skirt and blouse and hung them up in her bedroom closet when she came in. She wanted to keep her skirt fresh for another day. She was moving about in the kitchen in her slip and brassiere, making tea. Having put the kettle of water on the stove to heat, she sat down, crossing her legs. The sun coming through the upper panes of the kitchen window, which part of the window was not covered with curtains, warmed her lap and lay a golden finger on her bare knees. She leaned to one side on the kitchen table, her elbow propped, her head on her hand, feeling drowsy. Her thoughts became disconnected. An image of Minnie, soft, undressed to her brassiere, appeared. Allison was lying gently upon Minnie's breasts. Minnie's arm was tenderly caressing her shoulder.

A blast of steam from the tea kettle brought her to her feet. She went over and pulled the kettle off the burner. Her heart was racing. Whether from the sudden fright of the whistling steam or something else, she didn't know. She did realize she had an uncomfortable feeling about the image that had just been in her mind. It wasn't natural. Yet she'd had such moments before, which she'd always rejected. Now she confronted herself.

"Am I homosexual?" she asked, standing beside the stove. "Oh, I do love Minnie. I always have. But as a friend." An image of Minnie touching her passed through her mind again. It sent a warm feeling throughout her body.

"No!" She put the tea kettle back on the burner and went over to the table and sat down. "No, no, no!" she repeated, shaking her head, her hands upon her face. Warm tears wet her eyes. She wanted to cry. But the emotion within her heart was one of confused, unacceptable joy. It had an air of freedom to it, try though she might to construe it as wrong.

When it became obvious she wasn't going to cry, she went ahead and made her tea, though the water was becoming tepid. The teabag lay in her cup like a tiny white pillow, yielding very little of its essence. She stirred it, and the cup of water became lightly discolored, as though, at best, it contained a rusty nail.

"I've always had these feelings," she confessed to herself with something of surprise at the admission. "Certainly I have. I just didn't want to admit it." She reflected. "But I'm able to make love to a man. Or I was able to, until a few days ago. What kind of a grotesque monster am I?"

She took the dripping tea bag out of her cup, holding it by the string, and placed it on her saucer. She drank the nearly flavorless water. "Ugh," she remarked, putting down the half-empty cup. "Weak tea tastes like dirty dishwater."

She got up from the table, went into her bedroom, and threw herself face down upon her bed. She still thought she wanted to cry, but now even her eyes were dry, though they were hot. An intense anger arose within her, an anger with herself and with all the world besides. How was it possible she could go for forty years and never acknowledge she had such inclinations? Well, maybe she had at least partially acknowledged it to herself at times but just hadn't accepted it. She grabbed the bedspread in both her fists. "Damn it," she said. "Damn it, no!"

She sat up. I don't have to do anything I don't want to do, she thought. I've always been good with men. Happy with them really. I don't want to change. I … I'm afraid to. Poor Minnie. If she only knew. Well, thank God she doesn't.

Allison sat on the bed, staring at her knees. She looked at her brassiere. "I wonder if being flat-chested makes you queer," she said aloud. "Me a dyke?" She turned around and threw herself on her face on the bed again. "I'm not gay," she mumbled into the bedspread. "I'm not a … a lesbian."

She sat up. "I'll marry Todd. Yes, that's what I'll do. When he comes over tonight I'll tell him so. I don't have to torture myself like this. I'm in charge of my own destiny. I can choose to be who I want to be, just as I've always done."

She got up smiling to herself. Whatever possessed me? she thought. Everything was just fine now. She put on a pair of shorts and a blouse and went out to make dinner. A fancy dinner. Pork roast, gravy, biscuits and sweet potatoes. Todd was expecting to go out to eat, but she would have it all ready when he came over.

For the next several hours Allison was euphoric. She felt light as a daisy in summer wind. She could float like dandelion fluff, heedless of manicured lawns. Then the doorbell rang, the smell of good food filling the condominium. Her heart sank and her courage left her. "That's Todd," she told herself. She went to the front door and let him in.

"I thought we were going out," he said. He had already smelled the food outside the door.

"I … I wanted to surprise you."

"Oh." Todd smiled slyly. "I'm game." He came into the living room and sat down. Allison returned to the kitchen.

"What am I going to do?" she asked herself, leaning her back and head against the closed refrigerator door. Once again her heart was racing and she felt like bursting into tears. "He's expecting something, and now I know I can't. God please help me. God doesn't help queers!" she said to herself angrily, lifting her body off the refrigerator door. "God doesn't help queers," she repeated wearily.

"What was that?" Todd's voice came from the living room. She heard him get up and walk toward the kitchen.

Oh, please don't come out here, she thought, hurriedly straightening her posture, making herself look busy.

"Who you talking to?" Todd asked, coming into the kitchen.

"Myself," she said matter-of-factly.

"Well, I'd be jealous if I didn't think you loved me," he said.

She smiled at his humor as best she could.

* * *

Todd wanted to make love that night, but she told him she was starting her period.

"So soon again?"

"It seems to be irregular. I don't know why. Just stress, I suppose."

"About what?" Todd looked at her.

She thought she detected suspicion in his eyes.

"You all right?" he asked. He meant: Are you all right about me? She had seemed awful cold lately.

"Yes. Yes, I'm fine." A little later she told him she needed to be alone. She wasn't feeling well and wanted to go to bed. He left obediently but much perplexed, suspicious about her motives.

The next day was a Saturday, and she went straight to Meg's gallery. She needed to unburden herself and was desperate for someone to confide in. But Meg was a rather conventional woman. Unimaginative would perhaps be an unkind but truthful way of putting it. Allison thought better of her intended purpose the moment she arrived.

Shortly after she arrived, Minnie came in. "I was hoping I'd find you here," Minnie said upon seeing her. Allison was relieved to see her friend, but she didn't know why. It should've complicated things.

The two good friends left the shop together. As they strolled along Fifty-ninth Street, then down Fifth Avenue, Minnie was searching for words. "I told you I wanted to talk to you," she said. "Now I can't seem to …" She hesitated.

"To what?" Allison questioned, smiling. To reassure her friend, she took her friend's hand in her own. Minnie spontaneously tightened her grip, giving Allison's hand an affectionate squeeze. It was like an electric telegram that passed between the nerve centers of both of them. They were in perfect accord. Whatever she said, Minnie knew Allison would understand, that she wouldn't leap to an angry response.

For her part, Allison knew only this: that she felt supremely at peace for the moment, her doubts and fears folded away in a neat packet somewhere in a seething corner of her mind. All the rest of her was calm water.

"It's about our friendship," Minnie continued. She felt relaxed now, yet just a little apprehensive. It was only natural that she should be concerned, for Allison was looking at her with those incredible blue eyes. Minnie chose not to return the look. "There's something I've never told you," she said.

Allison did not interrupt.

"I'm not the kind of person you think I am. I never have been. I've always known it but … I didn't want to hurt our friendship."

Allison still didn't say anything, but she tightened her grip on Minnie's hand.

Minnie looked up, her dark eyes glistening. "You know what I'm trying to say. Don't you?"

Allison nodded, her own eyes filling with tears. They both stopped in the middle of the sidewalk, people going around them like wind-buckled water around a buoy. They looked at each other in silence. Then they turned and walked on down the street.

* * *

When Allison went home she had a mission. She had to tell Todd it was over. She had never felt more happy or more frightened. Nothing from here on was going to be easy. But for the first time in her life she was sure, in emotional terms at least, of what she wanted.

A Matter of Perspective

In 1972 the Schuylkill River rose above its banks in the city of Philadelphia. Of course, waters rose in other parts of southeastern Pennsylvania as well. A few people lost their lives, mainly due to entering their basements when they were flooded. The water, standing in those basements above the electrical outlets, was charged with electricity.

In Philadelphia a park runs along the banks of this river. The river, wearing its slender mantle of grassy meadows and trees, meanders through the north part of the city to join the Delaware River. It grabs hold of the Delaware by the flank, attaches itself unshakably to it like a hungry lamprey, and empties itself forthwith. All this under normal conditions.

In 1972 the Schuylkill bulged at the neck and sent its waters into the park. There it lolled about for several days before getting back into its regular course. Fortunately, the neighborhood nearest to the art museum, which latter institution was itself in the flooded area, rose on a gently sloping hill. For this reason, Art Robinson, who was unable to walk his dog in the park, which he was normally accustomed to do, was nevertheless fearless in the matter of the safety of his dwelling. It was securely above the reach of the flood.

Art Robinson was a gentle, pleasant, little man who had done a variety of things. Now in his fifties, he had as a young man traveled to California, where he had worked for a few months before the surprise attack on Pearl Harbor. Thereupon, he had immediately enlisted in the Navy and, in due time, sailed off into the Pacific aboard an aircraft carrier, or "flattop," as he generally referred to it. He had been aboard the Yorktown when it was damaged in the Battle of the Coral Sea near Australia in May of 1942. He was wounded, but not seriously, and remained in Hawaii when the Yorktown returned to action in June of the same year at the Battle of Midway.

Art went on to do other things, working as a welder and as a sheet metal worker in several eastern States and even in a brewery in Colorado. He eventually married and returned to Philadelphia, his home town. The marriage produced one child and then failed. His wife, a bitter woman, raised their daughter to dislike him. He never remarried.

By 1972 Art had been in Philadelphia a number of years. His earlier peregrinations had settled into routine work with the local southeastern Pennsylvania power company. He made a good wage, lived alone, and spoiled his dog.

This dog was a peculiar animal. It was of no particular breed, was short haired, mostly white with a few brown markings, and of a medium size. Its most notable characteristic was that it had a distinctive grin.

"No, dogs don't smile," a customer had once remarked during the latter stages of the above mentioned flood, while sitting in a barber chair. There was little one could do on a Saturday morning under such circumstances, other than get a haircut. The barber was tucking a white apron into the man's shirt collar. The man himself was a heavy, red-faced, leather skinned fellow who looked somehow choleric.

"I'm telling you, Bert, I've seen it. Ain't that so, Rob?"

Art Robinson was sometimes referred to in this way by a shortened version of his last name. He looked up from a magazine where he was seated reading, awaiting his turn from one of a row of chairs lined up against the opposite wall. The wall, a pale cream, showed grease stains from the many heads that had rested themselves against it over the years. The shop was small, having only one full-time barber and two barber chairs.

"Yeah, Petroleum's got a smile all right. Only it's more of a grin," he said.

"Look here," the man in the barber chair said. "I've seen lots of dogs. Got one myself. That beast don't ever smile. Nor any other that I've ever seen."

"Maybe he ain't happy," the barber said. He was smiling in fun, running his electric clippers through the man's hair. He didn't need to look at what he was doing, he'd done it so many times before.

"Hey, watch where you're cutting!"

"I'm sorry."

"I don't want to lose an ear. Not even a big red one." The man in the barber chair smiled at his own generous self-indulgence. It was true he had big red ears, and a matching nose to boot, with a kind of purple lining of the veins at the opening of his nostrils. It was said in the neighborhood that the man had a close relationship with alcohol, but he'd never done anyone any harm. He was a hard working plumber, or something like that.

Art was buried in his magazine. The former sea warrior and nation traveler had something of the air now of a timid man. He wore spectacles, usually half-way down his nose, and was balding at the temples and on the crown of his head.

The barber leaned over and whispered into Bert's ear. "The reason his dog grins is because he spoils it. Why, he treats that dog as if it were a person."

"Spoiled or not," Bert said aloud, "no dog can smile. Why, he might as well stand up on his hind legs and get a can of beer out of the fridge. I'm sooner like to see Crusher—that's my shepherd—do *that* than see him grin."

"Spoiled! Who said anything about spoiled?" Art looked up from his magazine.

"Now, don't take offense, Rob. You know you spoil that animal." The barber had put down his comb and clippers and was loosening the white apron from around Bert's big purple neck. He shook the hair off the apron with a loud snap. Then he got a broom and moved the hair into a pile over to one side to be dealt with later. Bert descended to the floor heavily, brushing the hair off his large belly and legs. He went over to the register with the barber, his head trimmed whistle clean on the top and sides in a butch, and paid his tab, then got a hat and coat off the rack by the door.

Art was already in the barber chair, his legs dangling, not quite reaching the foot rests. The barber came back and adjusted them. From inside the glass door of the barber shop, Bert watched him tuck the apron into Art's shirt collar.

"Hell of a flood out there," he said, glancing out the door toward the river, which of course he couldn't see behind several blocks of brown brick row houses.

"It's going down now," Art remarked. "I checked it this morning."

"Yeah. It's going down now," Bert repeated. "And we got dogs that smile now in this world."

"God's truth," the barber said. "I've seen it."

"Grin," Art corrected him. "The dog grins. I never maintained that he smiled."

"No," Bert mumbled, putting on his hat and adjusting his coat over his shoulders, shaking his head. He went out the door muttering something about the fine distinction between a grin and a smile in a dog.

The Schuylkill River did resume its normal placid course through the remainder of the year, and Art was once again able to walk his dog in the park. But he never seemed to come across Bert walking Crusher at the same time, so there never was, as far as anyone ever knew, a final settling of the dispute. You have to see a dog to know how it smiles.

Untitled: Acrylic on Pasteboard

The bullet had, as it were, turned a corner. It had no doubt come from a part of New York City where it was to be expected and had arrived where it was both undeserved and detested. Señor Ortega, who lived on the third floor of a large apartment building that was built thick and square like a fortress and had more TV antennas on its roof than a cactus has thorns, had not been home when the slug passed through his bedroom window. It shattered the glass.

"What is this!" he exclaimed upon entering the room with his wife, who had been over to Manhattan with him that Saturday afternoon. "This is a street where cars park side by side three in a row, but they do not fire bullets through people's windows, as some of those murderous fellows do down there in Flatbush."

The slug, a thirty-eight caliber, was buried in a stud of the wall opposite the window. There it was to remain a good many years, resting, as it were, covered over with plaster. The building owners were obliged to repair the window and cover the hole. It was in the price of the rent.

The Ortegas never discovered the source of that bullet. A passing car perhaps. The incident did not seem to auger any significant change in the neighborhood, which was a relatively good one for New York. Life returned to the usual snarl of traffic out front next to the laundromat and the rattle, shout, banter, ring and bang of cash transactions at the fruit and vegetable stand on the corner of Thirty-third Street and Ditmars Avenue.

Arturo and Emelia Ortega y Suarez lived in quiet peacefulness another five years and more in their apartment before the conversation recorded below took place. Arturo was a retired civil engineer of modest fixed income, and their four children were happily married or partnered (one was gay) and living in various parts of the Western Hemisphere. Arturo had come from the Dominican Republic as a young man, educated himself in a fine Eastern school with his parents' money, then hired himself out to work on various dam and levee projects in the green finger lake district of upstate New York. He had met his wife in Rochester. She was an Hispanic American, originally from the arid Southwest. Her ancestors had arrived in the New World before the Pilgrims.

"Now, here is what I am thinking, Arturo," she said to him one day. "Do you hear me? I would appreciate it if you would come out from behind that newspaper. You've hardly touched your toast, and your coffee is cold."

"I'm listening, Cecilia. Uh …"

"Cecilia! Are you thinking about an old girlfriend now? I will tell you that my name isn't Cecilia. Who is this Cecilia?"

"No one." Arturo set his newspaper down in his lap, a sheepish expression proceeding from beneath his bushy gray eyebrows. "I was reading an article and took the name from it accidentally."

Emelia looked sharply at her husband. Nearly forty years of marriage had not softened the pique of her jealousy. "Was she pretty?"

"Who?" Arturo had drawn his newspaper back up in front of his face like a shower curtain. Couldn't she see he was bathing in world events?

"This Cecilia of yours."

"What Cecilia? I don't know any Cecilias."

"Will you please put that newspaper down while I'm talking to you. It's wrong to keep it up like a screen."

"I'm bathing in the news."

Sensing defeat, or at least a stalemate, Emelia changed her tack. "Look, Arturo dearest …"

"Oh, so it's Arturo dearest."

"Yes."

"I'm listening—if you have anything to say that I could want to hear. No more of this Cecilia. I told you I accidentally …"

"I said I was thinking of something. A trip out west."

The newspaper came crashing down over the air hardened toast and cold coffee.

"Watch you don't spill what's in that cup!"

"It would not roll out of this cup if I put the cup to its side at a turn of ninety degrees," Arturo said dryly.

"If you don't like the way I make it, do it yourself."

"I cannot get in this little kitchen with you the way you are. You must diet, Emelia."

"Diet yourself."

"I can't. I'm too thin. What do you mean out west? That is thousands of miles."

"We can do it a few miles at a time. If you keep going in the same direction, it gets you there all the same."

"Maybe. Or maybe we'll end up in Canada or Mexico."

"I can read maps, even if you can't."

"I can read maps."

"Then it's agreed."

"No. I said nothing. What is out west?"

"My family."

"They're probably all dead."

"We just got a letter from my brother last week."

"At our age, Emelia," Arturo said, rolling up his newspaper, "a lot can happen in a week."

"All the more reason to go see him."

Wham! The newspaper hit the middle of the table. "Got him!" Arturo said with immense satisfaction.

"Oh! You frightened me. And look at your coffee," Emelia added in anger.

"It is the price of peace."

"You men are always at war."

"We will go."

"Yes? Oh, Arturo, you sweet man." Emelia got up and placed a large warm kiss on the side of her husband's forehead, throwing her arms around his broad shoulders. Even beyond middle age Arturo's shoulders were broad, for he was as solid and muscular as any bricklayer he might have worked with.

Within a few weeks Arturo and Emelia Ortega piled three suitcases into the trunk of their car and drove away in the direction of the fleeing sun. That is how they escaped the mean streets of New York City for awhile.

Phu Bai

At Phu Bai the food was terrible. I had been there before and knew about the powdered scrambled eggs that you covered with syrup. The heavy slices of Spam between thick dry crusts of bread were also memorable. All the comforts of home.

This time it was the rainy season and the sucking mud was the first thing I noticed. I had jumped off the back of a truck and sunk all the way to my knees in the muck. It was in this position that I heard over somebody's transistor radio that the war had gotten too tough for President Johnson and he'd decided to quit.

I had come to deliver two prisoners, both young and female. I told them to get down out of the back of the truck. The first one, the round faced and sassy one, flipped me the bird and told me to go screw myself if I could, but she doubted I was man enough. She got down muttering something like "American GI shit!" She was about sixteen. The second one was a little older and badly wounded. She had a hole in her back from shrapnel that was at least a few days old. Our corpsman hadn't treated it because she wouldn't let him near it.

I don't know how she got the wound. When we picked up these "Viet Cong suspects" in the village she was already in that condition. It was amazing she could even get around. I helped her off the truck. The other one said, "You touch Vietnamese woman. You dirt. Filthy imperialists!" She spit on the ground. This is the way she'd been all the way into Phu Bai.

I just wanted to get rid of these two, especially her.

"Where's G-2?" I asked. "Colonel Haskins."

Somebody pointed along the row of tin roofed hooches to a conglomerate of wooden buildings. "Over there. I just came from there. He's down in the Command Operations Center bunker with the General."

I knew that the Command Operations Center was a big underground bunker dug next to the wooden buildings. As I walked along behind my prisoners, I could observe some of the changes that had taken place since I'd been there a few months before. A lot of the hooches were gone, blown to splinters by rockets. Most of the mess hall was gone too. Only the galley was left. It was noon and I could see a sergeant standing next to the useless door. The seating area to the left of it was gone. Every now and then he'd hold up his hand showing five fingers. A good distance away there was a line of Marines holding mess kits. At the sergeant's signal five of them would approach and pass single file in front of the serving bins. Slop, slop. The different items offered, like green beans, canned peaches and cold powdered mashed potatoes, were piled one on top of the other in their mess kits. They moved away then and five more were called up. It was a slow process, especially in the rain. You could see scattered groups of two or three Marines eating together, some sitting on the ground out in the open weather, others crowded under the eaves of hooches with water running off the tin roofs onto their knees.

Sergeant Gunn in one of the wooden buildings took charge of the prisoners. I went down to report their arrival to the Colonel.

He and the General were in front of the big map in the main room of the command bunker. In a row on the opposite side of the room sat a bunch of office pogues manning field phones. Their one long desk faced the map.

"Sir, Corporal Tennial reporting. The prisoners are delivered. Sergeant Gunn is taking them down to the medical hooch. One of them is wounded. Our corpsman thought the other one might have gonorrhea."

"VC nurse?"

"Yes, sir."

Another colonel, a full colonel, walked in the door just then.

"General Johnson."

"Dave, how are you doing?"

"Lousy, Jim. What's this shit about pulling off the air cover for my men?"

"John thinks we're taking too many hits. He says the aircraft are too expensive for this kind of close in stuff. They're getting all shot up."

"General Jones?"

"Yes. Sorry, Dave. I tried to explain your position. He wouldn't see it my way."

"Damn it, Jim. I'm losing men right and left. First you pull off the tanks because the streets are too narrow and we might damage some sacred architecture, now this!"

"I'm sorry, Dave. You're going to have to go in there and slug it out alone."

On my way back down the dirt road beside the hooches, we suddenly got hit by a rocket and mortar barrage. The rockets came roaring in, one by one, like Phantom jets. After each one hit, there was a loud crack and a boom, everything shaking, shrapnel, wood and tin flying everywhere. Meanwhile mortars were being quietly walked from one end of the compound to the other. They don't seem as scary, so they do most of the killing. Down in a culvert, I was lying on my face in cold muddy water. Two or three rats were running back and forth, one over the back of my legs. They were upset because of the ground shaking and all the noise.

Spring Freshet

It had been a mild, warm day. The rose bush in the front yard was putting out healthy, green shoots, with the dark soil damp and freshly worked over its roots. There had been a pleasant afternoon rain. The Spokane River was brimming, rushing between huge granite boulders north of the city, and sparkling clear.

The screen door slammed as Charles Anders entered his house. Outside, dusk was falling and the street light on the corner boulevard had just come on.

"Matthew," Mr. Anders called from the foot of the stairs. "Matthew!"

"Yeah Dad." Fifteen year old Matthew appeared at the head of the stairs. He was a towering, gangling boy, toweling his smooth face.

"Come down here. I want to talk to you."

"I can hear you, Dad."

"Face to face. Get down here, son."

Matthew threw the towel over the banister and slid it along with his left hand as he descended the stairs. He seemed almost to be whistling as he came, and irritation visibly increased in his father.

"Your friend Billy is out front waiting for you," Mr. Anders said shortly, as his son reached the bottom landing.

Matthew turned to go have a look through the front door.

"Hold it, son." Mr. Anders grabbed his son's shoulder. Outside, Bill honked his horn on the city neighborhood street. He gave it two short bursts. The street was otherwise quiet.

Matthew dropped his head. He knew what was coming.

"You know," Mr. Anders said, slowly framing each word, "this is the fellow who hurt your sister."

"I know, Dad. Sue shouldn't have gone out with him. She wasn't ready for someone like Bill."

"You introduced them."

"I didn't know they'd take an interest in each other."

Mr. Anders studied his son's face. Matthew was still avoiding his father's eyes, and his shoulders were rounded against intrusion. He was playing with the end of his belt.

"What is your interest in this fellow?" Mr. Anders asked.

"He's my friend."

"He's a bad influence."

"Oh, Dad," Matthew started to protest, then fell silent. He cast his eyes on the floor, on the little gray rug at the foot of the stairs. Finally he asked, "Can I go?"

Without responding, Mr. Anders turned and walked into the living room. He flicked on a table lamp. It gave a warm glow inside the room. He picked a newspaper up off the armchair next to the end table the lamp was on, then sat down in the chair with it. It was dark outside now. Bill honked again three times. Matthew went over to the front door, pushed the screen door open, stuck his head between it and the dark blue doorjamb, and shouted, "I'll be right out." Then he went back, picked up his towel, which was damp and lying on the floor at the foot of the banister, and went upstairs with it.

When Matthew Anders left the house a few minutes later that evening, his father was still in the living room, reading the paper. Matthew shut the front door quietly as he went out, leaving his father in the warm lamp glow.

Shortly after midnight, Matthew returned. He, his older friend Bill, and two other boys had spent the evening cruising the downtown streets of the city. Bill had earlier that afternoon crossed the State line from Spokane, Washington into northern Idaho, near Coeur d'Alene, where he was able to legally purchase a case of beer. The four boys had drunk the beer in the car while driving slowly around the customary downtown loop followed by all the Saturday night cruising teenagers. A number of girls were out on the sidewalks in front of the shops, all in short skirts, though they wore sweaters and jackets against the cool of the spring evening.

In front of his house, Matthew got out of the car and very carefully, quietly shut its passenger side door. Bill drove away, gunning the engine, which irritated Matthew. "Damn it, I told him not to do that," Matthew muttered under his breath. He was surprised to see none of the downstairs lights were on in the house, though the curtained window to his parents' bedroom upstairs was lit up. Sue seemed to have already gone to bed.

Matthew opened the front door carefully. He felt a little drunk and was making an extreme effort to be in control of his every move. He shut the front door and screen, crept quietly up the stairs and went into his room, closing the bedroom door gently behind him. "Whew!"

"Good night, Matthew," his father's voice boomed.

"Good night, honey," his mother said. "You were out awfully late."

"Good night, Mom, Dad."

Matthew got undressed and lay on top of the blankets on his bed in his underwear. He had opened his bedroom window. He was a slender youth, and the cool night breeze coming in the window felt good on his bare, almost hairless chest and legs. He had, at this moment, an erection. He reached down and touched himself there, putting his hand inside his shorts. His penis felt hot, and when he pressed it, a good feeling went through his belly and thighs.

All night Matthew and his friends had cruised the same streets, hoping to find girls. Of course, they didn't. Who would get into a car with four drinking youths? But the effect of the alcohol in his brain, combined with the mere prospect of finding someone and the imagined results that might follow, excited him. His heart was still racing.

Matthew thought of his sister. What had happened that night she had gone out with Bill? She was so upset, but Bill swore nothing important had occurred. Well, he was sure nothing had. He believed his friend.

Matthew thought of Deborah. She was Sue's best friend. She also happened to be their cousin. She was so good looking! What he wouldn't give to see her in a bath towel, or without one. She always seemed a little shy around him. Was that a sign of interest? Wouldn't it be nice! Sue had simply said, "Don't mind him. He's just my brother," as if Deborah couldn't make up her own mind about her cousin.

Matthew fell asleep, the light of a full moon on his bare, white, bony chest and legs. Later he woke up freezing, put on his pajamas, top and bottom, closed the window, and got under his sheet and covers. It felt good just to be warm and comfortable. Like being with a girl maybe. With Deborah. He went back to sleep.

Max

A cloudless blue sky just after a rain, the sun having broken through and swept the clouds to the rim of the world. Yet, dripping from rooftops, the water seems still to be pouring from that distant horizon. But all in the center is bright, yellow with sun, crisp with the smell of green things, pungent with the nitrogen odor of wet sidewalks, and red with birdsong. It is a Virginia morning.

The child is alone. He is inside a fenced area. There are discarded tin cans lying about the grassy enclosure; an old car seat with torn upholstery of some now unidentifiable, soiled brown or tan color; and treadless, synthetic rubber tires. Large black tires, full of old and new rain water, mosquitos. The lids of the tin cans, whose labels are mostly worn off, are rusty and, along their sharp edges, ruffled from the bending action of a can opener.

The child is three. A large white nanny goat occupies the fenced area with him. For the goat supplies the only milk he can digest. The goat is cropping grass. The child is watching the goat, uncertain of what it will do. He has been told that goats will eat tin cans.

Inside the old farmhouse, two women sit in the sun room. This solarium is a converted porch. The two story house is surrounded by porches, but this one is twice enclosed, once with screen, now removed, then with glass. It is warm in the sun room, for the sun, a large summer sun, is sitting at ten o'clock in the open sky, shining directly into those large, east facing windows.

"Mother, I'm sorry. But if you and Dad could watch little Maxwell … I have no one else to turn to. It will only be for a year or so."

"Max will be fine, dear. I'm just glad you've found work. But Africa? With lions and cobras?"

"I will be in *North* Africa, Mother, teaching at an Air Force base dependents school in French Morocco. The only snakes or beasts of prey I'll have to worry about there are the two legged kind."

Mrs. Franklin Yeats looks at her daughter over her small, gold rimmed, reading glasses. She has an aged, puffy, white face. Resting her crewelwork in the broad apron on her lap, she muses: Poor Thelma has had so many troubles in her young life. Two husbands come and gone. Thank the Lord, the first one gave her no children. "You must be careful, dear," she remarks simply.

"Yes, of course, Mother."

Outside, little Max has become quite accustomed to the goat. A little bored perhaps. The shaggy animal has not attempted to eat a single tin can. On the other hand, the goat has not charged and tried to butt him either. This is another thing he has heard about goats.

Max has a new preoccupation. He is hanging on to the chain link fence with both hands, looking up toward the tops of the nearby pine trees and the blue sky, and bawling loudly. Max's diaper is not only full. It is overflowing, and the hot, sticky, strong smelling substance running down the inside of his leg is uncomfortable in the extreme.

Moments later, it is quite pleasant to be lying on a sun warmed table in the sun room, having one's diaper changed by two babbling women who seem to hold a special affection for him. He is being gently scolded by his grandmother for not waiting to use the potty. His mother points out in his defense that they probably did not hear his cries from outdoors.

"Yes, I know, dear. I was really chiding the two of us. We should have been more attentive. Poor thing."

Max smiles. The clean, dry diaper feels good. He doesn't speak. He rarely speaks. His father being French Canadian, he was raised in Quebec City by a spinster aunt who lived with her brother and sister-in-law for most of his life. So he has learned French instead of English. This in spite of the fact that his mother has only a rudimentary grasp of the language. Both his parents worked, his mother teaching in an English school. This was, of course, before the separation and divorce. After the divorce, his mother, who had relocated to Toronto, returned with him to Virginia.

Outside again a little later, Max is left free to run about the yard. He is, much to his relief, not confined again with the nasty goat. The stubborn animal has, so far as he can see, steadfastly refused to eat anything remarkable. A plastic pool, already inflated, has been filled with nearly a foot of water. But he is not interested. They may as well have left his second diaper on, instead of outfitting him with these unpleasant, tight-fitting trunks.

Near the white plastic pool, with its gay pattern of Donald Duck and nephews, is a large purple clover blossom. Upon the blossom, weighing it down, is a big, clumsy, black and yellow bumblebee. It crawls about, head up, head to one side, then head down; it buzzes up into the air, then lands again on the same flower.

"Bumblebee," Max remarks with philosophical interest. He moves closer, now on his hands and knees, and looks directly into the flower. Up above him, from an open window of the sun room, he can hear his mother and grandmother talking. Grandmother is still something of a stranger to him, for he has only recently met her and does not remember ever having seen her before. Still, it is pleasant to have her about, since she appears to be a friend of his mother.

"Bee. Sting!" Max suddenly observes, crawling back several feet and standing up. "Bee stings." The weighty consideration sinks into his mind.

At this moment, a line of six half grown chicks appears. They come around from the north side of the house. They are a strange lot, for they had been Easter chicks—white leghorns died pink, purple and other bright colors in the egg. Some of the original pigmentation still remains in their feathers. Their legs and feet, however, are of a natural flesh tone. Accompanied by nervous cheeping and pecking in the grass, their activity absorbs Max's attention. In these interesting animals is somehow concentrated all the light and freedom of the morning. Every fresh scent that blows toward him from flower, yard and field only heightens his sense of the living wonder before him.

One of the chicks finds an unlucky grasshopper. Clamping the insect in its beak, it begins to hammer it to pieces on the ground. This attracts several of its fellows, and a quarrel ensues. Max sits down rapt and watches, having forgotten the bumblebee. The wind is gently moving the green sweet pea pods swelling on a trellis beneath the peeling white paint of a window sill on the east wall of the sun room.

"Are you sure this will be alright?" he hears his mother ask. "This is so hard, Mother. What will Max think when I leave?"

"He'll be fine," Mrs. Yeats answers soothingly. "Don't you worry, honey."

"I won't, Mother. I know I won't," Max's mother says, almost in tears.

But Max understands only a few words of the English language. And the gangly chicks, with their half-feathered wings, big beaks and long legs, have for the moment got all his attention.

Young Womanhood

She awoke at seven in the morning. The curtains were drawn closed, and the semidarkness of her apartment descended upon her like a cloud. Her heart felt like a stone in her chest. She lay perfectly still, unable to move.

"This is crazy!" she said aloud after several minutes. She slipped a leg out from under the bed sheet and touched the floor with her left foot. It was like reinventing the earth. Then she got up. Her nightgown fell over her private parts but left her legs bare. They were plump legs with young, very smooth skin. In fact, she rarely had to shave them. And they were light brown, giving her the pleasant appearance of always having a tan. But she wished they were thinner.

"I had to do it," she said to herself, again out loud, slipping her feet into a pair of fluffy pink slippers that were tucked under the bed. The slippers were like old friends. "I don't love him." She had, on the night before, broken a four year engagement which had begun in her second year at City University's Queens College. She had actually known the young man since childhood.

The apartment which Anita Sanchez rented south of Astoria, not far west of Flushing where she grew up, was unbelievably small. Her third floor windows (bathroom and combined living room/bedroom, for there were only those two rooms and a kitchenette) were not more than thirty yards from the Queensborough subway platform. Every few minutes a train came through and shook the walls. But she was used to it.

Anita stretched out in the warm bath water she had just run for herself. There was a shower head six feet above her, but it didn't seem to work. It never had since she'd moved into the apartment. And the unwashable, dirty cream-yellow paint on the ceiling was peeling away. That's probably from the moisture, she thought. The bathroom window was stuck shut. The ceiling looked dirty enough anyway, peeled or unpeeled.

The warm water soaked heat into her childishly unblemished body and relaxed her. It especially soothed her thighs and pelvis, which ached in a way she had learned to recognize in her early teens. For she knew her period was about to begin, and now she made a mental note to carry the extra tampons she would need in her purse. Men are lucky, she thought.

Then she thought of Alex again. "I had to do it," she complained aloud. "I had to do it for him because I don't love him." She leaned her head back in the water soaking the short dark hair. The warm water felt good as it worked into her scalp among the roots. Actually, the water could be more accurately described as hot. It was beginning to put her to sleep.

Anita's mind slipped into reverie. In her imagination she saw a very handsome young man she'd recently met. He was softly kissing her, tantalizing, touching her lips and beyond with his tongue. His hands, so warm, so eager, strong and gentle … She opened her eyes and found her own hands on her breasts caressing the nipples, which stood out firm and dark.

"All right!" She got up, hair, arms and legs streaming water, stepped out of the tub, soaking the floor, and began toweling herself. She rubbed her sides and buttocks so hard with the rough cloth that they began to hurt. "I can't think about that," she said determinedly. "I mustn't. It's wrong."

At the breakfast table, a tiny table indeed, where she hungrily consumed two pieces of unbuttered toast and one poached egg, which she limited herself to to keep her weight down, she reassured herself that she had only acted in Alex's best interest. I couldn't let something go on that I knew would never end in marriage, she told herself mentally. It wouldn't be fair to either of us.

But how did you suddenly know this? a voice from another corner of her mind asked.

Because I don't love him.

You thought you loved him before.

"All right, all right, I love someone else," Anita shouted, getting up and throwing a half eaten piece of toast down on her plate.

Maybe it's just lust, the other voice said.

"Okay, so maybe it's only lust. What's wrong with wanting a man?" Doesn't all love begin with desire? she asked herself mentally. She waited for an answer, but her mind offered no response. It was like a silent judgment.

Anita went into the bedroom/living room and hurriedly dressed. She needed to get out of that apartment, go somewhere. She would catch the train into Manhattan, look in the shops. That's what she would do. It was Saturday. She had all day to do as she pleased.

Just before Anita left the apartment, she pulled the curtains back, allowing the sun to burst into the room. It seemed to separate the walls, pull them apart, fill the empty space with air. I should have done this in the first place, she thought. She felt much better as she went out the front door. But it was only because her guilt had been temporarily buried. Alex was, after all, her family's choice and their proud, safe expectation for a future husband.

Soft Light

He had not been a success with his life, and that was bad enough. But his wife had grown hard and unsexual. At least, that's the way he had come to think of her. And now the young man next door had decided to blast him out of the neighborhood with rock music. He simply could not find any peace of mind in this world.

Jeff Ryan went drearily off to work five days a week at the offices of the Franklin Corporation in downtown Seattle. He hated the diesel and damp moss odor of this condensed, waterlogged city, though he should have gotten used to it by now. He'd lived in it for better than twenty years. The place never grew on him. Nothing ever did, he supposed.

One day, while on the nauseating, diesel smelling bus coming home from work between five and six in the evening, he decided to do something about the Tolliver kid. Maybe he could reason with him, or with his parents at least. He'd give it a try.

The doorbell rang several times before anyone came to answer it. It was the boy's fifteen year old sister. She had red hair and blue eyes. She was slender, developed for her age, rather pretty in her tight blue jeans and short top. The girl flashed a smile at him. She had small, white teeth.

"Uh. Hi. I'm your neighbor Jeff Ryan."

She nodded prettily. There was a slight hint of moisture on her lips and teeth. She had smooth, clear skin and very lovely eyes.

"I was wondering if I could speak to your brother or your parents for a moment."

"They're not home. Nobody's home but me." She flashed him another big smile.

His heart skipped a beat. Why am I doing this? he thought. He felt his pulse was suddenly rising. "Thank you. I'll come back," he answered awkwardly, and walked away.

In Ballard, an old neighborhood in the heart of Seattle, the houses are very close together, but he had never seen the young girl before. Not up close anyway. He had just heard her brother's infernal music, now almost always played at top volume with the bedroom window open. Even on those rare occasions when both his and the Tollivers' windows were closed, it didn't matter. The damned bass beat of it crept underground, like a monstrous heart throbbing, and burst into whatever room he was in, rumbling through the very walls. At such times he felt as if the whole world were filled with maddening rhythmic thunder and there could be no escape from it. The very clouds must've shook and the sun been aglitter with a fibrillating motion. To make matters worse, Betty complained incessantly and wanted to know why he didn't do something about it. She of no sex and the refrigerator door always open, eating.

At the job Jeff, an accountant who'd failed to rise out of lower middle management in twenty years, tried to keep his mind on his work. Work, for the most part, consisted in making sure the mail and supply room was running smoothly. It ran like a conveyor belt. As long as the rollers were oiled, what could go wrong? The mail moved. Supplies were ordered and used. It was as simple as that.

The trouble with such a job was that it left plenty of time for your mind to wander, and he didn't think he should be fantasizing about a fifteen year old girl. "She's just a kid. Jail bait," he said to himself, laughing. But it was not a laughing matter. He couldn't get her off his mind. That lithe little body, the sweet face, that open, caressing smile. I'm beginning to think I'm in love with her, he thought, then laughed at himself again. Why did the thought of her make his heart feel so light? He hadn't felt like this in years.

Three days after the first attempt, Jeff went back to the Tolliver house at the same time of day and rang the bell. The mother answered the door. She was not bad looking herself, somewhat resembling her daughter, but without the freshness.

"Mrs. Tolliver?"

"Yes." She smiled warmly, but again, not in the way her daughter had.

"I'm your neighbor Jeff Ryan. I believe we've met a few times out by the mail boxes."

"Yes we have. Won't you come in, Mr. Ryan."

He stepped inside the door. The downstairs of the compact two-story frame house was warm and tastefully furnished. A deep indigo blue rug set off the living room to the right, and surrounding it were chairs made of Philippine mahogany, dark and rich with deep cushions. The walls were pale yellow. Beyond the living room was the dining room and then adjacent to it the kitchen. Only a corner of the former could be seen from just inside the house entrance. But it revealed a cabinet of fine china.

"I don't wish to bother you …"

Mrs. Tolliver's expression lost its warmth, though there was nothing hostile in it. Just concern. She seemed to read something in his face. Jeff wondered if she knew why he'd come.

"What I mean is that your son …"

"That awful music!" he heard a girl's voice reply. He recognized it. It was sweet as birdsong to him. "I told you it was too loud, Mom."

Jeff felt himself flush, and the very lovely young daughter suddenly appeared by her mother's side. She met him with the same sweet, interested smile. She was dressed in the same way she had been before.

Mrs. Tolliver went immediately, impatiently upstairs to find her son, who had just turned his stereo on for the evening. Full volume, of course. The girl and Mr. Ryan were left alone.

What does she see in me? he thought. What a foolish question to ask myself! What presumption! His heart was throbbing in his veins, and he knew his face must be as red as the girl's lovely hair, which hung soft and natural over one shoulder, shining like silk in the lamplight from the living room, for the curtains were shut. She looked at him with guileless blue eyes, parting her full shapely lips in a warm smile. How mature for her age she seemed.

The matter of the music was quickly resolved. The volume was turned down.

Back downstairs Mrs. Tolliver apologized and said she would see to it the volume was kept low from now on.

Jeff thanked her rather dryly or absentmindedly and left. He had not exchanged one word with the girl, yet he felt she was affectionately his somehow. What foolish rot, he told himself. I must clear my mind.

He had a drink when he got into his own home. The place felt unusually dark, so he turned on all the front room lights. The drink soothed him, but it did not do away with the images he saw. He sat down in an overstuffed armchair and had very tender thoughts. He was sure he would like to help this girl in some way. He hadn't the vaguest notion how or what for. He just wanted to do something nice for her. He wondered if he wasn't deeply in love. As he relaxed in this strange reverie, under the glow of the drink, he was beginning to feel as if he were framed in soft light.

Song of Youth

Tomás Archuleta operated a wine and beer distributorship in Albuquerque, New Mexico. From this he supplied Santa Fe and many lesser towns in the central part of the State. Being a shrewd businessman in a limited sort of way, he knew how to obtain small lots of Spanish, Portuguese and Latin American—notably Chilean—wines at reasonable prices. Thus, with relatively light inventory costs and a growing list of local restaurants willing to trust him alone, he could compete with the larger concerns. He called his business The Spanish Wine List, and advertised it as such in the yellow pages, though, of course, he dealt in more than Spanish wines. He also imported Mexican beer. And his Portuguese port was of the finest quality. He had been to Portugal itself, circumventing the West Coast import houses, to seal this deal.

Tomás, a man in his late twenties, had never married. He had been too busy building up his enterprise. He was five seven, slender, dark with a heavy mustache that covered his upper lip and extended out beyond the corners of his mouth. He dressed a bit too well, and this gave him the appearance of a dandy. His eyes were set like burning coals in his face and were known to make some women tremble.

Now there was a restaurant on Canyon Road in Santa Fe called La Parroquial. Though unassuming in its external appearance, it had a certain indefinable ambiance within. It felt as though one were in a New Mexican adobe church, the type that are seen in so many rural communities of Spanish origin. Perhaps it was the light:

airy but muted and cool. Perhaps it was the simple, rough cut, square wooden tables that made one think somehow of pews made by seventeenth or eighteenth century settlers out of huge cottonwood planks. Or maybe it was the foot high, carved, wooden images set in niches in the thick, whitewashed adobe walls. They were not religious images but seemed suggestive of such. What it was, in fact, that gave the restaurant this ambiance, no one really knew.

Tomás generally made his rounds to this place once a month, the second Tuesday. It belonged to one Hortensio Romero, who was never there, it seemed. Tomás would come in at nine or ten in the morning and find Mrs. Romero in the kitchen overseeing the preparation of lunch, which, when it was served, was the time at which the restaurant opened. Lunch consisted almost exclusively of tapas, or snacks, which could be ordered directly from the kitchen or chosen from a long table where they were set out on blue and white enamel saucers.

It was Alicia with whom Tomás had most of his dealings. This young woman of nineteen had a very level head and knew her business with wines. She was the only daughter of the Romeros. Her two brothers were attending the State university.

Conversing at a wooden table in a corner of the front dining room, Romero and this young woman sat one morning going over the wine list. The mother could see them through a window slot in the kitchen, though they were partially hidden in shadow. She did not completely trust this Tomás. He was too slick in his manner of dress, and why was he still unmarried, this supposedly great wine merchant? Bah! It wasn't the wine sales that concerned her. She knew her daughter couldn't be cheated in business. She kept one eye on the window.

Alicia leaned back in her light, canelike, wooden chair and laughed. The laughter of this young woman was like the flight of a robin through the room.

Tomás was laughing too, holding the wine list up to the muted light streaming in from the front door and pointing to something on it.

"What are those two up to?" Mrs. Romero thought. She was helping the morning prep cook prepare enchiladas and forgot to put the chicken in one. The laughter rang out again and she left the cheese out of another one. These enchiladas were among the New World offerings that were served among the tapas. You could apply the chili sauce from the table.

Now the two young people had their heads together. They seemed to be sharing some sort of secret. It did not look like normal business. But what was a mother to do, but worry? Wasn't Alicia old enough to know her own mind? And her own heart?

Finally Tomás got up to leave. He called goodbye cheerily across the room to Mrs. Romero, whose piercing eyes and grave expression could be seen through the narrow window slot, and went out the front door. Alicia passed through the kitchen on her way to the "wine cellar." This was a small room at the rear of the building. It was kept at a temperature varying between fifty and seventy degrees Fahrenheit.

"Alicia!"

"Yes, Mother."

"What do you and that gentleman find so funny?"

Alicia walked over toward her mother, wine list in hand. Tony, the cook, winked at her. She pretended not to notice.

Her mother's eyes made a rapid survey of her blouse and blue jeans. Then she turned back toward the fresh cloves of garlic she was presently mincing. "Your way of dress is much too provocative," she muttered, head bent over her work, as though she were talking to herself.

"I'm sorry, Mother," Alicia said. She had been taken completely by surprise. Why did her mother seem so upset?

"Go on," Mrs. Romero said gruffly. "We can talk later. I am busy here."

Alicia glanced up and saw Tony leering at her. She felt a warm flush in her face and anger across her shoulders.

Inside the wine cellar Alicia stood still with the light on and the door closed. The light was a single naked bulb in the center of the ceiling with a long string hanging down for turning it on and off. To her left was the cooling unit, blowing cold air into her thin cotton blouse, chilling her. It felt good just now. In front of her were the rows of wine bottles, mostly red, lying on their sides, canted slightly downward towards the corks to keep them from drying out. To her right were the stacks of Mexican and American beer.

Alicia felt a hot flush of tears start from her eyes. Her shoulders shook for several minutes. Then she straightened up and put the wine list and copy of her new purchase order away in a small box hung on the wall to the left of the wine bottles. She looked down at her blouse, adjusting it, smoothing the material about her neck and shoulders. The blouse was light, frilly, low cut. She felt a certain warmth and tenderness in looking at her own breasts and the pleasant full curve of her hips in tight jeans. I'm not a bad sort of woman, she thought. In looks or intention. But I won't always be young and pretty either. I have a right to be who I am.

Outside, on the freeway headed back toward Albuquerque, beneath the bright glare of the morning sun, which was glancing off bare hills and pouring out of a wide, blue sky, Tomás Archuleta squinted and whistled a tune as he drove, listening to Spanish language radio. His thoughts were on the lovely Alicia. He had, in fact, considered her for some time, and today he was certain he would be happy. His heart sang like a meadow lark that one hears but does not see.

Casualties of War

The stench was something awful. I tell you, never dig a man up after he's been dead for awhile! I don't know how the villagers finally found him or where they got the stuff to put in your nose to keep out the odor. It was a matter of one thing stinking enough to overpower the other.

He was a South Vietnamese Regional Forces soldier and had been out with some others on a joint patrol with American Marines. They had been ambushed and somehow in the firefight he'd been separated. It was thick, low growing jungle brush country. Hard to see, and they were in some kind of a swamp near a banana plantation. After the Viet Cong pulled back they never found him. His name was Mien Ngoc Chau.

His wife discovered through the village grapevine that he hadn't been taken prisoner but was dead. One of the strangest things in Vietnam was the way the villagers knew what was going on on both sides of the war. But they didn't know what had been done with his body. We searched for weeks, thinking he was still alive at first and checking the hospital in Da Nang. We thought he might have been one of the wounded medevacked by helicopter. Then his wife told us what she'd learned, and there wasn't anything we could do until the villagers themselves located the burial site.

It turned out that, just as we'd thought, he had been only wounded at first and had been medevacked by one of our choppers to the Vietnamese Hospital in Da Nang. Never mind that the hospital officials didn't know he'd ever been there when we checked. Their record keeping was on the level of their sanitation.

We supplied the truck. The driver, myself and another Marine went with a handful of villagers, including the wife and the man's father, to retrieve the body and bring it back to the village for proper burial. We went all the way to Da Nang and out into the sand dunes. He was buried in the sand only a few feet down in what looked like an oversized orange crate. When we uncovered him, he was bloated and resembled a very fat little man with his legs folded up under him to get him into the crate, which was too small. He really stunk! His skin was stretched tight with the swelling of decomposition and was hard, brittle, dark, almost a burnt orange color, and shiny in the bright sun like plastic.

Bright sun on white sand. This guy smelled really bad. I was trying to help several of the villagers get him out of the hole when I heard a scream. I turned around and his wife was headed right for him. She was going to jump into the hole with him. Ugh. He probably would have popped. I tackled her and with the help of one of the village men dragged her back to the truck, which was parked about thirty yards off. Ngoc Chau's father was squatted on his heels beside the truck, drinking a bottled orange soda. He said something in Vietnamese and she squatted beside him, holding herself with her arms crossed over her chest and shoulders, rocking and moaning. Her long black hair glistened in the white light. The old man kept talking in a low voice, almost a moan himself. There were tears on his dark crusty old face. He never once looked in the direction of the makeshift grave while we got the body out, put it into a decent coffin and loaded it onto the truck.

On the way back the wife was quiet. She sat by herself in a corner of the bed of the truck with a blank look on her face. The old man moved over beside her, and they both sat there without saying anything all the way back to the village. The other younger men talked and laughed, making jokes with me and finishing off the pop we'd gotten in Da Nang to replace the river of sweat that was now covering us with a layer of dust as we rolled and bumped down the road. I was in the back with the villagers because I could speak Vietnamese. The other Marine and the driver were up front.

After we'd dropped off the villagers with their cargo and helped the wife down off the truck—I never saw her again—we returned to our hilltop firebase. As we entered the compound, we came upon a group of villagers. Some were standing, others were gathered in a semi-circle, squatting on the ground. As soon as we stopped the truck, I went over and had a look.

The night before we'd been mortared and some of our own counter-mortar fire had landed in a nearby village. That was where the VC mortars and small arms fire were coming from. There had been civilian casualties, and that's what these people wanted: compensation. We usually shelled out money, called solatium payments, for our accidents. But the ones who brought the bodies to us were never the immediate next of kin.

Several of the women—they were all women—were keening. The ones who were squatting had set a straw basket on the ground in front of them. It looked to be full of banana leaves. When I walked up, they pulled the leaves back uncovering the cold body of an infant. His skull was gone at the level of his eyebrows, leaving a jagged edge all the way around. What was left of his head was hollow inside and the blood was dried to a kind of dark purplish brown. It looked like an inverted plum.

A Simple Farewell

The hearse moved slowly along the winding path of the cemetery. It was a wagon drawn by one horse bearing a single casket. Seven soldiers accompanied the casket. Behind them the family members.

The hearse came to a stop. The small, dark animal stood patiently in harness. It had done this before. The paved walkway, or narrow road, where the wagon had settled to a standstill, was very near the grave site. A Protestant minister was already waiting beside the grave. The family of the deceased, Army Lieutenant Robert Jackson Lee, had requested a simple service. Nothing but a few scriptures read at the place of burial. No eulogies, no commentary of any sort. Bob would've wanted it that way and had intimated as much in his last letter from Vietnam:

* * *

Dear Barb,

I've only got enough time for a few words. The choppers are already waiting, blowing sand everywhere with their prop wash. My platoon will go in with the second wave.

The sand is awful. It stings. I've got it in my eyes, ears and nose, even on my tongue and teeth, and can hardly see to write this. We're camped out next to the helicopter landing zone in full field marching gear: packs, helmets, knapsacks, ammunition—well, you know. It's kind of strange to be carrying all this, when you consider the nature of our mission. But I guess they figure we're going to be there for awhile.

I hope you don't mind having dirt mixed into the pages of this letter. I'm going to hand it to the Company First Sergeant, after I put it in an envelope and address it. He's staying behind.

The helicopters are lifting off now with the first platoon. They'll go in first and set up a defensive perimeter. Then we'll come in behind them. The worst problem will be getting in. The jungle canopy is thick in the mountains northwest of here. That's where we're going. There's already a company up there taking it pretty bad. They're pinned down and have sustained some casualties. A good many, I believe, but there's no definite word. We're going in to reinforce them.

There's a partial clearing on a mountaintop near the valley where they're located. We'll try to go in there, then link up with the beleaguered company if we can. As I say, the jungle canopy is so thick they can't be seen from the air. Just an ocean of green down there.

The choppers are out. Ours will be coming in in a few minutes. The clouds of sand are finally settling. At least we can breathe for a bit.

Hot! You wouldn't believe how hot it is, Barb. My fatigues are already soaked. It's not yet eight o'clock in the morning. There isn't a cloud in the sky. Just a big burning sun.

They're coming in again. I've got to go.

Barb, I know I shouldn't, but I want to say it. To warn you, I suppose, if going in there is really bad. I've had a funny feeling about it ever since we got word before dawn this morning. I'm afraid I might not be coming out. Please don't be upset with me for telling you this. If I'm wrong, if you get this letter and haven't heard anything worse by then, that means I'm okay. But, Barb—

well, I just want you to know how much I love you and our pretty little Teresa. I know she'll be alright. She's just like her mom. If anything does happen—well, just keep it simple. It'll be better that way.

Love always,
your Bob

* * *

The family was now gathered around the freshly dug grave. There were only six people present, besides the minister and soldiers. Barbara, her three year old daughter and her mother stood together in a small group. Next to them were Bob's parents and an older sister of his. They were all gathered near the foot of the grave. At the head of it was the minister with his Bible. To his right and their left, a pile of freshly dug soil. The thick, brown odor of it, damp from the spring rain, blended with the surrounding fresh green smell of lawns and trees. Spread out in every direction around them were even rows of simple white gravestones, some of them lit up in the morning sun, others darkened by the shadows from the trees. There were fields and fields of them, neatly arranged on gentle, rolling hills and softly sloping meadows. The stately trees were large and old.

The minister, a young man, read in a high tenor voice from the prophet Isaiah. Just a few words to be gathered quickly into the trees with the early morning sounds of the birds. These mourners were gathered at about the same hour of day as that in which Robert Lee had written his final letter. Word of his death had come before the letter arrived, as he had said it would.

The soldiers, having already removed the casket from the horse-drawn caisson, were standing at military attention a little apart on the right side of it. When the minister finished, one of them raised a trumpet and played taps. Barbara stood dry-eyed, as did her mother and uncomprehending daughter. There were dark circles under her eyes. Bob's sister could be heard crying softly, her thin shoulders gently shaking. His mother lowered her head. His father stood erect in military fashion, like the soldiers. He had been one himself.